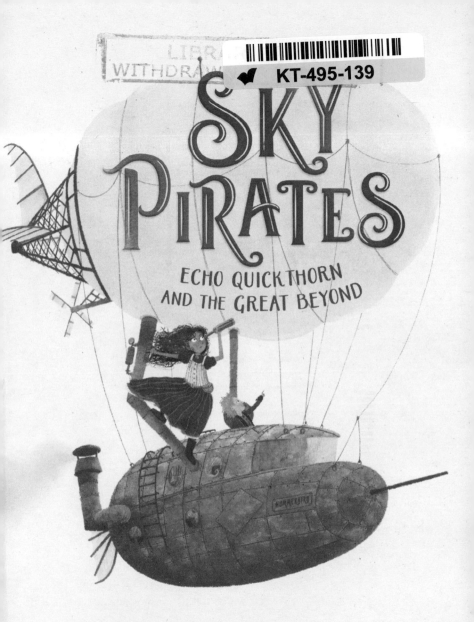

SKY PIRATES

ECHO QUICKTHORN
AND THE GREAT BEYOND

ALEX ENGLISH

SIMON & SCHUSTER

First published in Great Britain in 2020 by Simon & Schuster UK Ltd

1 3 5 7 9 10 8 6 4 2

Simon & Schuster UK Ltd
1st Floor, 222 Gray's Inn Road
London WC1X 8HB

www.simonandschuster.co.uk
www.simonandschuster.com.au
www.simonandschuster.co.in

Simon & Schuster Australia, Sydney
Simon & Schuster India, New Delhi

A CIP catalogue record for this book
is available from the British Library.

PB ISBN 978-1-4711-9077-3
eBook ISBN 978-1-4711-9078-0

Printed and bound by CPI Group (UK) Ltd, Croydon, CR0 4YY

For Freddie, George and Rik,
my very own band of sky pirates

A wall can keep you safe from harm,
From 'them' and 'who-knows-who'.
But walls that keep outsiders out,
Keep you a prisoner too.

PROFESSOR MANGROVE DAGGERWING

CHAPTER ONE

'Ready or not, here we come!' Echo scanned the castle ramparts for any sign of the evil king.

'Can you see him, Gilbert?'

Gilbert clung to her shoulder, his golden scales gleaming in the early-morning sunlight. For a lizard, he made an excellent lookout, and he bobbed his head and chirruped, as if to say, *There!*

'Yes! By the turret,' she whispered. 'Let's get him!' Echo raised a rolled-up tube of paper, ripped out of her history book when her governess hadn't been looking, took a pea from her pinafore pocket and inserted it in the end. She grinned to herself, shed her embroidered slippers and crept forward, barefoot, with her pea-shooter poised.

As she rounded the eastern tower, she aimed the pea-shooter at the imaginary king and tiptoed on. She took a deep breath. *And fire!* The pea flew through the air in a green blur. Gilbert

1

leaped from her shoulder and scampered along the parapet, catching the pea in his mouth with a soft squelch.

'Got him! Now let's capture the castle!' Echo sprinted along the walkway towards the northern turret, Gilbert racing alongside her on the wall. It was going to be close! Echo put on a last desperate burst of speed and threw herself at the turret wall.

'Capture the castle!' She slapped her hand on the stones and collapsed on to the parapet, panting. 'We did it, Gilbert. The king is defeated!'

Gilbert caught up with her and flumped down with an exhausted chirrup. Echo found another pea in her pocket and tossed it to him. 'Let's have a break, then one more game before lessons?'

Gilbert bobbed his head in a way that Echo knew meant, *You're on.*

She grinned and leaned on the parapet wall, her gaze drifting to the city streets below, where a group of blonde, barefoot children scooted a ball to each other in the dust. 'Hey, look – I wonder what they're playing.' She leaned over and cupped her hands around her mouth. 'Hello down there!' she shouted. But the children were too far away to hear. She sighed and shaded her eyes, scanning the city streets, as she always did, for a head of dark, curly hair. But, as always, there was nobody like Echo to be seen, just person after person with straight fair hair, peachy-pale skin and, if she'd been able to see closely, not a single freckle between them.

'One day I'll see someone like me out there,' she said in a small voice.

Gilbert scuttled up to her shoulder and gazed out too, his pea clasped in his front feet.

'I suppose there are no lizards quite like you either.' Echo smiled and tickled his chin. 'Maybe that's why we go so well together.' *Although*, she thought, as she watched one of the girls shoot the ball into a makeshift goal to yells of triumph from her sisters, *I do wish I could go outside, just once.*

Gilbert swallowed his pea with a gulp and butted her cheek with his snout.

Echo laughed and stroked his golden scales. 'Oh, Gilbert, of course you're my *best* friend. But we'd have even more fun with some other children to play with.' She glanced down at the girls again. 'I bet *they'd* like to play Capture the Castle. We could have a whole army to defeat the evil king!'

She looked out further over the city of Lockfort. It was the same old view. The castle towered in the centre, surrounded by a greenish, weed-filled moat. Outside, the streets expanded in rings of identical grey, cone-roofed houses right up to the city walls. Beyond the walls she could just about see the Barren, a wide, rocky, bare expanse that stretched out to the horizon. Beyond that there was nothing but the end of the world.

There was a shriek of delight from the girls below and Echo looked down again. With a jolt, she saw a woman, the girls' mother, emerge from one of the little round houses, carrying a tiny, blanket-wrapped bundle. The woman beckoned to the girls and they gathered round her.

'They've got a new baby sister!' Echo breathed. 'Or I suppose it could be a brother?' She leaned as far as she dared over the parapet, wishing she could get a closer look.

Down below, the woman enveloped all three girls in a hug and Echo's heart ached. Gilbert nuzzled her cheek and wrapped himself round her like a scarf.

'I'm so glad I have you, Gilbert. You're the only one who understands.' She took a deep breath to steady herself and he butted his head against her neck.

'What, you want another game?' Echo squinted up at the sun. The castle gong hadn't rung yet, which meant there were still a few minutes of freedom before the endless boredom of lessons. She cast a last longing glance at the girls and their mother as they disappeared inside their little grey house, before covering her eyes. 'Okay. Ready or not . . .'

The evil king was harder to find this time, but Echo finally spotted him lurking by the eastern turret doorway. She took a running jump, putting her pea-shooter to her lips as she leaped through the air. *Fire!* She shot the pea, but just as she did so the turret door flew open with a bang. Gilbert shot into a hole between two stones, Echo felt her skirt snag on the wall and suddenly she was tumbling through the air, head over heels, her skirt flying over her head and something tearing with a resounding *RRRIP!*

With a thud, Echo landed on the flagstones in a heap.

'What in all Lockfort is going on up here?'

Echo's heart fell into her stomach. She'd know that voice anywhere. Her governess, Miss Brittle!

Echo pulled her dress back down and looked up in horror to see that the pea had hit Miss Brittle between the eyebrows and was now dripping greenly down her long, pointed nose.

She crouched, frozen, as the governess slowly drew a handkerchief from the pocket of her long black dress and wiped her face. Miss Brittle frowned into the handkerchief. 'And what exactly is this?'

Echo swallowed. 'It's a p-pea, Miss Brittle.'

'I know it's a pea,' said the governess. 'I can see very well that it's a pea. But tell me, why is a pea flying through the air on the castle ramparts rather than being in the kitchen where it belongs? And why are you –' she extended a long finger – 'gallivanting about up here when you are needed by the king? I must have searched a hundred rooms for you!'

Echo's stomach clenched. The king? This couldn't be good.

Echo hurried down the endless twisting corridors to the king's rooms, wiping down her skirt as she went and hopping to jam her slippers back on her feet. She blinked as the door opened and her eyes adjusted to the dim light. It always seemed like evening in the king's study, with its heavy burgundy velvet drapes, dark wood panels and flickering oil lamps. The king sat behind his desk, his bejewelled fingers steepled and his face stern beneath its thick thatch of blond hair. What could he want?

'What happened to your dress?'

'It . . . it ripped, Your Majesty.'

'And the green stains?'

'I fell. I had peas in my pocket.'

'Peas?' The king's nostrils flared and he took a deep breath, then muttered something to himself and shook his head.

'Isn't Horace coming too?' Echo asked, looking around.

'Prince Horace,' said the king, 'is on bed rest. With a sprained ankle.'

Echo swallowed. So this was why the king wanted to see

her. But she couldn't possibly be in trouble this time. It wasn't even her fault.

'I would like you to explain to me how my son ended up injuring himself in your company. What were you both doing?'

'We . . . we were exploring,' said Echo.

'Exploring,' said the king.

'Yes,' said Echo.

'Exploring in the library?'

Echo twisted her skirt between her hands. The library was one of the many parts of the castle that were out of bounds, along with the kitchens, the dungeons, the stables and the dignitaries' private quarters. But it looked like she and Horace were in trouble anyway so she might as well tell the truth.

'Horace wanted to find a book—'

The king shook his head. 'Horace tells me it was *your* idea.'

'No! I was helping him. He asked me.'

'I understand you forced him to go.'

Forced him? The liar! Echo clenched her fists. 'I didn't. I—'

'The library is out of bounds for a reason.'

'I know. I—'

'I sometimes wonder why I ever took such an ungrateful child into my care. You have everything an eleven-year-old girl could want! What more could you ask for?'

Echo bit her lip. *My real family*, she thought glumly. *People who care about me, not about how neat and polite I am.* All the fine food and four-poster beds in the world couldn't compare to that. Why couldn't he see?

'Well?'

Echo twisted her hands together. She'd learned long ago not to speak her mind to the king, and she knew it was useless to even think about asking about her parents. 'Nothing, Your Majesty.'

'Very good.' The king sat back in his seat. 'You are a ward of the monarch of Lockfort. Your life is in this castle. It's a life most people out there can only dream of and you would do well to behave accordingly. Now for your punishment.' He gave a smile that showed his teeth but didn't reach his eyes. 'I will have Miss Brittle remove all your storybooks.'

'I don't have any storybooks left, Your Highness.'

'And why not?'

'You . . . you took them away last time.'

'So I did.' The king thought for a moment. 'In that case, I will remove your rooftop privileges.'

'But . . . but you can't!'

The king slammed his fist on the table. 'I am the king of Lockfort! Do not tell me what I can and cannot do!'

'But please, Your Majesty! It's the only time I get to see the outside—'

'From now on, the ramparts are out of bounds. You are confined to the interior of the castle. That is all.'

'But—'

'I said, that is all!' The king's face was an angry mask. He was still glaring as Echo ran from the room, tears stinging her eyes and his words ringing in her ears.

The injustice of the king's latest punishment spun through Echo's mind all day, through embroidery, history and deportment lessons. By the evening, she was still furious, and even Gilbert's gentle finger-nibbling couldn't cheer her up at all.

At bedtime, she sat miserably before her dressing table as Martha entered the bedchamber, brandishing a gilt-handled brush. As the door opened, Gilbert scuttled up the wall and hid in his favourite bedtime crevice.

Martha shook her head as she began untangling Echo's hair. 'Always in a mess, Lady Echo. I've never seen anything like it in all of Lockfort.'

Echo glanced in the mirror, looking from her own dark curls to Martha's smooth blonde hair. However hard she tried, she just didn't fit in. She sighed.

'What's wrong, Echo?' Martha's eyes were kind.

'Oh, nothing.' Echo stared at her hands.

'Now a problem shared—'

'—is a problem halved. I know!' Echo couldn't help a small smile, despite herself. 'It's just so unfair that I can't play on the roof any more. It's practically the only time I get to go outside.'

'Goodness knows why you'd want to, Lady Echo, when you have such riches inside.' Martha shook her head. 'I'd be happy never to go outside this place again. I remember the day I first got this job. It was the best day of my life.'

Echo fiddled with her nightgown. 'It's just ... I always thought someday I'd see someone like me out there. How can I do that now?'

'Oh, Echo,' said Martha, teasing a knot from one long lock. 'I've told you before. You're just the way you are, and there's nothing wrong with that as long as you're clean and tidy and well behaved. Now, do sit still.'

Echo curled her hands into fists to hide her grimy fingernails. 'I suppose I hoped one day I might see my parents,' she said in a small voice.

Martha shook her head in exasperation. 'Echo, we've been through this a thousand times! Who knows who your parents were or what they looked like? Your mother didn't even leave a note.'

But she did leave me this, Echo thought, reaching into the drawer of her dressing table and taking out a small parcel of purple velvet. She unwrapped it to reveal a golden hairpin. Strands of gold twisted and coiled to form a wolf's head, with a twinkling eye of deep green emerald. It was the only thing she had of her mother's.

Martha frowned. 'Do put that away. I'll be for it if someone finds out I kept it for you.'

'So why did you?'

Martha softened. 'Because your mother left it for you, and it's the only part of her you have. I couldn't take that away from you. Maybe she even thought she was doing the right thing, leaving you at the castle where you'd be taken care of.' She paused and glanced at the pin. 'Although what sort of mother leaves a sharp thing like that in a baby's basket, I don't know.'

Echo ran her thumb over the faceted stone. *A sharp thing but a precious thing,* she thought, her heart lifting for a moment. A mother who didn't care wouldn't leave her baby something as valuable as this, would they?

'And Lockfort only knows who your father was.' Martha gave Echo's hair a last exasperated stroke with the hairbrush. 'Just think how lucky you were to be taken in by the king! He doesn't do it for all the waifs and strays, you know. Now, put that away, and get to bed.'

'Goodnight, Martha.'

'Goodnight.' Martha gave Echo a quick peck on the cheek and left, closing the door softly behind her.

Echo carefully tucked the pin into its velvet cover, climbed into bed and hid it under her pillow. Her mother might not be here, but she had cared about Echo, and this was the proof. From now on, she was keeping the pin by her side at all times. After all, who knew what else the king might take away from her?

'Goodnight, Gilbert,' she whispered into the half-light and a drowsy chirrup came from the wall.

Echo settled down to sleep, one hand tucked under her pillow and her fingers curled tightly round the pin. Her parents were out there somewhere – Echo could feel it in her heart. They were out there and they were waiting for her.

Echo just had to find them.

CHAPTER TWO

Echo woke with a start, her heart racing. It was the dead of night, and although all was quiet in the castle, the only noise the gentle drip and whirr of the water clock in the eastern hall, Echo couldn't shake the feeling that something had woken her.

But what?

A prickle of fear ran down her spine. 'Gilbert?' she whispered, glancing up at his crevice. She heard the scratch of claws as he scuttled down the wood panelling, and a soft thump as he landed on her pillow.

'Did you hear it too?'

He bobbed his head and scrambled up on to her shoulder.

Echo took a shaky breath and listened. The moon shone through a gap in the curtains, casting a bright shard of light on to the floor of her bedchamber. A shadow flickered across it and—

There it was! Echo froze as she heard a gentle swish and creak from outside her window. Something was brushing against the stone turret walls. But what sort of something? A bat? A bird? A dragon-of-war ready to burn her to a crisp?

Don't be ridiculous, she told herself. Dragons had died out hundreds of years ago. No, she wouldn't let it, whatever *it* was, spook her.

'I expect it's an owl.'

Gilbert quivered in a way that Echo knew meant, *But owls eat lizards!*

'Don't worry, Gilbert. I'll protect you,' she said. She forced away the fear that was fizzing in her tummy, flung back the covers and crept out of bed, the polished floor cold beneath her bare feet. As she lit her candlestick and tiptoed to the window, the noise came again, closer this time. Gilbert's sharp little claws dug into her shoulder as she hitched up her nightgown to kneel on the velvet cushions of the window seat. Echo raised a shaking hand and, trying to ignore the rapid beat of her heart, took hold of the curtain. She wouldn't be scared, she just wouldn't.

Echo drew back the heavy fabric and gasped. Right outside her window a vast turquoise sphere bobbed and creaked against the glass, its surface gleaming in the moonlight. What in all Lockfort *was* it?

Echo forgot her fears for a moment, put down her candlestick and threw the curtains wider. The sphere was, in fact, a huge silk balloon, rigged with a network of ropes to some kind of peculiar horseless carriage that dangled beneath.

A flying coach? Echo placed both palms on the glass and peered down at it. No, that was ridiculous – coaches couldn't fly! It wasn't a coach at all; it had no wheels for one thing. And the round windows that studded its copper body made it look more like one of those little ships they sent out to clean the weed from the depths of the castle moat.

'Am I still dreaming?' Echo wiped the steam from the windowpane with the sleeve of her nightgown and pressed her nose back against the glass. 'Where's it come from, Gilbert? Whose is it? *What* is it?'

Gilbert scuttled down her arm and on to her hand, his yellow scales bright in the moonlight. He took a look out of the window with one conical eye, then rolled it in a way that said, *Search me.*

As she watched, a gust of wind caught the balloon and buffeted it in the breeze, and Echo saw that the rope rigging had snagged on the castle's ironwork. The strange vessel was trapped.

'Well, I suppose someone should do something,' she said. 'And it is outside *my* bedchamber.'

She pushed open the window and poked her head out, shivering at the rush of freezing air. '*H-h-hello?*'

No answer. She cleared her throat. 'Is anyone there? Should I fetch the guards to help you?'

A circular hatch at the rear of the vessel's roof popped open and a frizzy-haired ginger head appeared. A man's face, mostly obscured behind a huge pair of brass goggles, peered up at her from the shadows. 'Guards won't be necessary,' he said. 'I could do with a hand up though. Would you oblige? Blasted tethers are all tangled and my airship's completely stuck.'

An airship? Echo swallowed. Of course, she shouldn't help this strange man, whoever he was, into the castle in the middle of the night. She really, really shouldn't. She took a closer look at the man, who had climbed out of the hatch and now teetered on the airship's roof. She couldn't see the glint of a sword or dagger, and he had a friendly smile. 'I suppose he looks harmless enough,' she whispered to Gilbert, 'and I can always scream for a guard if anything terrible happens.'

Gilbert blinked and bobbed his head, in a *yes* kind of way, so Echo raced to her bed, tied two sheets together and secured one to the bedpost. She ran back and dropped the other end out of the window. The pilot hauled himself up and Echo stumbled backwards as he flipped over the sill and landed, panting, on the velvet cushions. He pushed his goggles up on to his forehead, making his halo of ginger frizz stand even more upright than before. 'I must apologize for my unscheduled arrival.' He grinned. 'Whatever would your parents say, eh?'

Echo swallowed, her mouth suddenly dry, and took in his strange green suit covered with gadget-filled pockets, his huge hobnailed boots and the wooden tube, thankfully not a sword, tucked into his belt. 'I don't have parents.'

The man's grin dissolved. 'Ah. Ah . . . I see.'

'Oh no. It's fine. I mean, it happened years ago,' Echo said, forcing down the heaviness that threatened to settle in her chest. 'I don't even remember them.'

'Well, oh dear. I do seem to have got off on the wrong foot, so to speak.' The man cleared his throat, jumped up and thrust out a large, freckled hand. 'Professor Mangrove Daggerwing – inventor, explorer, adventurer – at your service.'

An explorer? An adventurer? Echo opened and closed her mouth. Was this some kind of joke? Or a dream? Lockfort didn't have explorers or adventurers. 'I'm Echo,' she finally managed.

Professor Daggerwing grabbed Echo's hand and shook it so vigorously her teeth almost rattled. His palm was huge, warm and rather clammy.

'And who's this little fellow?' he said, peering down at Gilbert, who was back on Echo's shoulder, nestled among her curls.

'His name's Gilbert.'

'What a splendid chap,' said the professor, tickling him under the chin with his little finger. Gilbert's eyes rolled in delight and his scales flushed pink in the candlelight, in a way that said, *Why, yes, I am quite splendid, and thank you for noticing.*

The professor stood up straight again and glanced around, blinking at the opulent gold-and-purple fabric of Echo's four-poster bed, the wood-panelled walls carved with lilies and roses, and the hundred-candle crystal chandelier suspended, shimmering, from the ceiling. He cleared his throat. 'Perhaps I should be calling you Princess Echo?'

'Lady Echo, if you really have to.' Echo wiped her hand on her nightgown. 'Although I'm not much good at being a lady. I'm a ward of the king. You can just call me Echo.'

'Ah, the king. That would be the king of . . .'

Echo stared at him for a second. How many kings did this strange man think there were? 'The king of Lockfort, of course.'

'Lockfort!' The professor's jaw dropped for a moment, and then a slow smile spread over his face. 'Lockfort indeed. What luck!' He gave a sudden giggle and stifled it with both hands, then clapped them together in delight. 'Absolutely fascinating! I do wonder if I'm the first!'

'The first? What do you—'

He sprang forward and shook Echo's hand once again. 'Well, I do declare. Here I am talking to a real Lockfortian!'

'I . . . I don't know what you mean. We're all Lockfortians.'

He leaned closer and his voice dropped to a whisper. 'You were rumoured to be rather a hostile bunch, but I have to say that *I* think you're perfectly delightful.'

Echo grinned weakly.

'But I digress. The king! I must speak to him at once. Please take me to him,' said the professor.

'He doesn't really like to be woken.'

'Nonsense! When he hears the great explorer, Mangrove Daggerwing, has come from beyond the Barren—'

All the breath seemed to leave Echo's body in a rush. *Beyond* the Barren? Was that what he'd said?

'B-but there's nothing after the Barren,' she said after a moment. 'It's the edge of the world.'

'The edge of the world?' Professor Daggerwing's bushy ginger eyebrows shot up so high they almost disappeared beneath his hair. 'My goodness, is that what they tell you here?'

'Well, yes . . .' Echo trailed off. It *was* the end of the world. What did this strange man mean? She cleared her throat. 'At the end of the Barren, there's a great mist, and then if you go too far you . . .' She stopped, suddenly unsure of herself.

'You . . . ?'

'Well, I'm not exactly sure.' Echo felt herself flushing.

The professor grinned. 'I think someone must be pickling your peppercorns!'

'Pickling my . . . ?' Echo was completely confused. 'I don't have any peppercorns.'

'Joking with you?' The professor took a long look at her. 'No, maybe not. Here, let me show you what's really out there.' He removed the wooden tube from his belt, opened it and pulled

20

out a scroll of paper with a flourish. 'It's all here. Take a look.'

Echo grabbed her candlestick and leaned over the professor's shoulder as he unfurled the parchment and spread it out on her bedspread.

'We must be here,' he said.

Echo nodded, running her forefinger round the familiar ring of uninhabitable and treacherous land that was the Barren. Then she stopped. In the centre of it, where she'd expected to see Lockfort's orderly rings of streets bounded by the circular city walls, was simply a circle marked *Terra Pericolosa* in angry red ink.

Echo frowned, about to ask what this meant, but all thoughts were forgotten as the professor unrolled the rest of the map, opening it out right across the bed. For, outside the Barren, where Lockfort's maps had nothing at all and Echo had been expecting to see a blank space, this map showed snaking rivers and soaring mountain ranges. She looked at it in amazement. What were these places? Strange names were written in curling black letters – Cinnabar, Pomegranth, Dark Nordland – dizzyingly large numbers of them. And the map showed lakes and forests, deserts and valleys, moors and—

'That is the great city of Port Tourbillon,' said the professor, stabbing a large forefinger in the middle of the map.

'Another city?' breathed Echo. 'No ... There can't be!'

'Oh yes! There are many cities, and mountains, and—'

'An ocean,' said Echo, almost dropping her candle as she

spotted the pale blue expanse. She recovered herself, relieved at last that she was right. 'That proves it. This isn't a real map – it's just a drawing. The ocean's only in fairy tales.'

'Fairy tales? Not at all, my dear,' said the professor. 'There's a whole world out there just waiting to be explored.'

'What's the ocean like then?' said Echo, studying the professor's face for any signs of a lie, but not finding a single one. 'If it's real, that is. Have you actually seen it?'

'Seen it? I've swum in it! Soaked in the salty water, lazed beneath the star-palms, let the puzzle fish nibble my toes.'

'Puzzle fish,' Echo whispered, the words unfamiliar in her mouth. Despite herself, she felt a tingle of excitement. 'And what else?' she said.

The professor grinned. 'My goal is to explore the furthest reaches of the world and study their flora and fauna. Currently, I am on my way to the Violet Isles to assist Doctor Beetlestone with cataloguing her butterflies ... Such enormous creatures! You've never seen anything like them. Great strong wings that'll flap your hat right off your head. And they lick you like dogs, you know. It's a most peculiar sensation.'

Echo's mind spun. Was this strange man crazy? She thought for a moment. 'So why are you in Lockfort then?'

'Well ...' The professor flushed. 'Technically, we're not supposed to venture here; ever since the Great War, the place has been off limits. No, I was heading to the Violet Isles, here.' He pointed to the cluster of islands on the map. 'I came via

22

the Verdigris Plains. But I must have dozed off somewhere near Galligaskins and then the old girl's engines stalled and somehow I seem to have drifted here.' He gave her a beaming smile. 'But all's well that ends well, eh? A most fortunate occurrence, if I may say so.'

Echo's head whirled with all these strange new ideas. 'What's the Great War—'

They both jumped as Echo's bedchamber door burst open with a clatter of boots. The glare of a lantern dazzled her and she stumbled backwards.

'Drop your weapons!' yelled a guard, jabbing his spear at the professor.

Professor Daggerwing threw both hands in the air. 'Weapons, my dear fellow? I come in peace!'

'Are you hurt, Lady Echo?' Another guard barged into the room. 'What has this ruffian done to you?'

'I'm absolutely fine,' said Echo, pushing down a flicker of fear. Would the professor be in trouble? 'He hasn't *done* anything.'

The first guard clanked over to the open window. 'He must've got in through here,' he said.

'He didn't get in – I helped him in,' said Echo.

'You helped him—'

'What is going on in here?' The king appeared at Echo's door, his gold brocade nightcap askew on his mop of yellow-blond hair.

'An intruder, Your Majesty,' said the guard, bowing deeply.

'He's not an intruder.' Why did nobody ever listen to her? Echo folded her arms, feeling suddenly defiant in front of the king. The professor hadn't done anything wrong! 'I told you, *I* let him in.'

The king ignored her and glared at the professor, red-faced. 'Who *are* you?'

The professor gave a half-bow half-curtsy and almost tripped over his own feet. 'My name is Professor Mangrove Daggerwing, Sire.' He waved a hand at the map still spread out on Echo's bed. 'I come from beyond the Barren—'

'An outsider?' The king's blue eyes blazed. 'Treason!' He pointed a thick, shaking forefinger at the professor. 'Seize him! Take him to the dungeons!'

He marched to the door and turned, a complicated expression on his face that Echo couldn't quite read.

'And burn that map.'

CHAPTER THREE

Echo stared miserably into her coddled eggs as she sat at the banqueting table the next morning. The table was even longer and lonelier than usual; it seated at least forty, but had one measly place setting for Echo instead of the usual two, as Prince Horace was still on bed rest for his sprained ankle.

Martha clamped a plump hand on to Echo's forehead. 'Are you feeling well, Lady Echo? It's not like you to be off your breakfast.'

Echo brushed her away. 'I'm quite *well*, Martha. I'm just cross because you won't believe me.' Why had she ever teased Martha with tales of mushrooms growing under her bed or lied about eating Horace's marzipan bears? Now Martha would never believe her.

Gilbert wriggled in his hiding place in the pocket of Echo's gown and nibbled her finger, as if to say, *I believe you*. She waited until Martha turned away before slipping him a sliver of bacon, which he gulped down with a gleeful chirrup.

'Perhaps it was a dream, Lady Echo.' Martha came back with a gilt tureen and smiled kindly at her. 'You know, you do have them. Now, how about some nice sweet custard?'

'No thank you.' Echo folded her arms across her chest, wishing she'd never told Martha about a single one of her dreams. 'And I've told you a million times – it wasn't a dream. Ask King Alfons.'

'Oh, Echo, you can't just *ask* the king things—'

Echo sighed. Martha was right. The king wouldn't listen to a maid like Martha any more than he listened to Echo. He barely even passed the time of day with his son, Horace. But what if the professor's map *was* real? Why had the king had it burned? He'd called the professor an outsider. But Echo knew how it felt to be an outsider, and it wasn't fair. 'Maybe *I* should ask him.'

'You can't,' said Martha, putting down the tureen with a bang. 'Imagine! Bothering his Royal Highness with your stories. Remember when you told Lord Rolfe you'd seen a water serpent swimming in the moat? I didn't hear the end of it for days.'

'I was just trying to liven up that boring dinner.' Echo frowned. 'This time it's *not* a story, I swear it! There *was* a flying machine, with a balloon. An . . . an airship.'

'Airships indeed! You'll be telling me you've been on a flying carpet next.'

26

'It was right outside my window!'

'And where is it now then. This *airship*?'

'The guards took it away. I heard them.'

'I've never heard anything so silly in all my days, Lady Echo. You and your imagination! It'd be the talk of the turrets if something like that happened in the dead of night.'

'I'm not imagining this time!'

'Then you're playing tricks on me again.' Martha poured out a thick stream of creamy liquid into Echo's goblet. 'Drink your milk. It's good for your bones.'

'But there *was* a man—'

'Milk.' Martha put both fists on her hips.

Echo gave in and took a sulky gulp. Martha was clearly not going to believe her, whatever she said.

'Maybe you're right. It was a dream,' she mumbled into her milk. But her heart said there *was* an airship and a man and a map, and the king was keeping it all secret. But why?

Breakfast over, Echo left the banqueting hall and wandered back past the ballroom in the direction of her bedchamber. She took a quick look around, but there was nobody in the long, wood-panelled corridor, only the oil paintings of King Alfons's dusty ancestors frowning down at her from the walls.

'It's safe. You can come out now,' she whispered.

Gilbert emerged from her pocket and clambered up to her shoulder, where he draped himself round her neck like a scarf.

'You know I'm telling the truth, don't you?' she said.

Gilbert blinked and butted his scaly head against her ear as if to say, *Yes, Echo, always.*

'They must have hidden the professor's ship somewhere,' she murmured. But where? Where could they put it so that no one would find it? A thought hit her. *The ramparts!* Nobody ever went up there but her, and now, thanks to King Alfons, they were out of bounds to her too. Was there time to go up and look? She did some quick calculations in her head. It was Thursday, which meant history with Miss Brittle she realized with a groan. They would have to be quick.

Echo ducked into a side passage and ran all the way to the eastern turret staircase. She reached the top of the stairs and grasped the brass handle, expecting the door to the ramparts to swing open, as it always did. But today it wouldn't budge. She rattled it in frustration. 'It's stuck.'

Gilbert scuttled down her sleeve, over her hand and on to the door frame. He cocked a conical eye at the gap between the door and the jamb, as if to say, *Or rather it's locked.*

'Locked? Let me see.' Echo squatted down and peered at it. A metal block obscured the crack of light. Gilbert was right – the king must have had it locked.

Echo frowned. A lock wasn't going to stop her. Now, how could she get the door open? Echo glanced around, but there was nothing to help. She shoved her hands in her pockets in exasperation and her fingers found the velvet wrapping of her mother's emerald pin, carefully tucked into her pocket for safe keeping that morning.

Echo unwrapped it and looked at it for a moment. The pointy end might do it. Could she risk her mother's precious pin though? She thought for a moment about the deathly boring day that stretched out before her. What if the airship really was up here? No, she had a chance and she had to take it.

Echo opened the clasp, carefully inserted the point into the keyhole and jiggled it. There was a small click, and something in the lock loosened, but it didn't give. She pressed gently with the pin until she could feel the workings of the latch.

Gilbert's scales turned a shade of pale green, as if to say, *Be careful*, and he scuttled backwards along the wall, away from the door handle.

'It's working!' Echo said, easing it back and forth. Yes! Something was shifting. 'A little more—'

With a snap, the pin sprang out of the keyhole, fell on to the floor and shed its emerald, which went skittering across the stone.

'Oh no!' Echo chased after the emerald and the damaged pin and looked at them in dismay. 'I've broken it.'

Gilbert, who was fading back to his ordinary golden shade, scuttled back up to her shoulder and gently butted her cheek with his snout.

'What if I can't fix it?' said Echo, close to tears. She turned it over in her hands and saw with relief that the setting was still in one piece.

Gilbert suddenly sniffed the air, ran back down Echo's leg and over to the door where he peered at the crack beneath it.

'What . . . what are you doing?' Echo wiped her eyes on her sleeve and carefully wrapped the pin and the loose emerald in their velvet before tucking them back into her pocket. She squatted to take a closer look at the base of the door. A cool breeze came through the gap, which was almost as wide as two of her fingers. She stared at Gilbert and a thought came to her. 'Can you fit under?' she whispered.

The little lizard eyed the gap, seeming to size it up, then he squeezed his head under the door, flattened out his body and disappeared.

Echo blinked. It had worked! 'Hey, what can you see?' She jumped up and tried to peer through the keyhole. 'Gilbert!' She tapped on the door, then pressed her ear to the wood. Claws scrabbled on the other side. What in all Lockfort was he doing? She didn't have time to find out because there was a click and she suddenly fell forward on to her knees as the door swung open.

'Oh, Gilbert, you are brilliant!' Echo recovered herself, scooped the little lizard up and planted a kiss on his scaly snout. Gilbert rolled one eye and turned a very pale pink before jumping on to her shoulder and hiding himself in her hair.

Echo got to her feet and stepped out on to the roof, the cool wind blowing her curls loose and inflating her skirts like a balloon. She scraped her hair out of her eyes, leaned over the battlements and looked out across the city. As always, Lockfort's ringed streets of dingy grey roofs spread out before her. She looked round at the rooftop and shook her head. 'Maybe Martha was right. Maybe it *was* a dream.'

Gilbert nudged her ear and scuttled down her arm, hopping from foot to foot in excitement.

'What is it?' She turned to follow his gaze and gasped. Tucked almost out of sight behind one of the old guard posts was a shape covered in a mound of turquoise silk that was weighed down with stones. As she watched, the fabric billowed and flapped as if trying to escape.

The airship! So she was right! They *were* hiding it.

Echo raced over, removed a stone and released a corner of the fabric. The bright silk snapped and rippled in the breeze. The colour of an ocean, she thought. An ocean fringed by star-palms and teeming with puzzle fish. An ocean of adventure. A wave of excitement ran through her.

She pulled back the deflated balloon silk and found the airship huddled beneath. Up close, Echo could see that, while it was similar in size to the royal coach, its construction was completely different. Instead of polished wood, the airship was made of hammered copper plates fixed together with rivets. It had a large window of thick greenish glass at the front and smaller circular portholes dotted round the sides. Towards the front was a plate inscribed HUMMERBIRD. To one side a metal ladder led up to the roof.

Excitement fizzed in Echo's stomach. 'Shall we look inside?' she said, putting one foot on the ladder.

Gilbert jumped on to the ladder and started to climb with his sticky toes. Suddenly he froze and his scales blanched to white.

'What is it?'

Gilbert scampered back to her, his crest raised in a way that Echo knew to mean, *Danger!*

Echo turned as footsteps and voices came from the turret staircase. Fear shot through her. She grabbed Gilbert and shrank back behind the airship, where she peered out from behind the silk. Two guards, whose names she didn't know, appeared through the turret doorway.

'Someone's moved one of these stones,' came a voice.

'Why didn't you lock the turret door?' came another.

'Swear I did. Should we tell His Majesty?'

'Not unless you fancy a spell in the dungeons. Let's check no one's been inside, and make sure you lock the door next time you come up.'

Echo heard the dull ring of feet on the ladder rungs. One of them was getting inside! She slid back further behind the airship, praying they wouldn't decide to readjust its silk covering.

The guard landed with a thud and Echo heard slow footsteps

circling the cabin. Her heart thumped in her ears as the other guard's footsteps got closer to where she was hiding.

Please don't find me. Echo crossed her fingers, every muscle in her body tensed.

Closer still. Then the footsteps stopped. The guard was right beside her, so close she could see the toes of his big black boots beneath the balloon silk. Echo held her breath, dreading the moment she'd be hauled out by one ear by a furious guard and sent to the king for a new punishment. What would he do to her this time? Lock her in her room for a week? She swallowed.

'No sign of anyone in here!' came a yell from inside the airship. She heard the first guard groan as he heaved himself out of the hatch and the sound of feet clanging back down the metal ladder. There was a pause, and the boots near her clumped away.

'Perhaps the wind just blew the rock off,' came the first voice.

'Perhaps.' The other guard didn't sound convinced. 'But what about the open door?'

'Suppose I could've forgotten.'

'You'll forget your head next!'

Their voices grew quieter as the guards' footsteps faded away.

Echo sagged against the wall. Had she got away with it? She waited as long as she dared before unfolding herself and creeping out from her hiding place.

As the castle gong rang nine, she eased the turret door open and raced back down the spiral staircase, Gilbert tucked in her pocket and thoughts spinning through her head. The airship was being hidden, and Professor Daggerwing was too. But what did it all mean? She felt a sudden flare of anger at the injustice of it. The poor professor, shut away without his fantastic ship. All for being an outsider!

'I'm going to help him,' she whispered to Gilbert. She was the only one who would after all. But, to do that, she would have to go to the dungeons. Echo might have explored the furthest reaches of the castle, but even she had never dared go there before. She had to find a way in. And for that she'd need help from the last person she wanted to ask – Prince Horace.

CHAPTER FOUR

Horace was the only other child in the castle that Echo was allowed to mix with, the rest being servants or kitchen boys. Like Echo, he was motherless since the queen had died five years ago and, while she often despaired at his disappointingly cowardly disposition, he did come in useful for some things. He was the most bookish of bookworms; when it came to dungeons and punishments and the more gruesome aspects of the castle's inner workings, Echo knew he was an expert.

She ran up the stairs, only pausing to poke her tongue out at a particularly ugly marble bust of King Alfons looming in an alcove, and pushed open Horace's bedchamber door without knocking. She found him attempting to scale the side of his wardrobe. As the door burst open, he leaped down and scrambled into bed, his thick blond fringe falling over his eyes. He shoved a small book under his pillow. 'Oh, it's you,' he said, his face relaxing as he saw Echo.

'How's the ankle?'

'Terrible.' He scowled.

Echo perched on the end of the bed, scooping Gilbert out of her pocket and placing him beside her. 'Looked all right just then.'

Horace eyed Gilbert warily. 'Don't let him bite me.'

'I've told you a million times! He doesn't bite,' said Echo, with a small smile. 'Not unless I tell him to.'

Gilbert blinked innocently as Horace shrank back against his pillows.

Echo nodded towards the wardrobe. 'What were you doing up there anyway?'

'Getting this,' he said, waving the copy of *Spotter's Guide to Lockfort Butterflies* that they'd found in the library. 'I had to hide it or they'd take it away again. I told Father we didn't actually find a book.'

Anger flared in Echo's stomach again, but she bit her lip.

'He says butterflies aren't princely and I'm only to read about weapons,' he went on, with a grimace. 'You won't tell, will you?'

'Like you didn't tell on me?'

Horace turned scarlet. 'I was going to get into trouble.'

'So you got me in trouble instead.'

'You're used to it!'

Echo resisted the urge to take out her shooter and fire a pea at him. She had to stay focused. 'I need to know something.'

'What?'

She thought quickly. She definitely couldn't trust Horace to keep a secret. 'It's for history lessons,' she lied. 'I'm learning about the castle, as you'd know if you weren't up here, pretending to be injured.'

'Lessons? Since when did you worry about lessons?' Horace slumped back on his pillows again. 'Anyway, it's your fault I'm here.'

'You shouldn't have panicked!'

'You shouldn't have told me there were rats.'

Echo bit back a smile at the memory. 'I thought you'd like to know.'

'Anyway, what is it that you want?' he said, flushing. 'Something deathly boring, I suppose?'

'I want to know about the dungeons,' said Echo.

'Well, I don't think you'll get sent there for twisting a prince's ankle. Unfortunately.'

'Ha ha.' Echo looked pointedly at the butterfly book. 'You owe me, remember.'

Prince Horace frowned and studied the golden embellishments on his bedspread. 'They're beneath the castle. Father locks people up there if they say bad things about him.'

'I know *that*. But what would they do to you if you were down there?'

'What would they do to *you*?' Horace's eyes sparkled. 'They'd probably strap you into a squishing machine and

37

squidge you up until you squealed. Or chop off your toes with a rusty teaspoon. Or scoop out your eyeballs! They'd—'

Echo silenced Horace with a disbelieving look. 'You're making this up,' she said. 'They can't do any of that.'

'They might.'

'You've never actually been there, have you?'

Horace shrugged. 'Father got his dungeon plan out once during one of his dreary meetings. I saw it over his shoulder. There's a room marked *interrogation*. They probably do it there.'

A dungeon plan? Now this was interesting. Echo's mind whirled. 'Could you get hold of the plan? I . . .' She steadied herself. She couldn't tell Horace about the professor. 'I need to borrow it.'

Horace shook his head. 'Don't be ridiculous. Father would never let us borrow his plan.'

'You don't need to *ask* him.'

'He'd be furious though, if I got caught.'

'So don't get caught!'

'Why would I risk that for you?' Horace scowled at her.

'Because otherwise I'm giving Miss Brittle this.' Echo lunged forward and snatched the butterfly book from Horace's bedcover.

'Hey!' Horace opened his mouth to argue. 'You can't—'

'Lady Echo!' Miss Brittle's shrill voice rang up the turret staircase. 'Your lessons started three minutes ago!'

Echo silenced Horace with her most threatening look. 'Coming!' she yelled, shoving Gilbert into one pocket and the book into the other before sliding off the end of the bed.

'The plan,' she said to Horace. 'Bring it to me after lessons.'

Horace didn't get a chance to reply because Echo was already through the door and pelting down the spiral stairs.

'Four minutes!' came Miss Brittle's voice.

Echo clattered round the last bend and almost knocked over her governess, who was standing, thin-lipped and stern, at the bottom of the staircase.

'I'm sorry, Miss Brittle, I was—'

'To the schoolroom, immediately.' Miss Brittle stormed off down the hall, her long black skirts swishing. 'And I do hope that creature isn't with you.'

Echo jogged along after her and Gilbert gave a defiant wiggle in her pocket. 'Of course not, Miss Brittle—'

'Ladies do not have lizards,' snapped the governess. 'If I see him, I will have him put into the royal soup.'

Echo patted her pocket reassuringly and stuck out her tongue at Miss Brittle's bony back as she followed her to the schoolroom. Just a few lessons to get through, and with the king's dungeon plan she'd be on her way to finding the professor. His arrival had certainly spiced up castle life, Echo thought with a smile. Now she just had to help him.

In the schoolroom, Echo found her place in her book and felt her spirits drop at the thought of yet another dull lesson with Miss Brittle. Her venture into the depths of the dungeons seemed a lifetime away.

Miss Brittle settled herself at her little ebony desk. 'Today we will be learning all about the layout of the city streets and how to navigate them, where the farms are and the boundaries of the city walls. Please get your parchment and I will dictate.'

Echo took a new scroll and slumped at her desk. What was the point? She wouldn't ever get to use any of these tedious facts.

'Is there a problem, Lady Echo?' Miss Brittle gave her an icy stare.

'Well, I just don't see why I need to know the layout of the streets when I'm never allowed outside.'

'What is the point of going outside when you have everything you need in here?' Miss Brittle snapped. 'Let us start.'

Echo hunched over and dipped her quill in her pot of black ink. A thought occurred to her. The professor and his map! She glanced up at Miss Brittle, who was studying her papers. 'And will I be learning about places outside the walls too?' she said casually.

Miss Brittle didn't look up. 'The Barren? There's not a great deal to know. Ever since the Great War, it has been bare, lifeless and forbidden.'

The Great War. The professor had said something about that. 'When was the Great War, Miss Brittle?'

'One hundred and eleven years ago,' said Miss Brittle. 'That is when the city walls were first built, to keep our enemies out.'

So there were other people out there! Echo leaned forward, eager to know more.

'You seem unusually interested in my lessons all of a sudden.' Miss Brittle gave Echo a long look before continuing. 'And, after our enemies were all defeated, there was nothing left but the Barren.'

'What about beyond the Barren?'

'*Beyond* the Barren?' Miss Brittle's head jerked up. 'What do you mean, child? Have you learned nothing in my lessons?'

'No, I mean, yes, of course, Miss Brittle. But what if you, I mean we, were wrong?'

Miss Brittle's nostrils flared. 'Wrong?'

'I mean.' Echo swallowed the lump in her throat. 'I mean, what if there was something beyond. Another city or . . . or—'

'Another city!' Miss Brittle folded her arms and regarded Echo with a cold eye. 'Remind me. What happened to Beatrix Skitterbrook?'

'Beatrix . . .' Echo's mind was blank.

'Beatrix Skitterbrook!' Miss Brittle rapped her ruler on Echo's book. 'The Woman Who Thought the World Went On.'

'Oh!' Echo found the page and scanned it. 'She walked

across the Barren for three days and three nights and disappeared into the mist.'

'And?'

'And . . . was never seen again.'

'And why was she never seen again?'

'Because she fell over the edge of the world, Miss Brittle.'

'Indeed, and that is why, to protect the people of Lockfort, King Tybalt, the good King Alfons's grandfather, had the city gates locked, never to be opened again. People kept being curious and falling to their deaths. And it doesn't do to be curious,' said Miss Brittle, with a fixed glare at Echo.

'No, Miss Brittle.' Echo thought for a moment. 'But doesn't the prophecy say that one day the gates will open?'

Miss Brittle's nostrils flared again and she shook her head in irritation. 'Listen carefully at the Gate-opening Ceremony and you will understand that the prophecy is impossible to fulfil. Now, take your quill and I will dictate. *The city of Lockfort has an advanced system of streets that requires no maps to navigate . . .*'

Echo barely had time to think for the rest of the lesson, she was so busy scribing Miss Brittle's pronouncements; but, whenever there was a pause, her thoughts came back to the same thing. Could the professor's map be real? Had he really come from Beyond? It was the most interesting thing that had happened in a long time. In fact, the only interesting thing, unless you counted the time Miss Brittle had rearranged the desks and allowed Echo to sit by the window and Horace by the door. The very idea that there were other cities out there was almost too thrilling to be true. Echo desperately wanted the professor to be right. She didn't fit in Lockfort and neither did he. She simply had to get into the dungeons and help him.

Once she'd escaped from Miss Brittle, sat through a long, tedious luncheon with Marchioness Beauregard and suffered an hour of history with Martha, Echo went to find Horace, who was now reluctantly out of bed and back to lessons. Of course, Horace didn't have to learn anything as dull as needlework. Instead, he had fencing with a wiry, silver-haired man called Alfred. Echo loitered outside the courtyard, with Gilbert draped round her neck, watching Horace slash with his wooden sword as Alfred nimbly sidestepped out of the way. How she wished she could join in! Although she suddenly wondered why Horace had to learn to fight at all when he was never allowed outside the castle either. And, according to Miss Brittle, Lockfort had no enemies left to fight. Unless the professor's map was real, of course.

Alfred spotted her watching and grinned as she ducked back into the corridor.

'I think that's enough for today, Your Highness,' he said to the panting, pink-faced Horace.

'Thank Lockfort that's over.' Horace threw down his sword

and gasped in relief. 'I mean, thank *you*, Alfred.'

As Horace returned to the castle, Echo grabbed his arm and dragged him to a dusty alcove. 'Have you got it?' she said.

Horace looked over his shoulder. He nodded reluctantly and took out a browned scroll of parchment, creased with age.

'Thanks.' She took it from him and slipped it up one voluminous sleeve. 'See you later.'

'Wait! What about my book?'

'I'll give it to you after.'

'After what?'

Echo shook her sleeve at him. 'After I've been to the dungeons.'

Horace's mouth gaped. 'But Echo, you can't *go* there.'

'No such thing as can't.'

'But you'll get into trouble!'

Echo's tummy tightened, but she hid her nervousness behind a shrug. 'I'm still in trouble from when you told on me. A little more won't hurt.' She took the map from her sleeve and studied it. 'Where's the entrance?'

Horace shrugged miserably. 'The plan only shows the layout of the dungeons. It doesn't show how to get in there.'

Echo sighed. 'Don't you have any ideas?'

'Father goes through the grand entrance to the catacombs. But you'd never get in that way. That's just for ceremonial expulsions.'

'What?'

'When people are expelled from the city. Father sends them out into the Barren to perish.'

To perish? Echo's mouth dropped open in horror. 'To die? He really does that?'

'Only sometimes,' Horace continued. 'It's just for the very worst ones though. Like Mickermus Britch when he questioned Father's cutlery spending.'

'He was expelled for asking a question?'

Horace shrugged. 'It was treason. Father *is* the king. And he deserves nice spoons. Anyway, he hasn't expelled anyone for years. Mostly he just leaves them in the dungeons.'

Echo's thoughts turned back to the professor. Being trapped in the dungeons must be ten times worse than being trapped in the castle. She put her hand to her shoulder to stroke Gilbert's scales and the little lizard nudged her cheek.

Echo thought out loud. 'How do the servants get down there?'

Horace frowned. 'This can't really be for homework. What are you up to?'

'Someone has to feed those prisoners,' said Echo. 'And they don't go through the ceremonial entrance.'

Gilbert hopped from one foot to another and chirruped.

'Yes!' Excitement bubbled in Echo's stomach. 'The kitchens, that's it!' She slapped a confused-looking Horace on the shoulder. 'Gotta run!'

45

CHAPTER FIVE

Echo raced through the endless corridors, ducking into an alcove behind a bronze statue of a bear to avoid Greengrass, one of the more irritable castle footmen. She'd made it all the way to the western wing before Horace caught up with her.

He ran up, panting, and grabbed her arm. 'You can't go, Echo. I'm not letting you.'

'It's not up to you.' She shook him off, almost knocking over a vase painted with the face of King Valbert the Third. Were all of Horace's ancestors this annoying? They certainly looked it.

'I'm Crown Prince, and you're just a ward. You have to do what I say.'

Echo rolled her eyes and set off again. 'Oh really.'

Horace hurried after her. 'Well, I'm coming with you then.'

She turned to face him. 'You? Why?'

'It's my father's plan. If it's lost, he'll know I took it. I'm not good at lying like you are.'

Echo put her hands on her hips, not sure whether to be insulted or flattered. After last time, in the library, she didn't want him to tag along. But Horace was taught a lot of things about castle life that she wasn't and he might know something useful.

'Fine, I suppose you can come. But, if you tell on me again, I'll throw your book in the moat.'

'I won't,' said Horace, looking glum. 'Prince's honour.'

'Come on then.'

They made their way to the ballroom and Echo eased open the door to reveal a vast, gleaming space of pink-and-white marble columns, blond-wood panelling and an impossibly high ceiling hung with hundreds of mirrored chandeliers. The sunlight that came in from the tall arched windows reflected off the glass droplets, sending shimmering shadows dancing across the floor.

Horace followed her in, wringing his hands. 'Are you sure this is the way?'

'Yes!' Echo strode to the far wall, her footsteps ringing off the gleaming parquet, and ran her hands over the gilt-encrusted panels. 'Now, where's it gone?'

Gilbert ran down her arm from his perch on her shoulder and sniffed the air, then pointed his snout to the right, as if to say, *Here*.

Echo pushed and the whole panel swung open to reveal a dingy staircase leading downwards. She glanced back at Horace. 'Still coming?'

'Are you sure someone won't catch us?' Horace's voice wobbled.

'They only use the servants' stairs during mealtimes.'

'How do *you* know all this?'

'From exploring! Gilbert and I have been here hundreds of times. One day I was so bored I crept in and laced Miss Brittle's posset with white pepper, right under the pastry chef's nose. And another time I found a whole almond tart and sneaked it out under my pinafore.'

Gilbert's tongue flicked out at the mention of almonds.

Horace hesitated in the doorway.

'Come on, before somebody sees us!' Echo pulled him inside by the shirtsleeve and eased the door shut behind them. She set off down the stairs.

'I suppose you found that horrid old trout head down here too,' grumbled Horace from behind her.

'I don't know *anything* about a trout head.' Echo grinned to herself as she remembered the gleam of its cold, wet eye.

'The one that was in my bed on April Fool's!'

'No, still no idea. And keep your voice down.'

The narrow staircase twisted and turned as they descended towards the warmth of the kitchens. At the bottom of the stairs, Echo put her finger to her lips. Even Gilbert held his breath. She pointed to the jumble of grease-stained white jackets and caps on a counter outside the door.

'Child sizes are there. Stick some trousers on,' she whispered.

Horace screwed up his nose. 'But they'll ruin my new moleskin breeches!'

'You won't look like a kitchen boy in moleskin!'

'But I'm not a . . . Wait a minute! I thought we were going to ask someone here about the dungeons.'

Echo rolled her eyes. 'And have them tell Miss Brittle? We need to disguise ourselves and blend in.'

'But they'll recognize my face.'

'No they won't. They're all too busy preparing for the Gate Opening. Anyway, people see what they expect to see. And no one expects to see a prince in scullery-boy clothes.'

'I think I might go back . . .'

'Don't be such a lubberwort! Don't you ever want an adventure?'

Gilbert nudged her ear as footsteps echoed on the stairs above them, and flashed his crest.

'You said there wouldn't be anyone on the stairs!' Horace's eyes widened.

'Quick!' Echo threw a bundle of clothes at him. She yanked a jacket on over her bodice, placing Gilbert carefully in the pocket, then pulled on a pair of grease-spattered scullery trousers and shoved her skirts inside. The footsteps grew louder.

'Keep your head down and follow me.' Echo twisted her hair into a tight coil and jammed on a cap. She pushed open the door and burst into the heat and clatter of the kitchens.

Scullery boys scuttled hither and thither across the room,

where great copper pots boiled and steamed on the fire pits and enormous, ruddy-faced chefs bellowed orders. The air was thick with the smell of roast meat, smoke and sweat. Echo grinned. It was a place where things happened.

'I just know someone'll recognize me,' whimpered Horace from behind her.

'Don't look anyone in the eye and, if someone gives you an order, do it. And keep an eye out for where they cook the prisoners' food.'

'Oi, you two! Stop slacking! Take these to the pot wash.' A chef called Bartleby, with tiny, pig-like eyes, shoved a heap of food-encrusted pans at Horace and he staggered backwards under the weight. Echo kept her eyes on the floor and pulled a tangled handful of curls down over her face. Bartleby had caught her in the peach store once before and given her a hiding.

'Y-yes, sir.' Horace righted himself and wobbled away.

'To the pot wash!' bellowed the chef.

Horace turned. 'Which way is that again? I seem to have forgotten.'

The chef squinted at him. 'You look familiar. Don't I know you?'

'He's new,' said Echo, keeping the peak of her cap low and grabbing some of the pans from Horace. 'It's this way. Come on, er –' she grasped for a name – 'Bob.' She strode off across the kitchen, head down.

Horace followed. 'How did you know which way to go?' he panted.

'I told you, I've been here before,' said Echo. 'And, anyway, all the boys with empty pans are going this way.' She nodded as another scullery boy, carrying a stack of filthy pots, emerged from a row of stoves ahead of them. She followed him.

Everywhere Echo looked there was food. She passed a glistening hog roasting on the fire, fat spitting into the flames and sending up sparks. In the pastry section, great ham-handed chefs slapped and pummelled mounds of white dough, while others stirred bowls of quince aspic and poured the thick, shining liquid into jelly moulds. Knives flashed and whisks clattered. In one corner, she spied a chef plucking the feathers from an enormous swan and, in another, two chefs assembling a towering honey cake. She'd have to make sure she got a slice of *that* at the Gate Opening dinner.

'Mind your backs!' yelled a scullery boy.

Echo clung on to the greasy pans and swerved to avoid a procession of boys rolling barrels of mead. At the far end of the kitchen, she saw the pot wash – a vast copper tub of water surrounded by piles of dirty pans. A single scrawny boy, about Echo's age, scrubbed and sloshed furiously.

'Not more!' he gasped, as yet another chef arrived with an armful of grimy meat cleavers.

Echo saw her opportunity. She shoved her load down. 'We'll help you with that, One-Eye,' she said.

The boy turned to face them and Horace recoiled in fright. One of his eyes was completely missing, the skin patched together with stitches so large Martha would definitely not have approved. 'Echo!' he said in delight. 'You're back!' He looked at Horace. 'Who's yer friend?'

'This is Bob,' she said.

Horace put his pots down and gulped as he glanced nervously between the boy's face and the tub.

'Thanks,' said the boy. 'I'm One-Eye,' he said to Horace. 'On account of the . . .' He gestured at his face.

'Listen, we need to get to the dungeons,' Echo said. 'Can you help us?'

'Course! I still owe you for the seed cake.' One-Eye smiled. 'I have to warn you though – it ain't nice down there.'

'We don't care about that.'

'Echo, I'm really not sure about this,' said Horace. 'I want to go back.'

'There's no time now.' Echo glanced hastily over her shoulder. To her horror, Bartleby was striding across the kitchens towards them, a furious look on his face. 'There's no way back – we have to go on.'

'Quick, follow me.' One-Eye wiped his hands on his trousers and set off across the kitchen, with Echo pulling a reluctant Horace close behind.

They came to a smaller cooking area where vats of steaming porridge bubbled unattended.

52

'Get in,' said One-Eye, gesturing to a huge wooden barrel strapped with iron bands. 'They'll take that down to the dungeons when they do the next run.'

Echo scrambled inside and Horace peered in after her. 'In there?' he said.

'Yep.' One-Eye gave Horace a shove from behind and he tumbled in on top of Echo with a squeal.

One-Eye leaned in and grinned. 'Good luck, Echo. Don't get yerself lost down there.' He slammed on the lid of the barrel and everything went black.

CHAPTER SIX

Echo crouched next to Horace in the darkness, hugging her knees to her chest. Gilbert squirmed in her pocket. Through the wooden shell of the barrel she could hear the clamour of raised voices and the muffled clang of pans and ladles outside. Would someone guess they were in here? Echo's stomach flipped with fear. She'd been down into the kitchens hundreds of times before, but even she had never dared enter the dungeons. There were stories of rats, and ghosts, and worse, and she couldn't imagine what King Alfons would do if he found out.

But he wouldn't find out, she told herself. They'd be fine as long as she kept her nerve. And anyway she wasn't about to show Horace she was scared. She thought of the professor. Was he scared down here too?

Suddenly they pitched to the left and Echo was flung sideways on to Horace, who let out a muffled squawk.

'Shh!' she said, finding his sweaty palm and giving it a squeeze. She couldn't let him give them away, not when they'd got this far. The professor needed their help!

The barrel rolled and pitched again, then shuddered as it came to rest. Echo heard the squeak of wheels and her stomach lurched at the strange sensation of downward movement. A few moments later, there was the thud of a door opening and closing. Then the barrel rocked. They were on the move again.

'If one of the scullery boys opens this, we're toast!' whispered Horace.

'I know the scullery boys,' Echo whispered back, 'and most of them owe me at least one favour. Stop worrying.'

Let's just hope it is *a scullery boy*, she thought, with a shiver. *Not a dungeon keeper, or worse . . .*

When the barrel finally came to a halt, Echo spotted a small oval of yellow light in the side of the wood, knelt forward and pressed her eye to the hole. Flickering torches lit rough stone walls pitted with grey-green lichen. A tingle of fear ran down her spine as she saw a man in black disappear down the corridor. But there was no turning back now. She waited until he was out of sight before pressing her palms to the barrel lid and heaving at it.

'I think we're here,' she said. 'Help me push the lid off, would you?'

Horace wriggled next to her and Echo felt him put his weight against the lid too. Her muscles strained and something loosened. They continued to push and, with a *pop*, the lid shot off, landing on the flagstones with a clatter.

Echo waited for a few moments before daring to peer out of the top of the barrel, blinking as her eyes adjusted to the torchlight. They were really here. She swallowed.

'What can you see?' came Horace's petrified whisper.

Echo gathered herself. She had to stay focused if she and Horace were going to get out of here without getting caught. 'It's clear.' She gripped the top of the barrel and sprang over the lip to the floor.

Horace scrambled after her, catching his boot on his saggy scullery trousers and landing with an ungainly thud on the flagstones. 'Ugh.' He wiped one slimy hand on his trousers and wrinkled his nose in disgust. He looked around. 'I really don't like this, Echo.'

'Neither do I, but we're here now,' Echo said, trying to sound confident. Gilbert emerged from her pocket and draped himself in his favourite place round her neck.

'What do you think?' She showed the little lizard the dungeon plan.

'What . . . why are you showing him? Don't tell me he can read maps now?' Horace spluttered.

'It's worth a try,' said Echo.

But Gilbert cocked his head to one side, looked at the map, then curled his tail into a question mark, as if to say, *Who knows?*

56

'Come on, let's try this way.' Echo picked a path and crept into the damp darkness.

'But Echo, where are we going?' Horace trailed after her. 'What is this homework anyway?'

Echo ignored his complaints and kept going, shivering despite the hot, moist air pressing down on her. The torches cast strange shadows on the flagstones and strangled wails reverberated down the corridors. Every so often, a drip of slimy water landed on her head and slid down the back of her neck, but she pressed onwards.

Soon they came to the prisoners' quarters, where they passed cell after cell with thick bars of rusted iron. Inside, men with wild beards and wilder eyes lurked in the shadows.

'Brought me some porridge, boy?' A bald-headed man with three stumps of teeth in his red gums lurched at them out of the darkness and rattled the bars. He made a grab for Horace's sleeve.

Horace yelped and leaped backwards, knocking into Echo, who almost screamed in fright and dropped the dungeon plan in a puddle.

'Don't be such a pudding heart!' said Echo, half to Horace and half to herself. She fished the plan out and wiped it on her trousers. Horace had to be the worst possible exploring companion – his nervousness was catching. Why had she ever let him come?

Gilbert tightened his claws on her shoulder and cocked his head.

'What is it?' she whispered.

Up ahead someone was singing a melancholy song.

Horace wrapped his arms round himself. 'You've seen the dungeons now. Please can we go.'

'Shhh,' said Echo. She crept forward, her heart pounding in her ears, until she was close enough to make out the words.

> *'Oh, I sailed like a whale on the silvery sea,*
> *And I danced with a puzzle fish under a tree,*
> *And I sang to the moon and she sang back to me,*
> *By the light of the silvery, silvery sea . . .'*

Puzzle fish! Echo grinned in relief. It *had* to be the professor. She followed the singing and, as she rounded the last stone column, let out a gasp of delight at the sight of Professor Daggerwing, slightly bedraggled and with his hair in even more of a wild ginger halo than before, sitting cross-legged in a cell.

'Professor!'

Professor Daggerwing jumped and looked up, startled. Then his face broke into a broad grin. 'If it isn't the young Lady Echo! And her delightful reptilian friend.'

Gilbert hopped from one foot to another in glee.

'But what on earth are you—'

Echo beamed. 'I'm here to rescue you.'

'Hang on a minute.' Horace came panting round the corner.

'You never said anything about rescuing anyone. Who is he anyway?'

'This is Professor Daggerwing,' said Echo. 'And we can't just leave him down here.' She turned to the professor. 'This is Horace. He's not much good at exploring, but he insisted on tagging along.'

'And you insisted on taking my plan,' said Horace, folding his arms tightly across his chest. 'If it wasn't for me, you'd have been caught on the stairs before we even got to the kitchen!'

Echo scowled. But, before she could reply, Professor Daggerwing cleared his throat. 'Let me introduce myself, young man.' He stood and thrust a large, freckled hand through the bars. 'Professor Mangrove Daggerwing. Inventor, explorer, adventurer. I come from the great city of Port Tourbillon. Beyond the Barren.'

'Beyond the Barren?' Horace's pink face paled. 'Don't be ridiculous.'

'Why couldn't it be true?' Echo said, desperately wanting it to be. 'We've never been there.'

'But it's the end of the world!'

'What if it isn't though?'

Horace shook his head. 'You shouldn't speak of such things,' he said, his voice shaking. 'It isn't true. And if Father heard—'

They all froze as the sound of footsteps rang down the corridor behind them.

'That'll be Mortice – the dungeon master,' said the professor.

'A man heavy of boot and heavier of hand. You two should skedaddle.' He gave a mock salute as Echo and Horace scuttled round the corner and deeper into the dungeons.

The tunnels narrowed as Echo ran, as swiftly and as quietly as she could, Gilbert still clinging to her shoulder and Horace close behind. Once Mortice's voice had faded to nothing, she stopped.

Horace's face was flushed. 'You ... you tricked me! You didn't say anything about rescuing prisoners.' Even in the torchlight, she could see he was close to tears. 'If Father found out, he'd ... I don't even know, but it wouldn't be nice!'

'But the professor needs our help,' she said. 'He's got a map of places outside. He showed it to me!'

'There *are* no places outside,' said Horace. 'He made it all up, and you fell for it. Just because you're so desperate for it to be real. You want to think there's somewhere better where you don't have to play by the rules. Well, there isn't.'

Echo flushed at Horace's words. She swallowed. Perhaps Professor Daggerwing's tales *were* too good to be true. Down in the dungeons, other cities and rivers and oceans suddenly did seem unlikely.

'I want to go back upstairs right now,' Horace said, with a sniff. 'I can't stand it down here.'

'Fine,' Echo snapped. How *were* they going to get back

upstairs? In her haste to get to the dungeons and find the professor, she hadn't even thought about their exit route, and they couldn't risk going back up in a barrel with nobody to seal them in. She took a deep breath and examined the map, hoping Horace hadn't noticed her cluelessness. 'This way,' she said, pointing with fake confidence at one of the tunnels.

They walked onwards through the greenish-black puddles. In the torchlight, Echo made out walls covered with a stinking yellowish mould that made her grimace, Horace gag and pinch his nose, and Gilbert hide his face in the collar of her jacket. The air weighed down on her, damp and heavy. She stared deep into the gloom of one cell and jumped as a woman with a dark, shaven head appeared out of the shadows, the whites of her eyes glowing eerily in the darkness.

'I recognize you, girl. Now where have I—'

'Nowhere,' said Echo, hastily backing away and walking swiftly on into the shadows.

She was about to turn the corner back into the labyrinth of tunnels when the woman shouted after her, 'You're the very image of your ma!'

Echo froze. It was as if the woman's words had knocked all the breath out of her. She turned back. 'You knew my mother?'

The woman squinted at her. 'Dunno. I can't quite place her. I just know there was a woman down here who looked just like you. Had a baby with her.'

'Down here?' Echo shook her head. 'No, you're mistaken.

My mother wasn't down here. She abandoned me up on the castle steps. She wasn't a criminal.'

The woman chuckled and stared at Echo intently. 'Eyes like a stormy sea, she had, grey and gold, just like yours.' Suddenly she lunged between the bars and grabbed Echo's wrist. 'Her face shone like moonbeams, so it did.'

The look in the woman's eyes scared Echo. She snatched her hand away and stumbled backwards, then set off through the tunnels at a run, her heart pounding.

'Wait for me!' she heard Horace shout from behind her, but she couldn't stop her feet from moving. Every part of her was desperate to get as far away as she could from the strange woman and her intense stare.

'*Please* stop,' puffed Horace, after they had raced through tunnel after tunnel. 'We don't even know where we're going.'

Echo finally came to a halt, but she was still shaking. Stupid girl! For a moment, she had really believed that the woman had known her mother. That, for once, someone was going to tell her something about her parents. Anything! She fought back a sob. She'd been stupid to believe in any of it. Stupid to hope that there was something more to life than what she had. Stupid to come down here at all.

She suddenly realized Horace was talking to her.

'I said, are you okay?' he said. 'You mustn't trust the prisoners, you know. They're down here for a reason. What did she say to you?'

'Oh, nothing much,' Echo said stiffly. Horace was right. The woman had been confused; she must have been down in the dungeons too long. Why had Echo ever believed in the professor and his ridiculous fairy tales either? She'd risked another punishment to come down here.

Echo clenched her hands into tight balls. She wouldn't cry in front of Horace. She took a deep breath and steadied herself. 'You're right,' she said. 'I'm sorry I brought us down here. It was all a silly idea.'

Horace shrugged. 'I chose to come – it's not *all* your fault. Come on, let's go back.'

Echo nodded and stared blankly at the map. She blinked a few times and frowned. But Gilbert suddenly sniffed the air, ran up the folds of Echo's stolen outfit and leaped on to the wall.

'Gilbert!' said Echo, as the little lizard skittered away from her grasp.

'What's he doing?' said Horace. 'Looking for flies?'

'I don't think so,' said Echo. 'Quick. Let's follow him.' She raced off after him.

After following Gilbert along passageway after cramped passageway, they turned a corner and Echo suppressed a gasp.

Before her was a vast, stone-walled chamber lit with flickering torches. In the central wall was a huge, circular gold hatch ringed with skulls and at the far end of the chamber two tall metal gates hung open. Through the opening she could see torchlight and red-carpeted stairs leading upwards.

Echo ducked back into the shadows as a Royal Guard came into sight and began to polish the metalwork, humming as he worked. This had to be the way back to the castle – through the king's ceremonial entrance. If they could just sneak past the guard . . .

Echo grabbed Gilbert, tickled him beneath his chin and lifted him back on to her shoulder, where he curled his tail round her neck. She gestured to Horace and he popped his head out of the alcove to see.

'The ceremonial gate,' he whispered.

'*That's* our way out,' said Echo.

Horace nodded. 'We got lucky,' he said. 'They only open it when there's going to be an expulsion.' He pointed at the circular golden door with its ring of skulls. 'That's the chute.'

'That's where they throw them?' Echo's eyes widened as she gazed at the door. The eye sockets of the skulls that surrounded it glimmered red in the torchlight and she realized they were inset with rubies as big as gulls' eggs. She breathed in incense and mildew.

'Yes,' whispered Horace. 'Apparently, it leads right under the city and beneath the northern wall.'

'And they *really* throw prisoners down there?'

'Only for bad stuff like treason. I've never actually seen it though. Look, he's leaving.' Horace pointed. Echo stuck her head out again and saw the guard disappear up the stairs. This was their chance.

'Ready?' Echo whispered to Horace and he nodded.

'Come on,' she said and, hauling him by the sleeve, she ducked out of the open door, up the stairs and back into the safety of the castle.

CHAPTER SEVEN

Echo had only been back in her room for a few moments when the door burst open. Gilbert took a flying leap on to the bed and hid beneath the covers just as Martha appeared. 'There you are, Lady Echo! I've been looking for you all afternoon. You left this in the garden . . .' She held out Echo's embroidery kit, then stopped and gaped as she took in Echo's smeared face and creased skirts. 'You're filthy!' She strode forward and examined Echo's fingernails, then recoiled, her nose wrinkling. 'And you smell like you've been rolling in compost. What in Lockfort have you been doing this time?'

Echo snatched her hands away and shoved them in her pockets. 'Nothing much,' she said, still smarting with disappointment over her useless mission.

Martha sighed, putting the embroidery kit on the dressing table and disappearing into the bathroom. 'Of all the days. You know very well it's the Gate-opening

Ceremony tonight. Off with those filthy garments at once, and I'll draw a bath.'

Echo sighed. The Gate-opening Ceremony was so dull – a whole evening of ridiculous dresses, boring speeches, being on show as a grateful ward of the king. Although at least it meant she got to leave the castle for once and see the city close up. As always, a small glimmer of hope flared inside her. Would tonight be the night she'd finally catch a glimpse of dark, curly hair? A freckled face like hers?

'Echo, bath!' Martha called.

'Coming.' Echo pulled off her grimy pinafore and scurried into the bathroom.

After a hot soak and a rather thorough scrub from Martha, Echo dried herself in front of the fire and pulled on her undergarments. Martha came in with the armfuls of golden silk that made up Echo's ceremonial gown and laced her into the stiff fabric. Echo gazed into the mirror and grimaced as Martha tightened the stays.

'How lovely to see you so neat and tidy.' Martha stood back and admired Echo. 'Now, doesn't that feel good?'

Echo shrugged. 'I suppose.' She never felt comfortable in these flouncy dresses. She wrinkled her nose and examined herself in the mirror. She didn't feel or look like herself at all.

Outside her window, the whole city was abuzz with the

promise of tonight's Gate-opening Ceremony. Echo took a longing glance outside. What was it like, she wondered, living out there? Not having to be neat and obedient and polite, but instead playing football barefoot in the dust.

Her thoughts scattered as Martha gave the dress one final, rib-crushing tug and stood back, panting. 'Delightful, Lady Echo! Now for the Lockfort ruby, I think.'

She whisked out of the room, leaving Echo still staring at herself in the glass. The dress was beautiful, it was true, but it was like looking at a stranger. How she wished she could be in breeches and boots like Horace. A girl could hardly have much of an adventure in a dress like a sailing ship. Not that there was anywhere to adventure to.

She glanced back at her day dress, lying muddied and stained in a heap on the floor. With a jolt, she saw her mother's hairpin hanging out of the pocket. She quickly retrieved it and its wrapper, remembering with a pang of dismay how she'd broken it, trying to pick the lock to the ramparts. She took a closer look and found to her relief that the damage wasn't serious; the emerald had simply popped out of its clawed setting. The fitting was too tight to force the stone back in and the metal wouldn't give when she tried to prise the claws apart with her fingers. She needed something stronger. Glancing round the room, her eyes alighted on the embroidery kit Martha had left on her dressing table.

Echo took out the little pair of embroidery scissors and tried again to prise the setting open. As she twisted the scissors, she could feel the metal giving. Suddenly the blades slipped and the hairpin clattered to the floor, rolling across the bedchamber to the window. Gilbert poked an inquisitive head out from beneath the bedcovers as she raced over to grab it, hoping Martha hadn't heard. As she lifted the pin in the light of the window, she noticed something engraved in the setting that had held the emerald eye. She rubbed the metal on her skirt and squinted at it again. In tiny letters were engraved the words:

MESSRS EVERGREEN & SPRUCE,
GOLDSMITH'S LANE, PORT TOURBILLON

Echo frowned as she squeezed the emerald back into its setting. Port Tourbillon? She'd heard that name somewhere before, but she just couldn't place it. She quickly shoved the pin and its wrapper into her pocket as Martha returned with the ruby hairpin. Echo shook her head. What did the writing mean?

'Oh, do cheer up, Lady Echo,' said Martha. 'Most children would give their last crust of barley bread to see the Gate Opening from the royal table.' She softened. 'What's wrong?'

Echo turned the words over and over in her mind, but she still couldn't make sense of them. 'Martha,' she said, 'why would jewellery have writing on it?'

69

'Oh, probably just the maker's mark.'

'What's that?'

'The sign of the jeweller who made the piece. Look.' Martha took a pearl brooch from the jewellery box and turned it over so that a row of tiny letters caught the firelight: *Messrs Lock, Lockfort.*

'Of course, jewellery doesn't really need a maker's mark any more. There's only one royal jeweller's, and that's the Masters Lock. But it's traditional to engrave the name of the maker on every piece.' Martha gave Echo a last inspection. 'Now, I'm going to check on young Prince Horace. I'll come back for you in five minutes. Don't get dirty. In fact, don't do anything at all.'

But, for once, Echo didn't have to be told to sit still. She was frozen in thought.

She frowned at herself in the mirror. It made no sense. If there was only one jeweller in Lockfort, then who were Messrs Evergreen & Spruce? And Port Tourbillon? She'd heard that name before somewhere, but just couldn't remember when.

Echo took her mother's pin back out of her pocket and paced round the room. 'Port Tourbillon. Port Tourbillon. Where have I heard it?'

Gilbert emerged from the bedspread and gave a chirrup, and, with a jolt, she remembered Professor Daggerwing unfurling his map over her covers in the middle of the night.

'The map!' she breathed in wonder. *That* was where she had seen it. And the professor had mentioned it too.

The great city of Port Tourbillon!

Echo's mind bubbled with questions. What did it mean? Her mother's hairpin had been made by a jeweller in Port Tourbillon. *Could* the professor's tales be true after all? Could there really be a world beyond the Barren?

And, if his tales *were* true, how had her mother got hold of the pin? Had she been to Port Tourbillon herself? A prickle of excitement ran up Echo's spine. Could she even be somewhere out there now?

There was a soft knock at the door. 'Ready, Lady Echo?' called Martha.

'Coming.' Echo planted a kiss on Gilbert's snout. She couldn't risk him being seen at the Gate-opening Ceremony. 'I'll be back soon,' she whispered, before tucking the hairpin carefully into the pocket of her dress. A ripple of excitement ran through her. At last she was finally going to find out something about her mother. She had to get back down to the dungeons and ask the professor.

CHAPTER EIGHT

Thoughts of the hairpin, Port Tourbillon and her mother were still whirling through Echo's mind when she took her seat in the banqueting hall. She gazed round the table. All the richest families in Lockfort were there: Lord and Lady Rolfe sat proudly at the far end of the table nearest to King Alfons and Prince Horace; Sir Everett the Brave greedily guzzled a hunk of roast swan; Baron Hawkeswood guffawed as he clinked glasses with Marchioness Forthwind, who was primped and powdered and dressed in her finest jewels. None of them spoke to her though. None of them were *like* her.

Echo speared a juicy piece of quince pie on her fork and chewed it thoughtfully. She had to go back to the dungeons and talk to the professor about the pin. If only this infernal Gate-opening Ceremony would hurry up and finish. But there was always a long drawn-out meal where the king would drink too much mead and eat too much meat, and tell far too many boring stories, before they all were taken in coaches down to the city gates. Oh, when could she escape?

Eventually, the royal bugles blared and the gathered dignitaries began shuffling out of the banqueting hall. As she followed them through the hall and out of the castle gateway, Horace, dressed in a velvet suit and frilly-collared shirt, caught up with her and tugged on her sleeve.

'I managed to get the dungeon map back to Father's study.'

'Good,' Echo mumbled, not really listening.

'I crept back in and slipped it into the slot in his writing desk. And I didn't get caught. I don't think he suspects *anything*.'

'That's great.'

Horace stopped abruptly and the excitement dissolved from his face. 'Don't you even care?'

'What?'

'That I did it. That I didn't get into trouble?'

'I said it's good, didn't I?'

Horace huffed. 'I risked my hide to help you,' he grumbled. 'I've got other things to think about.'

Echo turned her back on him and scrambled into the royal coach opposite Martha. Horace got in next to Echo and was about to continue the argument when King Alfons appeared through the coach door in a swish of velvet robes and squeezed himself into the last seat next to Martha.

'Ah, the young Lady Echo,' he said, laying his emerald-encrusted sceptre across his knees and adjusting his crown.

'And how is the embroidery going? I hear you have quite a talent with the needle.'

Echo shrugged. 'It's all right. I suppose.'

'Hmm.' King Alfons gave her an appraising look. 'I see we still have some way to go with the etiquette lessons.'

He turned to Horace. 'And the swordsmanship?'

Horace squirmed under the king's gaze. 'Do I *have* to learn fencing, Father?'

'Of course you do. Boys have to fight. It's what they're made for.' King Alfons turned to Echo. 'Just like *girls* are made to learn the needle.'

'But *why*?' Echo couldn't help herself. 'I bet I'd be better at sword fighting than Horace.'

'Echo!' exclaimed Martha.

'I just mean . . .'

The royal carriage jolted off and Echo's words were lost in the clatter of hooves on the cobbles. The king leaned closer to the window and gave a gracious wave to the passers-by as the carriage rumbled off into the crowds.

Echo silently shook her head. Everything the king did was for show. She glanced over at Horace, who was flushing miserably beneath his own crown. Why should he be forced to fight when he'd clearly much rather be engrossed in a book about bugs? He didn't suit the role he'd been given any more than she did. It was all so stupid. What was the point of forcing them into these things that made them miserable?

Echo peered out of the carriage window, as always searching the hundreds of faces in the crowd for one like her own, but there was nothing. She put her hand in her pocket and squeezed the hairpin in its velvet wrapping. Her mother was out there somewhere: she could feel it. And, when Echo found her, she would finally belong.

The coach rumbled through the streets of grey-roofed houses towards the city walls and before long they were drawing up to the gates. Echo leaned out of the window and peered up at the great iron-studded wooden doors that towered above them. For so long, they had marked the edge of her world, but what if there was more out there?

The coach juddered to a halt and bugles blared to herald their arrival. The ceremony was the same every month: the king would go through the motions of unlocking the gate and, as always, find that it wouldn't budge. Tonight though there would be celebrations and fireworks to commemorate the thirty-year anniversary of the gates being locked. Echo remembered Miss Brittle's words about Beatrix Skitterbrook: *Listen carefully at the Gate-opening Ceremony and you will understand that the prophecy is impossible to fulfil.* There had to be some way though, didn't there? Nothing was really impossible.

A page opened the coach door with a bow and King Alfons led the way out of the coach, followed by Horace, Echo and finally Martha. The seated dignitaries all clapped politely as they passed, while those people standing in the rows behind whooped and leaped into the air to get a better look.

'Good evening, Your Majesty,' simpered Marchioness Beauregard, fanning herself with a black ostrich-feather-trimmed fan.

'A most delightful feast, Your Majesty,' said Baron Hawkeswood. 'You have outdone yourself.'

Sir Everett the Brave, Sir Garamond the Fearless and the other knights stood to attention as the group made their way to the royal platform.

'Good evening, good evening,' said the king, as he lumbered up the steps and everyone took their seats.

'Ladies and gentlemen,' announced King Alfons from his gilt-covered throne. 'Tonight is an important night. Tonight we celebrate the thirtieth anniversary of the gates of Lockfort being locked for good. These gates protect our city. They protect us! Now, let the ceremony begin!'

The crowds hushed as the Royal Reader stepped up to the podium and Echo sat up in her seat as he read the prophecy from the Great Book.

> *'When Tuesday arrives on a Sunday night,*
> *When a she-wolf soars by dragon flight,*
> *When the king's blood turns from red to white,*
> *Then the gates of Lockfort shall open.'*

Echo had never really listened to the prophecy before; she was usually too busy searching the crowds for a head of dark hair. Tonight though she was listening intently. And, as she did, she realized with dismay that Miss Brittle was right. Dragons, wolves, Tuesday on a Sunday? It just couldn't ever be.

'Well,' said the king, swinging a chain of three huge, bejewelled keys, 'I'm afraid it's a *Thursday* night tonight, but I'll do my best.' He grinned as the crowd laughed and cheered at his joke, then strode over to the gates.

A hush fell as he inserted the first key, made out of gold encrusted with pink tourmalines, into the lock. As he attempted to turn it, the crowd drew a breath. King Alfons turned to his audience, shook his head and shrugged.

The audience seemed to sigh as one. He turned back to the gate and inserted the second key, this one covered in scarlet rubies.

Echo leaned forward in her seat in expectation, willing the gates to open this time. She slumped in her seat as, for the second time, the key didn't turn.

Finally, the king flourished the last key, studded with glimmering white diamonds, before grunting with effort as he attempted to turn it in the lock.

As he turned back to the crowds and made his way to the podium, the king gave a mock grimace. 'The prophecy holds!' he said. 'The gates of Lockfort shall not open tonight. Let us celebrate these closed gates. These gates of tradition and keeping Old Lockfort alive. These gates that keep us, the people of Lockfort, safe from harm.'

The crowd cheered and the royal bugles blared again as King Alfons lumbered back to the carriage.

The journey back to the castle through the city streets was a blur. Echo had never really been interested in the Gate-opening Ceremony before – after all, it was the same every month. But Professor Daggerwing's arrival, and the map and the hairpin, had shown things in a different light. What if there *were* other cities out there? And rivers, and mountains, and the ocean. What if the prophecy was meant to be fulfilled and the gates did open? What if Beatrix Skitterbrook didn't fall off the edge of the world, but had found somewhere new out there?

Echo climbed out of the carriage and into the castle courtyard in a daze, her mind still whirling with possibility. Then she stopped. Usually, everyone filed straight back into the castle, but something different was happening tonight. The king, a huge goblet in his jewel-encrusted fingers, stepped into the centre of the courtyard and addressed the assembled dignitaries. The chatter hushed.

'Gentlemen, ladies.' King Alfons gazed proudly round the courtyard. 'We are celebrating not one but two great events this evening.'

A murmur reverberated round the walls. Echo blinked. What was going on?

'Not only is it the thirtieth anniversary of the closing of the gates . . .' There was a great cheer and clinking of goblets from around the courtyard. King Alfons gestured for quiet. 'I am also pleased to announce that only a few hours ago I was able to personally expel a traitor to the throne from the city.'

Echo was suddenly cold with shock. *A traitor? Expelled?* She tried to catch Horace's eye, but he was staring resolutely forward at his father.

The king continued. 'This individual was a danger to the crown and a danger to the very foundation of Lockfort. He was a troublemaker, a rabble-rouser and had dangerous ideas that have no place in a society such as ours.'

A murmur of agreement rippled through the crowd. Echo's heart filled with fear. *No, no, no! Not him! Please not him!*

'And not only that,' the king went on, 'but he was caught breaking into the castle in the middle of the night.'

There were gasps in the crowd. Echo fought back the urge to cry. It was Professor Daggerwing. It had to be. But expelled? Surely King Alfons couldn't have thrown him out into the Barren?

'Worry not, worry not.' The king waved a hand lazily in the air, his ruby signet ring twinkling in the candlelight. 'He has been expelled from the city. I saw him slide down the chute with my own eyes. He is now outside the great walls in the Barren where he can do no harm to anyone.' He clapped his hands together. 'And now – fireworks!'

A great cheer went up in the crowd and people leaped to their feet. But Echo was frozen where she stood. The professor would die out there in the Barren! How could they leap around, squealing about fireworks, as though nothing had happened? She clenched her fists until her knuckles turned white, unable to stop the terrible thoughts filling her head. The professor, alone in the Barren, stranded without even his ship. What would he eat? What would he drink? What would become of him?

And how in all Lockfort would she find her mother now?

CHAPTER NINE

Echo let herself be carried along with the crowd to the outer courtyard, where the ladies and gentlemen of distinction would watch the firework display. Everyone was gazing up at the night sky, drinking mead and chattering. Horace was talking animatedly to Lord Rolfe. Even Martha was completely preoccupied with the show that was about to start. And that, Echo suddenly realized, meant nobody's eyes would be on her. Echo knew how to recognize an opportunity when she saw one. And she had to help the professor. But how?

Echo gazed up at the darkening sky above the castle ramparts, where the last tendrils of evening sun were disappearing. The ramparts – that was it! Daggerwing's airship was up there. What was it called? The *Hummerbird*. An idea was bubbling up inside her. The professor was alone in the Barren without his ship. But what if he *had* his ship? If someone took it to him ... Did she dare?

Echo plunged her hand into her pocket and closed her fingers round the familiar metallic shape of the pin. This was her only chance to find her mother. She couldn't go her whole life without getting answers to her questions, and nobody in Lockfort was going to help her, not even Martha. No, there was only one way out. She had to take Daggerwing's ship and find him! If she slipped out now, while everyone was watching the fireworks, nobody would even notice she was gone.

Echo felt a tap on her shoulder. It was Horace. 'What are you up to?' he said.

'Nothing,' lied Echo.

'You seem all . . . happy or excited or something.'

She tried to look nonchalant. 'It's just the fireworks.'

'You? Excited about fireworks?' Horace snorted. 'I don't believe it.'

Echo turned away from him and pretended to be waiting impatiently for the show. As soon as it started, she'd give Horace the slip and race up to the rooftops. Then, once the fireworks had finished, she'd fly off in the airship and find Professor Daggerwing. He'd be so grateful, he'd take her to Port Tourbillon, she'd find Evergreen & Spruce and then . . . Well, she didn't quite know. But what she did know was that saving the professor was the first step to finding her mother, and she wasn't going to let Horace, or anyone else, stop her.

There was a boom and the first firework crackled across the

82

night sky. Echo slipped backwards into the crowd. There was a tug at her sleeve. It was Horace again.

'What now?' she snapped.

'What *are* you doing?' whispered Horace.

'Nothing! Nothing to do with you anyway,' she hissed back.

'You're going to do something stupid.'

'What's it to you?'

Horace swallowed, his cheeks reddening. 'Echo, you *can't*.'

'Can't what?'

'You're going to try and rescue the professor, I know it.'

Echo shrugged. 'None of your business if I am.'

'But Echo, it's dangerous!'

'I'm not asking *you* to come.' Echo pulled her sleeve out of Horace's hand and pushed her way into the crowd towards the eastern entrance to the castle. She glanced back, but Horace was hidden in the mass of bodies. Good. She didn't have time to deal with him and his nerves.

Echo inched open the heavy oak door and slipped inside the castle. She crept as quietly as she could past the rows of suits of armour lining the corridor, their polished metal reflecting the sparks in the sky outside, and over the grey flagstones to the turret archway.

She stopped on the bottom step and stared up at the staircase as it spiralled away into darkness. Was she crazy? Maybe. She paused for a moment, struck all of a sudden by the madness of her idea. Could she really hope to fly the airship? And, even if she could, would she be able to find the professor? Sparks of fear and doubt rocketed through her like the fireworks outside. Maybe she should turn back. Outside, the sky flashed red, then blue, then gold.

Echo felt again in her pocket for the hairpin, turning it over in her fingers. She might not have much chance of success, but she had to at least try. And there wasn't any time to waste.

She hitched up her skirts and ran up the stairs.

Echo took the ruby pin from her hair and used it to pick the lock before racing across the ramparts to the *Hummerbird* and rolling away the stones that held down the deflated balloon. She scrambled up the ladder and pulled open the entry hatch with a *pop*. As she glanced out over the Lockfort rooftops, each ring of houses twinkling with lanterns as golden sparks exploded across the sky above, it hit her that perhaps this would be the last time in a long while that she would see the city. She felt a sudden pang of sadness and took a deep breath to steady her nerves.

Down below, the royal bugles blared. The ceremony must already be more than halfway through. She had to get going before it finished. She put a hand to her shoulder for Gilbert, then suddenly remembered. She'd left him in her bedchamber for the Gate-opening Ceremony!

Echo slid back down the ladder and clattered down the

staircase, across the hall and back to her room without stopping for breath. She had to find him before someone noticed she was gone! She flung the door to her bedchamber open.

'Gilbert,' she hissed. Oh, where was he? 'Gilbert!'

There was a rustle, and the little lizard emerged from under her covers, blinking in confusion.

'Quick, on to my shoulder!'

Gilbert shook himself in a way that said, *What? Now?*

'Yes, now. Come on!' The fireworks outside were getting closer and closer together. How long would they go on for? Echo rushed over and slung him on to her shoulder.

'Hold on,' she said, and flew back out of the door, through the empty castle, up to the roof and over to the airship. Without a further glance, she clambered up to the entry hatch and slipped in, slamming the hatch shut behind them, her heart hammering.

Inside the airship, Echo blinked as her eyes adjusted to the gloom, then shivered in awe. 'Gilbert, look!' she breathed.

Copper pipework snaked and coiled all over the walls. Towards the rear of the ship, a hammock, a battered enamel saucepan and a pair of brass binoculars hung from hooks above a low cupboard. In front of the large window at the fore stood two worn leather seats, a dashboard covered with dials and buttons and a large, spoked wheel of polished red-brown wood. A real airship.

Echo climbed into the pilot's seat and clasped the wheel in

both hands. It seemed to fit her grip perfectly. She scanned the dashboard, her heart beating a wild rhythm in her chest. Now she was here, things suddenly felt a whole lot more real. And a lot more dangerous. If only she'd had time to make a plan. She peered more closely at the dashboard. How in Lockfort would she even get the ship started? There were so many dials

and buttons and levers. Sweat prickled on her forehead and she pushed her hair back, her fingers closing on the ruby hairpin. She quickly ripped it off and replaced it with her mother's. She could do this; she had to.

Echo took a deep breath and pressed each button in turn. 'Surely one of them has to start it,' she muttered.

Gilbert ran down her arm and on to the dashboard, where he scuttled up and down, squinting at the dials. Through the windscreen, a shower of gold burst into the sky with a bang that made them both jump. Far away she could hear the cheers and whoops of the crowd and the bugles playing the royal salute.

'The show's nearly over,' she said, fear sparking through her. She frantically stabbed at the buttons, grabbing at levers and flicking switches, her hands growing slippery with sweat. 'Nothing's happening!'

She took a hasty glance outside, and saw to her horror that the fireworks had slowed and the night sky was filled with drifting clouds of gunpowder smoke. Time was running out. Martha was bound to notice she was gone soon. Perhaps Horace had even told on her already. A terrible thought hit her. What if the ship had been damaged and couldn't fly? After all, when Professor Daggerwing had arrived, he'd drifted into her window. Echo slammed her palms down on the steering wheel in frustration. 'What do we do now, Gilbert?' she said.

Suddenly the airship shuddered and something above them whirred into life. Echo jumped. She glanced at the dashboard. Gilbert was sitting on a button she hadn't tried. A button with, when she looked closely, a tiny brass inscription beneath it saying INFLATE. Echo's cheeks burned. Of course! How had she been so stupid?

'That's it, Gilbert, you've done it!'

Gilbert sat up proudly on the dashboard as the whirring continued and the balloon silks pulled up and away from the portholes.

'Yes!' Echo punched the air in delight. The floor rocked and bobbed beneath her as the airship began to float. Excitement bubbled in her chest. 'It's working!'

'Hey!'

They both jumped at the sound of a shout from outside. Somewhere a door slammed and Echo heard the clatter of boots on stone. She raced to the rear porthole and made out two guards with lanterns marching across the ramparts towards her. The airship was floating only a little above the ground. Close enough, Echo realized, for the guards to grab the bottom of the ship and drag it back down. She couldn't let them!

Echo ran back into the cockpit and scanned the controls, settling on a lever marked THRUST. She pulled it, there was a roar and the airship surged forward, throwing Echo back into her seat and leaving Gilbert dangling from a control handle by the tail, his feet scrabbling for purchase. Through the windscreen, Echo saw the stone of the castle rooftop disappearing as they gained height. Yes! This was it! They were getting away!

Something hit the hull with a metallic clatter. Echo jumped.

The guards! They were firing at the ship! But what would happen if they hit the balloon? Would it hold?

Echo shuddered. She wasn't going to find out. She leaned hard on the thrust lever, the engines hummed with life and the little ship surged forward. There were more muffled cries from behind and the clang of a spear as it bounced off the hull, but they were gaining speed now. Climbing up, up and away from the rooftops, into the open sky. Into the night, over the city and beyond.

'Look,' cried Echo. The city's streets spread out before them, the little grey-roofed houses as small as toys. Gilbert ran over the dashboard to the windscreen and peered out too.

Below, city dwellers were returning home from the firework display, weaving through the streets, their lanterns bobbing ahead of them like fireflies. At the hum of the airship engines, people turned to look skywards. There were shouts as city dwellers stopped, pointing up at the *Hummerbird*, open-mouthed.

Echo gazed back down at them. *I'm leaving*, she thought. *I'm really leaving.* She snatched one last glance at the upturned faces below her, then fixed her gaze on the northern wall, where the flames of the north beacon flickered in the breeze. She put her shaking hands on the wheel and held her course steady.

She was going beyond the Barren, and she would not be afraid.

CHAPTER TEN

As they neared the city wall, Gilbert let out an urgent cheep and Echo jerked her gaze up from the dashboard to see that the *Hummerbird* was surging dangerously close to the north beacon, with its bowl of flickering flame. Echo was pretty sure that flames and balloons didn't mix. In fact, if they kept on going this way, they were going to crash right into it!

She grabbed the steering wheel with both hands and swung it to the right. The airship bucked and jerked and Echo was thrown to the floor. The wheel spun wildly as she was thrown this way and that. A cupboard above the pilot's seat flew open and a little brass telescope tumbled out, hitting a button at the top of the dashboard and barely missing Gilbert, who scrabbled to stay upright. An amber light began to flash and dials whirled.

'Hold tight, Gilbert!' Echo struggled to her feet and clung to the dashboard. She glanced out of the windscreen and gasped as she realized they were racing straight towards the flames of the beacon again. The wind must be against them! They were getting far too close. Echo grabbed the wheel and wrenched it to the right once more. Gilbert's scales glowed danger red and his tail stood to attention as he let out a panicked squeak and hung on to the dashboard with all four feet. The airship turned, but too late. Flames surged up the windscreen; there was a crackle and a hiss from above.

'Oh no!' To her horror, Echo saw smoke billowing above them. 'We're on fire! What should I do now, Gilbert?' She pulled the wheel hard to the right again. 'We're going to crash!'

The pressure gauge spun wildly, an alarm blared and the dashboard lit up in a sea of flashing red lights. Echo heaved on the thrust lever and the little ship surged forward over the city walls and into the Barren.

The *Hummerbird* began to drop towards the rocky ground. Echo grabbed Gilbert and strapped herself into the pilot's seat before pulling in vain on the thrust lever. Her heart pounded in her ears in time with the shrieking alarm. They were falling!

They dropped further and the ship spun in the air. Echo saw the greyness of the Barren and the starlit night sky flying past the portholes as the ship tumbled faster and faster.

'Aaagh!' Echo gave up on the steering wheel and flung both hands over her eyes. Her stomach turned and she braced herself against the dashboard as the ship bounced and skidded over the Barren. There was a horrible scraping noise as they juddered across the rocks, then suddenly they were falling again. Cupboards burst open, showering saucepans, jars of strange vegetables and copper-plated instruments over the floor.

Finally, the ship came to a stop, the charred silks deflating over the portholes with an empty sigh.

It took several minutes before Echo could relax her grip on the dashboard. Gilbert scrambled up and nudged her cheek.

'I'm all right, Gilbert. Are you?' she croaked.

Gilbert bobbed his head, chirruped as if to say, *Fine and dandy,* and shook the dust out of his scales.

Echo gingerly raised her head and surveyed the scene. 'What a mess!' The windscreen and portholes were obscured by the deflated balloon silks, but in the gloom she could see that the floor was littered with the brass instruments, cooking implements and jars that had fallen out of the cupboards.

'Let's look outside.' Echo released her seat belt and wobbled out of her seat, Gilbert clinging to her shoulder. She picked her way over the spilled paraphernalia, scaled the ladder and released the exit hatch with a pneumatic hiss. The stench of burnt hair hung in the air as she pushed her way out from under the balloon and slithered down the hull to the ground.

She emerged from the charred fabric and looked around. They'd rolled into a rocky crater so deep that the city walls could barely be seen behind them. At least that meant that they couldn't be spotted from the city, Echo realized with relief. But her relief turned to dismay when she examined the balloon. Even by moonlight, she could see it was well and truly ruined, its turquoise silk blackened and crumbling into ash around a gaping hole.

'Oh, what are we going to do, Gilbert?' she said. This rescue mission was not going well.

Gilbert nuzzled her cheek, but Echo could tell he was out of ideas too.

To the north, bare grey rock stretched out as far as she could see. She squinted at the horizon, but could only make out silvery clouds of mist. Was there really anything beyond? A lump of panic threatened to form in her chest, but she put her hand to her hair and grasped her mother's pin to steady herself. Of course it was real. It had to be. Just because she couldn't see it yet, that didn't mean it wasn't there.

There was a rustle of fabric behind her. Echo jumped in fright and spun round to find a familiar rumpled blond head appearing from under the balloon.

'Horace!' She opened and closed her mouth for a moment. Why in Lockfort was he here? He'd followed her again! She bit her lip in fury. How dare he? He was bound to ruin everything! Although, she had to admit, looking around at the emptiness of the Barren, it was comforting not to be completely alone out here. She sighed. 'What are *you* doing here?'

Horace flushed as he fought his way out from under the

balloon. 'I didn't think you were going to make it *fly*. Are you quite mad?' He glanced around. 'Where in all Lockfort are we?'

'We're not *in* Lockfort.'

'We're not ...' Horace's face turned pale as he took in the grey rockiness of the Barren. 'Oh no! Echo! What have you done?'

Echo's relief turned to irritation and she scowled. 'I'm going to find the professor and ...' She considered for a moment. She couldn't tell Horace about going to Port Tourbillon yet. 'And help him.'

'But the professor's a criminal! And now we're stuck out here like criminals too.' His voice rose to a squeak. 'We'll perish! We'll wither away to skeletons! We'll—'

'No, we won't.' Echo clenched her fists to keep her voice from trembling. She had to be brave. She mustn't let Horace panic her. 'We're *not* stuck. We'll find the professor and he'll fix the airship and ... Where were you anyway?'

'In that cupboard at the back. I just wanted to see what you were up to, and then I heard footsteps and I ... I got spooked.' Horace sniffed. 'Oh, I wish I'd never looked inside this stupid contraption!' He kicked the side of the ship with a dull, metallic clank, winced and hopped away. 'Ow! And now I've hurt my toe!'

Echo shook her head in exasperation. This was all she needed. Horace must have followed her and hidden when she'd come back with Gilbert.

She sighed. 'Look, we're here now, and it's no good panicking,' she said, more gently. 'We need to find the professor. He'll know how to fix things.'

'Are you sure?' asked Horace.

'I'm certain,' said Echo, not feeling very certain at all. 'I'll go and find the end of the expulsion chute and see if he's there. You wait here, where it's safe.'

She scrambled up the side of the crater on her hands and knees, Gilbert clinging to her back. When she got to the top and looked out, she could see the high stone city walls and the bright bowl of flame that marked their exit from the city. At the base of the wall, directly below, gaped the dark mouth of the expulsion chute.

She squinted in the moonlight, but there was no sign of the professor. 'Can you see anything, Gilbert?' she whispered.

The little lizard ran forward through the grey dust and cocked his head up at the wall as if to say, *Look*.

'Not up there . . . Oh!' As Echo followed his gaze up the city wall, she saw dark figures emerging, frantic dark figures, more and more of them appearing by the moment, waving bows and arrows. Even in silhouette, they looked very unfriendly indeed.

Echo shrank back below the edge of the crater. She swallowed, suddenly full of doubt. Maybe she'd been wrong. Maybe it wasn't the professor who had been expelled at all. Maybe it was someone worse, somebody dangerous! And now she and Horace were alone in the Barren with a broken airship and no way forward, and no way back. And all of it her fault.

'Echo!' Horace yelled from below in the crater. 'Echo, I see him!'

Echo glanced back down towards the airship. Horace was waving a little pair of brass binoculars.

She half climbed, half fell back down and ran up to him, panting, and covered in a film of grey dust. 'Where'd you get those?'

'They were on the floor,' he said. 'I thought they might come in handy.'

'Can I have a look?' Echo took them and scanned around. Everywhere she looked was bare grey rock.

'There!'

Echo focused the binoculars where Horace was pointing and grinned in relief. Beyond the far side of the crater, small but getting larger, a figure with a distinctive halo of frizzy hair was walking towards them.

CHAPTER ELEVEN

'It sounds like you've had quite the adventure!' said the professor, with a grin, after Echo had explained what had happened. 'It's just as well the *Hummerbird* doesn't take flammable lifting gas!'

Echo grimaced. 'I'm sorry about your ship.'

'No need to apologize. I should be thanking you both for being daring enough to come out and find me. That expulsion chute is quite the ride, you know, although those rivets are murder on the old posterior.'

Echo took a sidelong glance at Horace, who had his arms tightly crossed and was watching the professor suspiciously.

'Luckily, I have a spare balloon envelope,' the professor went on. Then he scratched his head. 'Unluckily, I punctured it during an unfortunate incident with a barbed albatross.'

Echo frowned and went back to examining the balloon, wishing beyond all wishes that she could undo the damage.

Gilbert ran down her arm and hopped on to the fabric. He sniffed the blackened silk and recoiled with a squeal.

Echo shook her head sadly. If only she hadn't gone so close to the beacon, they'd be on their way to Port Tourbillon already.

The professor continued mumbling to himself. 'Perhaps we can mend the puncture in the old envelope. Let me get the repair kit.'

He disappeared into the *Hummerbird* and returned with a small zipped suitcase. As he opened it, Echo realized it was just a bigger version of her own embroidery kit, complete with a gleaming pair of long-bladed scissors, several bulky needles and a large spool of thread.

'Now, we just need something to patch it with,' said the professor, releasing the ropes and rolling up the charred turquoise silk. 'But what?'

Echo glanced down at her ceremonial gown and wriggled out of her voluminous petticoat. 'How about this?'

'Perfect!' said the professor.

Horace cleared his throat. 'I suppose I could help with the sewing too,' he said. 'The sooner we mend it, the sooner we're back to Lockfort. Can you show me what to do, Echo?'

Echo nodded. 'Take one of these.' She passed him a needle and thread and started sewing, trying to ignore the guilt that niggled at her. She had no plans to return to Lockfort any time soon, but Horace didn't need to know that yet.

Between the professor, Horace and Echo, it didn't take long

to repair the spare balloon. As Echo cut a rectangle out of her petticoat and deftly secured it to the tear in the fabric, she had to admit that her embroidery skills were finally useful for something. It turned out that Horace had the knack too, and, as they worked together through the night, their squabbles were forgotten. The first light of dawn was emerging on the horizon as Echo put the last stitch into the patch, knotted the silk thread and held it out for Gilbert to bite through. The balloon didn't look too smart, but it would do.

'A marvellous job!' said Professor Daggerwing. 'Now, let's get her hitched up and inflated.'

After several minutes of struggling with ropes and buckles, they managed to attach the balloon to the airship gondola.

Professor Daggerwing stood back and admired it. 'Now, I really should get you two as close to Lockfort as I dare,' he said.

'No!' Echo shook her head in horror. He couldn't! Not after she'd got this far. 'I don't *want* to go back,' she said.

'What?' The professor stared at her. 'Surely you want to go home?'

'Lockfort doesn't feel like my home,' said Echo. 'I want to go to Port Tourbillon, with you.' She didn't want to tell him about the hairpin, not yet. 'I just need you to fly me there. You don't have to do anything else. I'll do chores, mend sails, scrub dishes, anything.'

'Well, that's a lovely offer, but—'

'Hang on a minute. What about me?' said Horace. 'You

100

two might be prepared to fall over the edge of the world, but I'm not.'

'It's not the edge of the world!' exclaimed Echo. Why did he always have to ruin everything? Couldn't he understand that this was important to her? 'You'll see – there are other cities out there.'

'I don't care if there are. I want to go back,' said Horace, turning to the professor, who was looking between the two of them with his eyebrows knotted together in a frown. 'I only came by accident. I didn't know she was going to fly out here.'

Echo set her jaw. Everything was going wrong. But she wasn't about to go back to Lockfort again after coming this far. She took a deep breath and put on her kindest voice. 'You're here now, Horace. You'll just have to come with us to Port Tourbillon. We'll bring you back straight afterwards.'

'But I don't *want* to go to this Port Toblerone place, even if it does exist,' Horace said. He folded his arms and pouted. 'If it's so good, why haven't we ever heard about it?'

Echo looked at Horace's obstinate face in despair. How could she convince him?

Gilbert cocked his head at faint voices and a rumbling coming across the Barren from the city walls.

That was it! Echo remembered the armed soldiers gathering. She turned to the professor. 'We can't go back, even if we wanted to. It's not safe.'

She told the professor and Horace about the figures she and

Gilbert had seen. 'We're hidden while we're in this crater,' she said. 'But I have the feeling that, once they see us, they won't be welcoming us back into Lockfort.'

The professor nodded gravely as he listened. 'I'm certainly not popular with King Alfons.' He considered the situation for a minute. 'Going straight back in daylight would be risky.'

'More like certain death,' said Echo.

'Don't be ridiculous,' said Horace. 'You're exaggerating. They won't shoot at children.'

'The young lad does have a point,' said the professor. 'I should take you back right away. Let's hope there's enough lifting gas in the tanks to get us airborne.' He clambered up and disappeared inside the *Hummerbird* before Echo had a chance to argue. They followed him up the ladder.

In the airship, the professor sang under his breath as he flipped switches and adjusted levers on the dashboard. There was a *whoosh* as the patchwork balloon inflated and the engine hummed into life.

'Aha!' The professor looked upwards with a grin on his face. 'We have lift-off!' The floor wobbled beneath them as they rose once more into the air.

Echo ran to the back of the ship and pressed her nose to the porthole, then peered through the binoculars. She squinted through the brass eyepieces and swallowed. As the *Hummerbird* rose from its hiding place in the crater, there was a shout from atop the city walls. Three guards were positioned behind the parapet. As she watched, she saw more emerging, wheeling a low black cylinder.

'What is it?' asked Horace.

'I think,' said Echo, passing him the binoculars, her heart thudding in her ears, 'it's a cannon.'

'A cannon!' Horace peered through the binoculars. 'I've never seen the royal cannons taken out before.' He paled. 'But why would they—'

'To shoot at us, stupid!'

Horace gaped in dismay. 'But Father wouldn't . . .'

'Father?' Professor Daggerwing spun to face them, his eyes as round as the *Hummerbird*'s portholes. 'Do I need to add kidnapping a prince to my list of misdemeanours?'

But Horace was too busy staring through the binoculars to answer. As he passed them to Echo, she took in his terrified face and softened. 'He can't know you're in here,' she said. 'He won't actually shoot at us, like you said.'

But, as she put them to her eyes, she saw that slowly, very slowly, the guards were turning the cannon to face them, its mouth a gaping black hole. A fourth guard staggered forward with a huge cannonball in his arms.

'Quick, Professor, fly!' she shouted.

'Change of plan! Port Tourbillon it is! Hold tight!' yelled the professor and the little airship surged forward.

Echo staggered sideways and Horace grabbed on to a nearby pipe as the airship tore out of the crater.

The professor held the wheel steady, murmuring to himself as he adjusted levers and turned dials.

The *Hummerbird* soared upwards, making Echo's stomach lurch. Something large and bright whistled past and exploded beneath them with a dull boom. Horace let out a yelp and fell into a cupboard. Echo held tight to the pipework, Gilbert clinging to her neck and hiding his head in her hair. The professor flicked switches, his brow creased in concentration.

Echo scrambled into the co-pilot's seat and glanced back at Horace, who had crawled back out of the cupboard with a look of utter horror on his face. 'He's ... he's *shooting* at us!' he whimpered.

'Probably just a warning shot,' said the professor, rubbing his nose and studying the controls intently. 'No need to panic.'

'Yes,' said Echo, with fake brightness. 'I'm sure they weren't really trying to hit us, Horace. Look, sit here.' She shuffled to the left and made room for him.

Horace wedged himself in next to her and stared listlessly out of the window.

Echo cast a sideways glance at him and found his face so miserable that her insides swirled with guilt. He hadn't wanted any of this. He hadn't known what her plans were. And, whatever she might have said earlier about the Lockfort guards not trying to hit the little ship, she was pretty sure King Alfons had been aiming straight at them. She turned back to search the horizon for a glimpse of the world beyond the mist, but ahead of them was just an endless grey emptiness, and the bare, rocky terrain of the Barren spread out as far as she could see.

'Are we safe?' said Echo, as the boom of the cannon faded into the distance.

The professor nodded. 'Yes, we must be out of range by now.' He ran both hands through his hair. 'Oh dear, we are in a pickle though. It doesn't look like I'm going to get you two back home after all. Not for the moment anyway. Those rumours about Lockfortians being inhospitable are certainly true!' He cleared his throat. 'Present company excepted, of course.'

'Let's get to Port Tourbillon,' said Echo. 'To . . . to fix your airship. It would be risky to try to sneak back to Lockfort with the balloon all patched up, wouldn't it?'

The professor nodded thoughtfully. 'Well, yes . . .'

'And we could stay with you. Just for a couple of days until the king cools down.'

The professor opened and closed his mouth, then gawped at them as if they were strange specimens in a jar. 'I don't really know how to look after children.'

'We'll look after ourselves,' said Echo. 'We won't be any trouble at all. Will we, Horace?'

Horace, who was still looking rather green, gave a glum shrug.

'I suppose it's the only course of action,' said the professor, looking slightly dazed by the turn of events. He took in Horace's pale face and suddenly clapped his hands together. 'I don't know about you, but I'm parched. Who's for a nice cup of sweet tea?'

The professor jumped up and pulled a nearby lever. A little copper table unfurled neatly from the wall. He found a kettle rolling about on the floor and filled it from a tank of water stowed behind the entrance ladder. 'Now, I'll need some assistance with this. Safety first and all that.' He strode to the rear of the aircraft, popped open a porthole and began to wriggle out.

'What are you doing?' yelped Horace, over the hum of the engine.

The professor chuckled and shouted back over his shoulder, 'The engine's the hottest part of the ship. Perfect for boiling kettles on. Grab my boots, will you?'

Horace and Echo looked at each other, then took a boot each and held on tightly as Professor Daggerwing dangled out of the porthole to balance the kettle on the engine exhaust.

A minute later, Echo and Horace hauled the professor and a steaming kettle of water back into the *Hummerbird*, where the professor found a teapot and passed round cups of the strong brew.

'I'm afraid I'm all out of cake,' he said, riffling through the cupboards. 'I got rather peckish on the journey over, you see.

However, I do have these.' He brandished a large jar. 'Anyone for a pickled squibnut?'

'A pickled *what*?' said Horace, looking horrified.

'I'm all out of pickled lily livers,' said the professor. 'I do have pickled sweetroots, but I tend to save those for dire emergencies. They are a rather, er, acquired taste.'

'Do you have anything that isn't pickled?' asked Echo.

'I'm afraid not.' The professor searched his shelves. 'Anyway, pickles are an explorer's best friend.'

'They are?' said Horace, wrinkling his nose.

The professor threw his head back and broke into song:

> *'Oh, pickles are not fickle, they will always be your*
> *   friend,*
> *And, when I'm in a pickle, on a pickle I depend!*
> *Oh, they won't wilt or wither, they stay scrumptious*
> *   in their jar,*
> *Preserved for years and years and years with lots of*
> *   vin-e-gar!'*

Echo gaped in amazement at the professor's unexpected musical outburst, almost spilling the cup of hot tea she was holding. Then she broke into a grin. Professor Daggerwing was different from anyone in Lockfort, that was for certain. 'Okay,' she said. 'I suppose I'll try a squibnut.'

She nervously bit into the slippery little nut, which

was rather like chewing a dried-up, vinegary slug. Echo was hungry after the evening's adventures though, so she gulped several handfuls, swilling them down with the dregs of her tea.

Gilbert slurped some tea from her saucer, but took one bite of the squibnut, turned green and shivered in a way that suggested he was not a fan at all. Horace wouldn't even try one.

'How are they?' asked the professor.

'Er . . . vinegary,' said Echo. 'Very vinegary.'

'Vinegar is one of nature's wonders,' said the professor. 'A natural weedkiller. I often use it to keep the blondweed at bay in my window boxes when I've got any left over from pickling. It's marvellous stuff.'

'Do you live in Port Tourbillon?' asked Echo, trying to imagine what sort of house the professor's window boxes might be attached to.

'Why, yes. Although I do spend a lot of time in the skies, of course, exploring and documenting. The Explorers' Guild will be astonished when I tell them about Lockfort! I do believe I'm the first person from outside to have set foot in the city since the Great War.'

'But why?'

'After the Great War, it was agreed that Lockfort would be a no-fly zone. Of course, this was all more than a hundred years ago.' He unfurled the map and pointed to the red-inked words *Terra Pericolosa*. 'It's considered *dangerous lands*.

Although it seems that on *your* maps the outside world has been entirely erased.'

'That's because it doesn't exist,' said Horace, folding his arms. 'All Lockfort's enemies were defeated during the Great War. Nothing was left except the Barren. That's what really happened.'

'I know that's what they've told us,' said Echo, thinking back to her lesson with Miss Brittle, 'but I think they're wrong.'

Horace shook his head. 'I don't believe any of it. It can't be true.'

'Now, now, let's not argue,' said the professor. 'Horace will see soon enough. We're all tired,' he added, as Echo stifled a yawn. 'We should get some rest.'

'Rest?' said Echo, looking round the cockpit. 'But where?'

The professor gave two sharp tugs on a chain and two hammocks sprang from hatches in the ceiling to join the one already there. Echo climbed into hers and Horace reluctantly took the one next to her.

'I won't be able to sleep,' he said, pulling a blanket over himself. He lay back in the hammock, then suddenly jerked upright, almost toppling on to the floor.

'Wait, who will drive?'

'Autopilot,' said Professor Daggerwing, adjusting a lever and reducing the engine hum to a soft purr. 'We'll be in Port Tourbillon by breakfast.'

Echo relaxed into the soft fabric, Gilbert curled in the crook of her arm. The hammock was surprisingly comfortable and soon the gentle loll and sway of the airship made her drowsy. Port Tourbillon by breakfast! She'd find Evergreen & Spruce and show them her mother's hairpin. Perhaps someone in the jeweller's would remember her mother. And then ... Echo was about to think of something else, but the excitement of the night caught up with her and she slipped into a deep and velvety sleep.

CHAPTER TWELVE

Echo woke before the others to find the airship humming its way steadily through a silvery-grey dawn. She climbed out of her hammock, moving a sleepy Gilbert on to her shoulder, and crept past Horace, softly snoring, and Professor Daggerwing, who breathed loudly, with his mouth hanging open. She settled herself into the pilot's seat, drawing her knees up to her chest, and stared out into the endless grey of the Barren and—

Echo gasped and leaped out of her seat. 'Gilbert, look!'

In the distance, through the hazy clouds, higgledy-piggledy rooftops formed a jagged silhouette against the rising sun. Towers soared into the sky, a wide arched bridge curved from east to west and above it all – could it really be? Yes, there were hundreds and hundreds of airships, as tiny as flies, hovering and darting through the air above the city. Was this it? Was this Port Tourbillon? She gazed, open-mouthed, unable to tear herself away.

'Oh, Gilbert, it's real,' she breathed. Somewhere, deep down inside her, she had always felt there was something missing. That she belonged somewhere else, but she had never dared believe it was really true. Some part of her had feared it would all – the airship, the professor, the hairpin – turn out to be an elaborate hoax, or a dream, or . . . She couldn't help grinning. But it *was* real. Port Tourbillon was there before her. And every inch closer they flew was an inch closer to finding out about her mother.

Echo wiped her eyes on her sleeve, before leaping out of her seat and running to shake the others from their slumber.

'Horace! Professor! I can see it! We're almost there!'

Horace flailed his arms, tried to sit up, twisted his hammock upside down and landed on the floor. 'What's wrong?' he spluttered. 'Are they shooting at us?'

'Look! I can see Port Tourbillon!'

Horace stood up and rubbed his bleary eyes, then went to the cockpit and squinted out. 'Where? I can't see it ... Oh!' He froze and, for a moment, just stared. 'It's ... it's another city,' he finally said.

'I know! Port Tourbillon! That's what we've been telling you this whole time. Here, take a look with the binoculars,' said Echo, passing them to him.

Professor Daggerwing swung his legs out of his hammock, leaped gracefully down and strode to the cockpit. 'Port Tourbillon indeed,' he said, gazing out of the windscreen and settling himself in the pilot's seat. 'And just in time for breakfast.'

Echo gazed out of the windscreen as a thousand multicoloured rooftops spread out before them. Smoke curled from chimney pots and early-morning light gleamed on roof tiles. Down in the streets she made out tiny figures darting back and forth, some of them on foot, some of them riding in strange horseless contraptions. And, everywhere above, airships flew. Huge great Zeppelins gliding grandly through the sky, mid-size ships setting down and picking up deliveries, and tiny vessels even smaller than the *Hummerbird* buzzing here and there like bees at work.

'Isn't it wonderful?' Echo said, almost hopping from foot to foot in excitement. 'What do you think it'll be like?' She glanced at Horace.

'But, but that means ...' He trailed off, dropping the binoculars on to their strap around his neck. 'But Father said ...' He blinked a few times. 'It was all lies, wasn't it?'

Echo didn't know what to say to this. In her excitement to get to Port Tourbillon, she hadn't thought what it had all meant. But Horace was right: someone had been lying about it all. She took in his dazed expression. Horace had always believed his father so completely, it must be a huge shock. She gave his arm an awkward pat. 'I think it must have been,' she said softly.

The professor looked up from the controls. He cleared his throat. 'I'm sure your father had his own reasons for keeping this from you. Perhaps he was trying to protect you.'

'Perhaps,' Horace said, but his shoulders slumped and he sat down in silence, chewing his thumbnail.

Echo shook her head. If only Horace hadn't stowed away in the cupboard! She set her jaw. She would have to make sure the professor somehow returned him safely to Lockfort once this was all over. First though she had a mother to find.

Echo gazed out of the windscreen as they descended,

thoughts of Horace's predicament soon forgotten as she took in the sights below. Unlike Lockfort, with its identical low grey-roofed houses, Port Tourbillon was a jumbled mass of brightly painted buildings. Here a skinny townhouse in buttercup yellow jostled next to a wide indigo cottage painted with stars, while across the street a turquoise building with triangular windows and a spiralling turret leaned at a very peculiar angle indeed. No two houses were the same. It was as if a giant had crammed them in any which way, and then hurled his paintbox at them. Echo had never seen anything like it.

'Here we are – twenty-seven Hawthorn Square,' said the professor, pointing down at a skinny purple-painted building with a jumble of little white-framed windows and snaking copper drainpipes. 'My humble abode, where I will rustle us up some breakfast. I do hope the cats haven't given up on me while I've been away.'

'Cats?' said Horace, stirring from his silence.

'Cats,' said the professor. 'I have seven of them. An explorer's best friend, don't you know?'

Echo gave Horace a quizzical look. 'Isn't that ... er ... pickles?'

But the professor was too busy adjusting levers and turning dials to reply. He released the balloon pressure gauge, there was a low hiss and the airship began to descend gracefully towards the rooftop of 27 Hawthorn Square.

A prickle of excitement ran down Echo's spine, and she

hugged Gilbert to her chest. Port Tourbillon felt like a city where things happened. Where things would happen to her. Where she'd find answers.

She shook her head in awe, then felt a new stab of pity as she took in Horace's shell-shocked expression. There was a whole amazing world out here. Why had King Alfons ever wanted to keep this from them?

Once the *Hummerbird* was tethered to the rooftop landing dock, they descended through a hatch on the roof into the attic of 27 Hawthorn Square. Professor Daggerwing's house was just as skinny on the inside as it looked from the sky, with high ceilings and a multitude of small, boxy rooms spread over its five storeys. Echo loved it at first sight.

'Now, who's for breakfast?' said the professor.

Gilbert gave an enthusiastic chirrup from his foothold on Echo's shoulder.

'Me too,' said Echo, about to take the staircase down.

'Not that way,' said the professor, pulling a lever. 'The slideway goes directly to the ground floor. Avoids all those stairs, you see.'

There was a whirr of springs and a clank of metal parts and a trapdoor sprang open in the floor to reveal a dark hole.

'Follow me,' said the professor, grabbing a cushion from a pile and leaping into the opening, feet first, with a, '*Wheeeee!*'

Echo and Horace looked at each other with a shrug, then Echo took a cushion and jumped in too.

'Eek!' she squealed as she slid into a clear, curving tube that spiralled down the centre of the house. Room after room flashed by until she finally landed, giggling, in a huge pile of cushions. A few seconds later, Horace arrived with a *flump*.

Echo sat up and looked around. They seemed to have landed in a corridor in the basement. 'That was fun!' she said.

Gilbert shook himself and chirruped in a way that Echo was sure meant, *Let's do it again!*

Even Horace had a smile on his face as the professor took his hand and heaved him up. 'All my own invention,' he said proudly. 'I used to have a pulley system in both directions, but I decided sliding down was much more fun. The kitchen's this way.'

As they made their way to the kitchen, Echo couldn't stop staring at everything. What she really loved about Hawthorn Square was the homely messiness of it. There was no Miss Brittle here to tut or tidy. Every surface was covered with either paper or cats. Or sometimes paper *and* cats. There were diagrams, notes and maps. There were drawings and charts and newspaper cuttings. But most of all there were cats. All seven of them.

'May I introduce you to Beetlecrusher, Foxtrot, Dandelion, Sugarsnap,

Pumpernickel, Stargazy and Fred,' the professor said, when they arrived in the kitchen with a throng of purring, leg-twining felines. 'It seems the good Mrs Milkweed has been keeping you well fed and watered,' he said, as he stroked all seven mewing heads in turn.

'Ah, Professor! You're home!' Echo turned and goggled as a tiny woman with rainbow-striped hair and a huge, sparkling diamond in her nose appeared in the doorway. The woman's own eyebrows shot up when she spotted Echo and Horace. '*Children*, Professor?'

'Ah yes.' The professor fumbled for words. 'There was an occurrence. Well, an incident . . . a number of incidents in fact. Echo and Horace will be staying for a night or two. It's . . . ah, something of a long story.'

'Isn't it always?' The woman's eyes sparkled. 'I'm Meera Milkweed.' She thrust out a hand to shake Echo's and her armful of silver bracelets jangled. 'I'm the professor's housekeeper, cat keeper and sometimes cartographer.' She looked them up and down. 'I suppose, if you're staying, I'd better make up some beds.'

She disappeared out of the room in a whirl of colour.

'Now for breakfast,' said the professor, opening cupboards and examining jars.

Echo's eyes widened and she hugged herself in glee as she took in all the strange foods and spices that filled the professor's shelves.

'I really hope it's not pickles this time,' whispered Horace.

In fact, the kitchen *was* full of jars of pickles, stacked up to the ceiling in an array of colours. It seemed the selection in the *Hummerbird* was only the start. The professor had just pulled out an assortment of jars when Mrs Milkweed returned, carrying armfuls of sheets.

'Oh, Professor, you can't feed children on pickles,' she said, rolling her eyes in amusement at Echo and Horace. 'There's fresh wildeboar bacon in the larder. Now, you put these sheets on the top-floor beds and let me deal with breakfast.'

The four of them were soon sitting companionably at the large wooden table, tucking into huge plates of eggs, smoked wildeboar bacon and crisp, sugary waffles dowsed in hazel syrup. It was a world away from the bland coddled eggs and goblets of milk Echo and Horace were used to. The professor poured out generous mugs of tea for all of them, while explaining their adventures to Mrs Milkweed, who seemed to be used to tales of undiscovered cities, dungeons and daring escapes. 'So,' he said, 'it'll take a couple of days to get the old *Hummerbird* fixed before I can take these two home.'

'If we can *get* home,' said Horace, staring glumly into his mug.

'The professor will find a way,' said Mrs Milkweed, patting his hand. 'There always is one, however difficult things seem. Now, what can we do to cheer you up in the meantime? There's lots to see in the city.'

'I don't know,' said Horace. He absent-mindedly broke off a piece of waffle and tossed it to Gilbert, who was sitting in the middle of the table, ready to nab any leftovers. Gilbert caught it with a snap and swallowed greedily.

'There must be something.' Echo wiped the syrup from her mouth with one of the professor's butterfly-print napkins. 'That's it,' she said. 'Butterflies! Horace loves butterflies, don't you?' She turned to the professor. 'You said you were on the way to study them before.'

The professor nodded sagely. 'Indeed, I was. The best butterfly country is out in the Violet Isles, but here in the city there is, of course, the Tourbillon Butterfly House, and the Great Library has plenty of reading matter.'

Horace brightened slightly and nodded. 'I suppose that does sound interesting.'

'Take a look at this.' Mrs Milkweed took down a worn purple book from one of the overcrowded shelves. 'This'll tell you about some of the varieties we have out here.'

121

Horace opened the book and immediately lost himself in its pages and Echo saw her chance to ask about the pin.

'I was wondering, Mrs M,' she said, casually nibbling on a waffle, 'if you've ever heard of somewhere called Evergreen and Spruce?'

'Want some jewellery, do you?' said Mrs Milkweed, jangling her bracelets with a grin. 'I get all mine from Ginshi Flux at the market. Tell her I sent you and she'll give you a discount.'

'No, I mean thank you, but I need to find that particular shop,' said Echo. 'I . . . I just want to look in the window.'

'I don't blame you! They've got some beautiful things, but they're pricey. You'll find it on Goldsmith's Lane.'

'Can you show me where that is?' asked Echo, stuffing the last piece of waffle into her mouth and jumping up from her chair. 'I'm going to go right away.'

Mrs Milkweed looked at her for a moment and cleared her throat. 'We'll have to get you kitted out first. Your clothes make you a bit . . .' She paused and searched for the right word. 'Conspicuous.'

Echo looked down at her crumpled golden silk gown. 'Oh.'

'And I think young Horace could do with wearing something more . . . practical too.' She turned to the professor. 'You'll need to go to the Mech Market to order a new envelope for the airship anyway. Why don't you get them some new clothes while you're there?'

'Clothes shopping?' The professor almost choked on his tea. 'But Mrs Milkweed, I hardly think—'

'Nonsense, Professor. These children rescued you. The least you can do is take care of them for a few days while they're here.'

'But I can't . . .' He trailed off in dismay.

Mrs Milkweed took his plate. 'If you can care for seven cats, Professor, then two children should be a doddle.'

'But I was hoping you would—'

'I'll be far too busy redrawing the map you lost. Now, off you go, all of you!'

CHAPTER THIRTEEN

As they walked to the market through the streets of Port Tourbillon, Echo stared in awe around her, at the crazy kaleidoscope of buildings towering above, their chimneys snaking towards the sky; at the steam carriages rumbling over the cobbles; at the hustle and bustle and people and dirt and *differentness*.

But the differentness felt like home somehow. Like she'd been here before. Like she belonged. She gazed around her with a huge grin on her face. No longer was she the only one with dark curls and freckled skin: Port Tourbillon shimmered with a whole rainbow of people. She had to stop herself from staring in wonder at the people she passed. A woman with tall studded boots and hair woven with pink feathers rode by in a steam carriage, waving in greeting to the professor; a boy with skin darker than Echo's and startling purple eyes rattled past with a barrow of strangely mottled vegetables; two white-moustached men with completely bald heads nodded to them as they strode along, arm in arm, swinging matching jewelled canes.

The professor seemed to know half the city. 'Good morning, good morning!' he cried, tipping his hat to a man with a waist-length, plaited beard, waving to three women pedalling a three-seated bicycle and shaking hands vigorously with a fellow in jingling cowboy boots who introduced himself to the children as Palomino Jones.

Echo soon realized what Mrs Milkweed had meant about her golden silk skirts being conspicuous though, as she raised quite a few eyebrows herself. Everyone wore such practical clothes in Port Tourbillon. There were no tight, rib-crushing gowns or swishing skirts to get in the way. In fact, most of the city's women wore breeches, Echo noticed with envy.

'Will I be able to have breeches too?' she asked.

'We can certainly obtain some ladies' breeches,' said the professor. 'I know a very capable tailor who will run you up a few pairs in no time.'

'He'll need to make sure there's a pocket for Gilbert,' she said, stroking the little lizard, who was slung round her neck, happily taking in their surroundings and enjoying being out in the open for once.

'Naturally! And how about you, young Horace?' said the professor. 'Do you have any special requests?'

'Can't I stay as I am?' said Horace, looking down at his velvet-clad legs. 'They're just ordinary trousers.'

'They might be in Lockfort,' said Echo. 'For a prince. We need to look normal here.'

'But ... but,' Horace spluttered, 'these are my best pair. Father will be cross ...' His face crumpled. 'I suppose that doesn't matter any more.'

Echo shook her head. Why couldn't he see how incredible everything was here? She found herself wishing once again that she'd noticed he had stowed away. Why *had* he followed her anyway? He knew he wasn't cut out for adventures. With some effort, she softened her voice. 'The professor will take you home, Horace, just as soon as the balloon's fixed. But for now we're here. Think of the Butterfly House! You can't go there dressed like royalty.'

'I suppose not.' Horace gave a half-hearted shrug and followed after them, but his shoulders drooped and his eyes stayed fixed firmly on the pavement the whole way there.

The Mech Market was a vast palace of a building, with a high arched roof of glittering black glass. As they entered, Echo saw huge gas lamps hanging overhead, their light reflecting off the stalls full of metallic machine parts – cogs and propellers, spanners and screws, flywheels and fenders and rusty old canisters of flying gas. There were compasses, barometers, star charts and navigation maps everywhere she looked.

'What is this place?' she whispered in awe.

'Welcome to the Mech Market,' said the professor, 'where engineers come to buy and sell everything they need. Port Tourbillon isn't the trading capital of the world for nothing, you know! It's famous for the best technology money can buy. That's why explorers like myself base ourselves here. It's the gateway to the whole world!'

The gateway to the world! Echo looked around in amazement. In her excitement to get to Port Tourbillon, she hadn't even thought about places beyond. Just how big *was* the world? She glanced at Horace, who was staring at everything with a dazed expression. 'What's wrong?'

He gave a tight-lipped shrug. 'It's all just so . . . so different.'

'I know!' Echo grinned and hugged herself. 'Isn't it wonderful?' She raced off after the professor before Horace could answer.

They continued past racks of scopes and eyeglasses, goggles and leather-flapped flying hats, stalls selling travelling provisions – tins of jellied rabbit, leathery strips of salted meat that made Gilbert's nostrils twitch, paper bags of boiled sweets (perfect for airsickness) and hard little sky biscuits – until they came to the fabric area.

'Now this is what I need,' said the professor, as he pointed to a stall of rainbow-hued silks.

As they waited for him to find exactly the right silk for the *Hummerbird*'s envelope, Echo stroked a bolt of purple fabric. 'I still don't quite see why it's called the Mech Market,'

127

she said, as he finally emerged from the stall, his order finished.

'Ah,' said Professor Daggerwing, 'let me show you. Follow me.' He strode off across the market hall.

Echo and Horace trotted after him. They came to the end of the hall, went through an archway of cogs and emerged into an outer courtyard.

Echo sucked in a breath. Everywhere spanner-wielding engineers tinkered with mechanical beasts. There was a stall full of clockwork pigeons, a table covered with glittering metallic beetles and a trio of robotic monkeys busily tapping out messages on typewriters.

But, most magnificent of all, in one corner stood an enormous copper dragon. Its metallic scales shifted over one another as its owner, a dark-skinned, oil-smudged girl with green ribbons woven into her black hair, fiddled with the controls to its hydraulic wings.

The girl, who looked a few years older than Echo, saw Echo's open-mouthed stare and glared at her, before returning to her work.

Echo quickly turned away and examined the table of clockwork beetles behind her. As she did so, Gilbert emerged from her pocket, cocked an eye at the robotic insects and, before she could stop him, leaped on to the table.

 'Gilbert, no!' Echo lunged forward, grabbed him and prised open his scaly jaws. 'It's not food!' she said.

Gilbert's crest crumpled and he forlornly spat out the beetle.

'Mighty smooth clockwork there,' said the stallholder, a portly man with a handlebar moustache and a rather battered-looking top hat. 'Mind if I examine its workings?'

'Workings? Oh!' Echo realized he was talking about Gilbert. 'Oh, he's not a toy.'

'Toy?' The man's eyebrows flew into the brim of his hat. 'These aren't toys, my dear. These are sophisticated pieces of communication equipment.'

'Postal pigeons and beetle bugs,' explained the professor, arriving beside her. 'The former are used to send and receive messages. The latter are for spying on people.'

'Surveillance,' corrected the man. 'They're very popular – can I interest you in one?'

'Oh, no thank you, my good man. My postal pigeon is still going strong.'

The man shrugged and went back to polishing his beetles.

Echo looked up and noticed that the girl with the dragon was staring at her. She hesitated for a moment before shyly walking over. 'This is incredible,' she said. 'Did you build it?'

'Yes,' said the girl, raising one eyebrow as she looked Echo up and down. 'Nice dress. Going to a costume ball, are you?' She went back to her work.

Echo flushed. Was the girl mocking her? She tried again. 'Can I have a look inside?'

The girl answered without looking up. 'No,' she said. 'You may not.'

Echo swallowed, starting to feel silly. 'What does it do?'

The girl put down her rag. 'You're not from around here, are you? *She* is a dragon mech and her name's *Smokesister*,' she said. 'Full hydraulic wing action, flexible talons, night vision. Plus, she does this.' The girl stood back and casually pressed a button attached to the dragon's belly cavity by a long cable.

The dragon's metal jaws opened, there was a *whoosh* of gas and suddenly flames burst out of the beast's mouth, almost singeing Echo's skirts. Gilbert hissed and hid in Echo's hair. Horace, who had wandered up to them, jumped backwards with a yelp, bumping into a pile of metal cogs, which went spinning away across the floor.

The girl laughed as Echo stepped backwards in alarm. 'Realistic, isn't she? Don't be scared though; she's completely under my control.'

Was the girl trying to upset her on purpose? Echo couldn't make her out. She dusted down her skirts to hide her nerves and forced a smile on to her face. 'Does she fly?' she asked.

The girl shook her head. 'Not yet, but she will. And three times faster than the fastest airship. Got to get the engine working on all cylinders before I can get her off the ground though. Then I'll have my name on a plaque at the Engineers' Guild – Abena Tuesday, master engineer.'

The burly man from the beetle stall grinned, a wicked glint in his eye. 'Gotta get her working first, Abena.'

'I will if you'd stop interrupting me,' Abena snapped, grabbing her spanner and going back to her work with a huff.

'Well, bye,' said Echo. But the older girl had turned away and disappeared beneath the dragon without a word.

Echo's cheeks flushed with heat. She glanced down at the glossy folds of her silk gown and felt suddenly foolish.

'Echo, come on!' called Horace.

Echo turned away and went back to the entrance, where Horace and the professor were standing.

'Ah, young Echo! Ready to go and buy some breeches?' said the professor. 'I think it's about time we got you kitted out Port Tourbillon style.'

Echo nodded and her smile returned. 'Definitely.' She wanted to get out of these Lockfort clothes right away; the sooner she looked the part, the sooner she'd be on her way to Evergreen & Spruce.

CHAPTER FOURTEEN

Back at Hawthorn Square, Echo found the room that the professor had prepared for her, and threw her parcels down on the bed, dislodging the dozing ginger-and-white Stargazy, who leaped down with an injured *miaow*. She stroked his head and took a look around. There was no chandelier or four-poster bed here. Instead, her room was small but cosy, with a neatly made-up copper-framed bed, a shaggy purple rug on the smooth-worn floorboards and a small circular window that looked out on the garden in the square. It was no palace bedchamber, but somehow it was perfect for her, she thought with a grin. She ripped open her parcels, peeled off the gold silk dress, now somewhat rumpled and torn, and discarded it in a corner, before pulling on her new clothes.

Echo bent her knees experimentally and grinned as she admired herself in the mirror. The new breeches fitted perfectly. She could be anything in breeches like these – an explorer, an adventurer, a pirate!

'Oh, Gilbert, I'm sorry!' Echo suddenly caught sight of the little lizard wriggling out of the folds of her dress. He gave a cross chirrup, which to Echo sounded like, *How could you forget me?*

'I didn't.' She scooped him up and slipped him into her specially designed lizard-sized hip pocket. 'Plenty of room for you in here.' She paused. 'I suppose we should check on Horace.'

Gilbert popped his head out and gave a chirrup, which Echo knew meant, *Let's go!* So, after a moment to ready her nerves, she grabbed a cushion and whizzed into the slideway back downstairs.

Horace was in the professor's library with a glossy black cat, Beetlecrusher, on his lap. He looked up from one of the professor's butterfly books as Echo came tumbling in. 'Can you believe it?' he said. 'There are over a thousand butterfly varieties out here. Lockfort only had twelve, and I'd already spotted eleven of them.'

'Wow!' Echo smiled, relieved that Horace had found something to occupy himself with. He was definitely less trouble when he was happy. Gilbert scuttled out and leaped on to the table, where he eyed the books curiously.

Miaow! They all jumped as a loud cry rang out from the ceiling. Echo looked up to see that the noise had come from a large metal speaker.

Horace sighed. 'That'll be another one of the cats wanting to come up. Can you do the honours?' He pointed at what looked like the rear half of a bicycle in the corner of the room. 'It's another of the professor's inventions – he calls it the cat-o-puller. Just pedal until the cat appears.'

Echo got on to the seat and pedalled. There was a whirring of cogs and a clanking of chains and finally a basket emerged from a hole in the corner of the floor with not one but two more cats inside, the sleek white Sugarsnap and the fluffy golden-brown Dandelion. They hopped lightly out of the basket and Sugarsnap jumped on to the table, where she circled Gilbert curiously.

'No! Shoo!' said Echo, waving her away from the little lizard in vain. 'Leave him alone.'

The white cat lowered herself on to her haunches, ready to spring, her blue eyes fixed on Gilbert. But Gilbert scuttled to the end of the table and took a flying leap on to a bookshelf.

Sugarsnap followed, scrambling up the shelves after him, showering books and papers all over the floor. Gilbert sprang for the lampshade and the cat followed, swinging wildly from it. Gilbert dropped down on to the table, leaving Sugarsnap dangling, and scampered up Echo's breeches and on to her shoulder. He gave a triumphant chirrup at the still swinging Sugarsnap. Dandelion, who was twining round Echo's ankles, unable to get to the little lizard, gave a dismal yowl and strolled off.

'Don't scare me like that,' said Echo, shaking her head at Gilbert. She turned to survey the mess. 'The professor's papers! Horace, could you help me with this one?' She knelt on the floor and began to roll up a huge map.

'It's so big,' said Horace, staring at it.

Echo nodded, taking in the scope of the world in pen and ink. She pointed. 'We must be here in Port Tourbillon and those are the Violet Isles,' she said. 'That's where the professor was supposed to be going to see the butterflies.'

'Cinnabar, Ratamacue, Ambercourt.' Horace shook his head as he read some of the place names. 'I can't believe how much there is out there.' He paused. 'It makes Lockfort seem so small.'

Echo smiled ruefully. 'It always felt small to me.'

They rolled the map up and stashed the professor's strewn papers back on the shelves.

There was a knock at the door and Professor Daggerwing poked his head round. 'The marvellous Mrs Milkweed had to go, but she left this for you.' He passed Echo a scrap of paper. On it was a little hand-drawn map showing the way to Goldsmith's Lane.

Evergreen & Spruce! Echo's heart raced. Now she'd get some answers. But what would those answers be? She swallowed down her doubts. There was no time to lose.

'Thanks,' she said to the professor, dashing past him with the map in her hand.

'An urgent matter, is it?' he asked, raising his eyebrows.

'Er . . . yes.' Echo stopped and bit her lip. What if she didn't find anything? The professor seemed nice, but she didn't want to tell him everything. She shrugged. 'Just something I need to do.'

'Well, be careful,' said the professor. 'Port Tourbillon is a meeting place for all kinds of people, and not just the nice ones.' He looked at his pocket watch. 'I can go with you if you can wait till three bells.'

'Thanks, Professor, but there's really no need,' said Echo. 'Why don't you get back to your maps? I promise I'll stay out of trouble.'

After leaving Gilbert with Horace, and strict instructions not to antagonize the cats, Echo raced down the steps and out on to Hawthorn Square. Following Mrs Milkweed's map, she soon found herself in a narrow, cobbled alleyway clustered with brightly painted shops. There were windows full of feather-plumed hats, tiny glass horses and carved wooden chests with gleaming brass hinges; there were shops selling boxes of marzipan fruit and sugared almonds, purveyors of strange crystals, flying goggles, even, to Echo's amazement, genuine antique dragon-skin umbrellas. But finally, finally, she came to a parade of jewellers.

Echo checked each shop name in turn:

138

GOSHAWK & SON

PENDRAGON ESQ.

BRITCH'S BUDGET SILVERWARE

MESSRS EVERGREEN & SPRUCE
(BY ROYAL APPOINTMENT)

Evergreen & Spruce!

Echo's heart raced as she approached the window, where a tall, skinny man with gleaming black hair was admiring the display. She peered through the glass at the delicate opal rings and ropes of sea pearls arranged on green velvet in the window, then put her hand in the pocket of her breeches and squeezed the hairpin to steady her breathing. It was the only lead she had. A chance to find out the truth.

'Lovely stuff, isn't it?' The man ran one spidery finger over the glass. 'I'd love to get my hands on some of these, wouldn't you?'

Echo swallowed and nodded.

'After you.' The man gestured to the door. Echo pushed it open and heard a bell tinkle somewhere deep inside. After a moment, there was the swish of a curtain at the back of the shop and a tiny woman with a neat bun of blue hair shuffled out of the shadows.

'Can I help you?' she asked, looking between Echo and the man over her half-moon glasses.

139

'You go first,' said the man. 'I'm just browsing.'

'Yes, I . . .' Echo tailed off and thrust her hairpin at the lady. 'I want to know where this came from.'

'Of course, dearie.' The woman took the hairpin and turned it over slowly in her hands before stopping to look sharply at Echo. 'Where did you get this?'

Echo swallowed. Why was the woman looking at her like that? 'I . . . it was my mother's.'

She went to take the hairpin back, but the woman snatched it away, came round the counter and grabbed Echo's arm.

'Hey, get off me!' said Echo, stumbling backwards in alarm. What had she done? The woman looked absolutely furious.

'Mr Spruce, some assistance, please!' the woman yelled, still glaring at Echo and holding her firmly. The black-haired man looked up, interested, as Echo tried to wriggle out of the woman's grip.

'Let go!' squealed Echo. 'I just wanted to know where it came from, that's all. The maker's mark said Evergreen and Spruce.'

A young man with bright red curls and a golden monocle emerged from behind the curtain.

'What is it, Lucinda? I'm really terribly busy back here—' His mouth dropped open as the woman – Lucinda – silently showed him the hairpin.

'Could it really be?' The man stepped forward and took the pin, adjusting his monocle to examine it. 'It is!' He took a step back, still staring incredulously at the pin as he let the monocle drop on to its chain around his neck. He passed the pin to Lucinda open-mouthed.

Lucinda nodded. 'It is. And the question is, how did *you* get hold of it?' She gave Echo a firm shake.

'I told you, it was my mother's,' said Echo, unease flooding through her. What was wrong? Why were they so angry with her?

'We should call the Queen's Guard,' said Lucinda.

'But why? I haven't done anything.'

'Calm down, Lucinda. You're scaring her.' Mr Spruce laid a hand on Lucinda's shoulder, then turned to Echo. 'This hairpin is part of the Black Sky Hoard,' he said.

'I . . . I don't know what that is.'

Lucinda snorted. 'Where have you been living for the last fifteen years? In a cave?'

Echo shook her head. *Almost*, she thought. 'I've never heard of it,' she whispered. 'Honest.'

'The Black Sky Wolves were a notorious band of sky pirates,' said Mr Spruce. 'Many years ago, they held up the Royal Zeppelin and stole the Crown Jewels, of which this is one. One of the least valuable pieces, but still.'

'But you haven't told us yet how *you* got your sticky fingers on it,' hissed Lucinda. 'And where's the rest?'

'I don't *know*. I . . .' Echo trailed off.

'Lucinda, I really don't think she knows anything about it.'

'Nonsense,' snapped Lucinda. 'Call the Queen's Guard. They'll soon make her talk.'

'You're being too hasty. I'll put the kettle on and we'll all sit down with a nice cup of tea.'

Echo shrank back, away from Lucinda and her steel grip.

'This is no time for tea. We're talking about the Crown Jewels, Mr Spruce! They've been lost for fifteen years.' Lucinda put the hairpin down on the counter and gestured crossly at it. 'No one has tracked down the jewels – or the Black Sky Wolves – ever since.'

Echo's eyes darted round the room. The black-haired man was looking intently over at them and the pin. Was he listening? Sweat prickled down Echo's spine. She glanced back at the arguing jewellers.

Mr Spruce studied Echo with folded arms. 'She doesn't look like a sky pirate,' he said, turning back to Lucinda. 'Perhaps it's all some kind of mistake.'

'It's thievery, that's what it is.' Lucinda narrowed her eyes.

Echo saw her chance as they continued to argue. She lunged forward and grabbed the hairpin.

'Hey! Stop, thief!' yelled Lucinda.

But it was too late. Echo raced for the shop door, dodged past the black-haired man and pelted off down the street, the hairpin gripped in her hand.

She sprinted helter-skelter through the alleyways, her heart hammering and her boots slipping over the cobblestones as she ducked and dived between the passers-by. Behind her she heard Lucinda cry, 'Get her!' and the shrill blast of a whistle. But she didn't falter, dodging this way and that, that way and this, through the crowd, ducking past a man with a great plume of peacock feathers waving on his hat, swerving between two women riding unicycles and narrowly missing a surprised-looking boy pushing a barrow full of lemons.

Eventually, she burst out on to the main street, almost under the huge brass wheels of a steam carriage. The driver blared his horn at her, but she didn't stop, just carried on running, running, running, tripping and stumbling over the slippery cobbles, not knowing where she was going, just that she had to get away.

Finally, she clattered past an arch of cogs and suddenly realized she had come to the back entrance of the Mech Market, where the strange metallic animals were displayed. She darted inside and stopped for a moment, her lungs burning and her breath ragged. The whistle sounded somewhere off behind her, but she knew she couldn't run for much longer. She had to find somewhere to hide. But where?

She put her head down and walked, as fast and as inconspicuously as she could, into the maze of the market, past stalls of clockwork dogs in various states of repair, gleaming brass postal pigeons, even a huge, wheeled, metallic tortoise.

There were shouts behind her. Were they getting closer? Echo caught a glimpse of a glossy blue bun in the crowd. She cast around desperately and spotted the stall of postal pigeons and beetle bugs unattended. She raced over and crawled beneath the tarpaulin where she crouched, panting.

Echo had not even got her breath back when there were footsteps and a pair of battered and oil-stained boots appeared beneath the edge of the tarpaulin. She'd been spotted! But whose boots were they? They were far too grubby to belong to one of the Queen's Guard.

'What *are* you doing under there?' an amused voice came from above.

Echo flinched as the tarpaulin was flipped back to reveal Abena, the girl who'd been so rude to her before, looking down at her. Great, that was all she needed.

'Put it back,' she hissed. 'They'll find me!'

Abena smirked and looked Echo up and down. 'I see you've got yourself some more practical clothing. I almost didn't recognize you out of your fancy ballgown.'

Echo ignored this slight. '*Please*, Abena, they're after me!'

'Who are?'

'The Queen's Guard! And a ... a mean woman with blue hair and glasses. Do you see her?' Echo glanced over her shoulder. There were shouts from outside the market entrance. 'I don't have anywhere else to go.'

'The Queen's Guard?' Abena gave Echo an appraising look that turned into a grin. 'I'm impressed. What've you done?'

'There's no time. Please—'

144

Abena suddenly seemed to understand Echo's desperation and her grin disappeared.

'Okay, I'll help. But you can't stay under there. Come with me.'

CHAPTER FIFTEEN

Abena reached out an oil-stained hand and Echo grabbed it. The older girl pulled Echo from under the table and across the courtyard to her dragon, where she pulled a lever beneath its wing. There was a pneumatic hiss and a hatch opened under its belly. Echo felt strong hands shove her inside before the door shut with a wheeze and a click. She crouched in the darkness, breathing in the smell of engine oil and rust, poised to jump out as soon as she had to. Outside there were muffled voices. Echo pressed her ear to the cool metal of the dragon's insides, her heart racing, but she couldn't make out who was talking or what they were saying.

She sank back on her heels in the gloom. Could what the woman had said about stolen Crown Jewels be true? And, if it was, how had her mother ended up with one of them? Echo silently shook her head. She'd thought she was going to find answers at Evergreen & Spruce, but all she had were more

146

questions, and now the Queen's Guard were after her too! She wrapped her arms round herself, her mind spinning with pieces of a very peculiar puzzle. Just where had her mother got the pin, and how did the Black Sky Wolves fit in? Echo clenched her fists in silence as she waited alone in the darkness.

Finally, after what seemed like hours crouching in the dragon's belly, there was a *swish* and the door opened, dazzling Echo with daylight. She jumped as Abena's dark, goggle-clad head appeared through the hatch.

'You can come out now,' Abena said. 'They've gone. Said they were looking for a jewel thief!'

Echo uncurled herself and half climbed, half fell out, landing blinking between the dragon's gilt-clawed forefeet.

Abena stood over her, hands on hips and a twisted grin on her face. 'So what, exactly, did you do?' she said, grabbing Echo's hand and pulling her to her feet.

'I can't tell you, not here,' said Echo, glancing around anxiously. 'They must still be *looking* for me.'

The smile slipped from Abena's face. 'You're right. Look, you've had a scare. You seem a bit peaky. Are you feeling okay?'

Echo tried to say that yes, she was absolutely fine, but only a croak came out and she staggered sideways.

Abena grabbed her arm. 'Come with me. I know somewhere the Queen's Guard *never* go. We'll get you something to eat and then you can tell me everything.' She turned and searched through a rusty old toolbox. 'Here, put these on.' She handed Echo a telescopic monocle on a brown leather strap and a battered brown aviator's cap.

Echo twisted her hair with trembling fingers, wound it round her head and secured it under the hat, pulling the flaps down over her ears. She set the monocle over her right eye.

'Very fetching,' said Abena. 'Now, come with me.'

Echo followed Abena out of the Mech Market and down a maze of alleyways until they arrived at a dingy old blue-bricked building with dirt-encrusted windows. A sign covered with clockwork parts swung from a high bracket over the door. 'Welcome to the Cog and Gasket,' said Abena, ushering Echo inside with a theatrical bow.

The Cog and Gasket was a vast dark tavern full of chatter and laughter. Echo breathed in the scent of woodsmoke and blinked as her eyes adjusted to the gloom. The place was full of goggle-wearing aviators: leather-clad men and scar-faced women.

In the centre of the far wall, a log fire roared and crackled. The walls were a dark lacquered red, covered in faded paintings of airships and aviators, engine diagrams in battered frames and newspaper cuttings of daring adventures. An old wooden propeller hung proudly above the fireplace. Echo noticed that even the door handles were cog-shaped.

They found a booth in a dark corner and Abena went to

the bar to order from the mechanical bartender. Echo gaped as the man-sized robot whizzed back and forth, taking orders and serving drinks, its cogs busily whirring. The professor was right – Port Tourbillon certainly did have some impressive inventions!

She was still watching the robot, fascinated, when Abena came back, holding a tray of tea and two huge slabs of cake.

'Can I take this off now?' Echo gestured to the monocle. 'It's making me feel a bit sick.'

'Of course.' Abena sat down. 'You don't need a disguise in here. Everyone's a criminal!'

'What?' Echo whispered in panic. She looked around, her eyes wide, taking in the bar, where men and women guffawed and slapped their thighs. Echo imagined them swapping tales of illegal exploits and derring-do. Another thought occurred to her and she scanned the room, her heart racing. Had the Queen's Guard followed her? What did they even look like?

'You okay?' said Abena.

'Surely the Queen's Guard will come straight here if they know it's where criminals hide?'

Abena shook her head with a laugh. 'Don't worry about that. Nobody in here is very fond of the Queen's Guard, and the back door's right there.' She nodded behind them to a trapdoor in the floor. 'Best stay here until nightfall, then make your way home quietly.' Abena took a swig of tea and a huge bite of almond sponge.

Echo did the same, the hot liquid and sugar warming her insides and soothing her frazzled nerves. 'Thank you for helping me,' she said, through a greedy mouthful of cake.

'You're welcome,' said Abena, eyeing her over the brim of her cup. 'I didn't have you down as a thief, you know. Not when I first saw you trussed up in that gown.' She cupped her hands round her steaming tea. 'So what exactly did you steal to have half of Port Tourbillon's Royal Guard on your tail?'

Echo swallowed her mouthful, her mind scrambling to make up a story and coming up with nothing. Could she trust Abena? She had rescued Echo after all. And anyway, did Echo even have a choice? She looked up at the older girl, who was still gazing unblinkingly at her with dark eyes. No, she could trust her. She had to.

Echo took a deep breath and explained everything that had happened. When she got to the part about the Black Sky Wolves, and showed Abena the hairpin, the older girl's mouth fell open.

'Keep your voice down!' she hissed, flipping a napkin over the pin, before taking a peek at it. 'Are you telling the truth?' Her voice dropped to a whisper. 'The Black Sky Wolves?'

'Yes!' insisted Echo. 'But I don't even know who they are.'

'Only the most notorious gang of sky pirates to have ever lived! The worst of them all! They chop off their enemies' fingers and toes and feed them to the cloud eels!' Abena's dark eyes sparkled as she leaned forward over the table and passed back the pin. 'How do you think your mother got it? Do you think she *met* them?'

Echo sighed. 'I don't know anything about her. I haven't seen her since I was a baby. And I don't see how she could be connected to the Black Sky Wolves. All I know is I have her pin and now all sorts of people are after me.' She drew in a shuddering breath. 'I thought going to Evergreen and Spruce would get me closer to finding out about her, but now I'm even further away.' Echo's eyes filled with tears. She'd had such high hopes for her visit. She'd really thought the jeweller would somehow remember selling her mother the hairpin. Have an address, or at least a name. Or something.

'Hey, I'm sorry. I really didn't mean to . . .' Abena trailed off, then awkwardly put an oil-stained hand over Echo's.

Echo rubbed her eyes on her sleeve and swallowed down her sadness. 'It's all right,' she said.

'I'll help you if I can,' Abena said. 'And you're not further away from finding out about her – the Black Sky Wolves are your next clue.' She smiled. 'When I was a little kid, my big brothers used to play at being the Heartless Violet Pilots or the Thunder Sharks all the time. I *dreamed* of joining a band of sky pirates.' She took a slurp of tea. 'Until I found out how horrible and violent they all were, that is.' She grinned. 'The captain of the Black Sky Wolves fires people out of cannons if she doesn't like the look of them.'

Echo swallowed. Had her mother been caught up in something dangerous?

'Sorry,' said Abena, catching the look on Echo's face. 'What I'm saying is, I bet one of my big brothers will know something about them. I'll ask them as soon as I can.'

Echo nodded gratefully and blew her nose on her sleeve. Maybe this wasn't the end of the trail after all.

'Come and find me at the Mech Market in a few days.' Abena drained her teacup and got up.

'Are you leaving?' Echo glanced around, inadvertently catching the eye of a tattooed woman with a gleaming gold tooth. She lowered her gaze and pulled her cap down. Would she be safe here on her own?

Abena nodded. 'It should be fine now.' She looked through the grubby window at the darkening streets, then tipped her hat at Echo. 'See you soon. And be careful with that pin. No one's ever found the rest of the Black Sky Hoard. You *don't* want people to think you might know where it is.'

Echo sat for a while as the tavern filled with the glow of gas lamps and the laughter became more raucous. She was about to risk leaving when she caught a glimpse of oily black hair and froze. It was the black-haired man from the jeweller's. And he was making his way from patron to patron at the bar, stopping to talk to each one. Was it a coincidence he was here, or could he be looking for her? Instinct made Echo shrink back into her seat and pull the monocle back down over her eye. Only when the man had reached the far corner of the bar and turned his back was she finally brave enough to slip out of her seat and scramble outside.

She ducked her head down and scurried through the back alleys, her heart racing, not daring to make eye contact with anyone she passed until she was safely back in Hawthorn Square.

CHAPTER SIXTEEN

'Where on earth have you been?' hissed Horace when Echo finally appeared in the professor's parlour. 'I haven't been able to concentrate at all. I've been rereading the same two paragraphs of *Bagshott's Animalarium* all night!'

'Sorry to ruin your studies,' said Echo, folding her arms across her chest. 'I've been on the run from the Queen's Guard.'

'Oh really,' said Horace, rolling his eyes. 'I fed Gilbert by the way. He seems to have made friends with the cats now.' He gestured at one of the baskets in the corner where Gilbert was curled up with Pumpernickel.

'Thanks,' muttered Echo, scooping the lizard up and putting him on her shoulder. 'And I really was on the run. There's a wanted poster stuck to a wall on Fortescue Street already. I had to hide out in a tavern for criminals until it was safe to come back.'

'You're really wanted?' Horace let his copy of *Bagshott's Animalarium* drop to the table with a thud. 'But what for?'

Echo was about to answer him when Professor Daggerwing emerged from his study, examining some papers covered in calculations. Beetlecrusher, Sugarsnap and Fred twined themselves round his ankles. 'Ah, the old Cog and Gasket, was it?' he said, without looking up.

'Do you know it?' Echo said, surprised.

'I do indeed. The nature of exploration means you sometimes need the services of the, er . . . less salubrious types.' Professor Daggerwing glanced at his watch and blinked. 'Gosh, it's jolly late. I must've been caught up in my calculations. How did you find the old place? I haven't been there in an age.'

Echo grasped for words. 'The cake was very nice.'

'Marvellous. And you're here now so all's well that ends well, eh?'

Echo bit her lip and nodded. How much had he heard? She didn't want him to know too much about her escapade. He might not let her stay if he thought she was a criminal. Her mind whirred. 'Just a misunderstanding at the jeweller's. Nothing to worry about.'

'Good, good,' said the professor, still absent-mindedly staring at the sheaf of papers in his hands.

Echo paused. 'Professor, have you ever met sky pirates on your travels?'

The professor put his papers down. 'I have had the odd

brush with a pirate, come to mention it,' he replied. 'Luckily, they don't bother too much with rickety little ships like mine. It's usually the big merchant vessels they're after. Or each other!'

'And have you ever heard of the Black Sky Wolves?'

The professor suddenly looked serious. 'Why do you ask?'

'Oh, just interested,' said Echo.

The professor sat down at the table. 'They were the most notorious crew of sky pirates around, got outlawed from the city after they hijacked the Royal Zeppelin and stole the Crown Jewels. That was years ago, of course. They escaped beyond the city limits and that's the last that was heard of them.'

'But where did they go?' asked Echo, trying not to let her desperation show. Abena was right – the Black Sky Wolves were her next clue. She had to find out their connection to her mother and somebody must know where to find them. 'I'm going to go out first thing tomorrow and—'

'You *can't* go out,' said Horace. He gave her a meaningful look. 'The posters, remember?'

'But how can I find out about them?' Echo clenched her fists in frustration. She couldn't waste time sitting around. She had a mother to find and the Black Sky Wolves were the only clue she had!

The professor rubbed his chin. 'Well, I suppose I could take you two along to the Explorers' Guild if you're so interested. Someone there might have more information about the Black

Sky Wolves.' He raised his eyebrows. 'Although I can't see why you'd want to know about such a violent bunch of criminals.'

'Can't we go now?'

The professor shook his head. 'I'm afraid it's not done to just show up at the Guild. It's strictly invite only. But there's not long to wait.' He picked up his diary from the bureau and riffled through it. 'Yes! The next meeting is tomorrow night. In the meantime,' he said, 'who's for a late-night snack? I've found a lovely jar of pickled bogplant that would be perfect on crumpets.'

The next day, Echo felt quite trapped at Hawthorn Square. Although Professor Daggerwing had made sure she had plenty to eat and a pile of books to read, he was busy in his study all day and didn't emerge at all. Meanwhile, Horace was either mooning over the butterfly eggs that he'd procured that morning from a sympathetic keeper at the Tourbillon Butterfly House, or losing himself in the professor's book collection, where he was reading everything on bugs he could find.

Unable to explore outside for fear of being caught, Echo had to make do with searching the professor's books too, but there wasn't anything on sky pirates. 'This is hopeless, Gilbert. I can't find anything helpful,' she said, as she slammed yet another dusty book shut.

Gilbert scuttled down from the top bookshelf with a dismal chirrup, as if to say, *No luck here either*.

Echo sighed. Maybe one of the professor's maps would give her an idea. He'd said the Black Sky Wolves had been outlawed from Port Tourbillon, so that meant they had to be hiding somewhere else. She pulled out Mrs Milkweed's latest work and took it into the dining room, where she unrolled it across the table.

'Oh, Gilbert, where do we start?'

The map took up the entire table. Lockfort was merely a small red circle in the south-west, surrounded by the grey of the Barren. And the rest of the world was so vast! Echo traced her finger from Port Tourbillon, across the Verdigris Plains to Galligaskins, where the professor had dozed off and got lost before arriving in Lockfort. But there were so many more places too: the cities of Cinnabar in the west, Bonneville and Ambercourt in the north, Ratamacue in the east and the cluster of islands that made up the Violet Isles in the great Stony Sea to the south. Beyond Ratamacue and Dark Nordland, Echo saw Mrs Milkweed had written *Dragonlands*, *Terra Incognita*. Lands unexplored. It was so much more than she had ever imagined. And it had been there all along! But how would she ever find her mother in a world so large?

'What are you doing?' said Horace, appearing in the doorway behind her. 'Trying to find the way back to Lockfort?'

Echo turned and took in his leather jerkin and boots. 'Something like that.' She frowned. 'You're going out again, aren't you?' she said. 'Without me.'

'You're wanted, remember.' He sighed. 'Only you could get into so much trouble so quickly. I can't believe the professor hasn't noticed all the posters. I saw them everywhere when I went out to the Butterfly House!'

'It wasn't my fault!' said Echo.

'It never is. I'm going to the library.'

'That's it! The library.' Echo grabbed her boots and began furiously lacing them up.

'What are you doing?' said Horace. 'You know you can't leave.'

'I can't bear being trapped inside,' said Echo.

'But what if one of the Queen's Guard sees you? They think you're a thief! It's too risky, Echo. They might arrest you.'

'They won't if they don't recognize me.' She tied her laces in a double bow, in case she had to run. 'How do they describe me on the posters?' she asked.

Horace bit his lip. 'Wanted. Jewel thief. Girl of between ten and fourteen years. Long, unruly dark hair. Grey eyes. Fierce demeanour . . . Hey, what are you doing?'

Echo had jumped up and grabbed a pair of scissors. She ran to the fireplace mirror and looked at herself carefully – eyes of grey flecked with gold, a wild mane of dark curls, almost down to her waist now. Did she look like her mother? Did she have her mother's eyes? Was this her mother's hair?

She shook herself. There was no time for this. If she didn't get out of here and do something, she'd never find her mother at all. She took a lock of hair in one hand and opened the scissors.

'Echo! You can't!' Horace gasped.

'Watch me,' said Echo.

She closed the blades and let the first dark lock of hair fall to the floor.

'You don't look like you!' wailed Horace when she'd finished. Gilbert merely cocked his head to one side and stared at her for a while, before shaking himself and taking his usual place on her shoulder.

'I do look like me,' Echo said, gazing at the strange new girl in the mirror and running a hand over her shorn curls. It felt so odd. Would she ever get used to it? Or stop feeling surprised every time she caught a glimpse of herself in the mirror? She smiled, and the strange girl smiled back. However peculiar it was, something about it just felt right.

'*This* is the me that was under here all along,' she said, finally tearing herself away from the glass.

'Well, I think you looked nicer before.'

Echo rolled her eyes and grabbed a scarf to conceal her face. 'You'll get used to it. Come on, let's go to the library. I'll even let you lead the way.'

Although the sun was bright outside, the morning air was surprisingly cold on Echo's ears now they weren't hidden under a tumble of curls. A chill ran down her neck, as if someone was watching her, but when she looked round there was no one to be seen on the street. She pulled the scarf across her face and quickened her pace until they reached the large wooden doors of the library.

Inside, it was dim and hushed, the tables lit with golden gas lamps. At the central desk, a robotic librarian whirred round on its single wheel, the rhythmic thud as it stamped books echoing round the room.

'I'm going up to the natural history section,' said Horace. He pointed at a spiral staircase that curled upwards beyond the bookshelves on the wall to their right, then looked nervously at Echo. 'You won't cause any trouble, will you?'

'Don't worry about me,' said Echo crossly. 'Go on.'

'Shh!' said an old man who was poring over a leather-bound book at a nearby table.

'Sorry,' whispered Horace. He gave Echo one last worried look, then scurried off up the stairs.

She waited until he was gone, then approached the desk and cleared her throat.

'May I help you?' The robotic librarian's voice was metallic, like the chime of an out-of-tune bell. It continued stamping books as it spoke to her.

Echo opened and closed her mouth for a second. She'd never spoken to a robot before.

'I . . . I'm looking for books on sky pirates,' she said.

The robot stopped, its stamp poised in mid-air. An amber light on its shoulder began pulsing. 'Sky-pirate materials are restricted access,' it said. 'What is your interest in this subject?'

Echo swallowed. Not again! She couldn't get caught now; she might not be lucky enough to escape a second time. Panic rose in her stomach and she swallowed it back down.

'Silly me, I meant ... I mean ... I meant to say ...' She scrambled for an idea. 'Parrots. Sky ... parrots. You know ... parrots that fly in the sky.'

'Parrots,' repeated the robot. Its amber light stopped blinking. 'Accessing memory banks. Please wait.'

Echo's heartbeat steadied. How could she get away with asking about the Crown Jewels? 'And also royal fashion. Dresses, you know. And ... and accessories.' She didn't dare say jewels, in case it set the amber light flashing again. Echo held her breath and heard the well-oiled cogs of the robot's innards spin.

The robot's eyes lit up. 'Parrots. Section 636.886. Upstairs,' it said. 'Royalty. Section 305.522. Across the hall.' Its head spun round as it extended a telescopic arm to the doorway on the left-hand side of the main hall.

'Thanks,' called Echo over her shoulder, already rushing past the towering stacks of books to the door.

Echo heaved down a huge, leather-bound book with the title

Royal Costume Through the Ages embossed in gold lettering on the spine. She set it down on the table where Gilbert was sunning himself beneath a warm gas lamp and flipped through the pages until she came to the section on the Crown Jewels. Echo pored over it, her heart quickening. A cough behind her made her jump and she turned round to find Horace standing behind her, looking sheepish.

'Finished with the bugs already?' asked Echo.

'I thought you might need some help,' said Horace. 'I mean, it's not like you usually spend much time reading.'

Echo scowled at him, then softened. Maybe two heads would be better than one, even if one of them did belong to Horace. He certainly knew books. 'Thanks. Take one of those and look for the Port Tourbillon Crown Jewels. Anything about a robbery or the Black Sky Wolves.'

Horace frowned and looked at her. 'Why *are* you so interested in the Black Sky Wolves? They're criminals, aren't they?'

Echo took a deep breath. If he was going to help, she would have to tell him everything. 'I think they've got something to do with my mother,' she said. For the first time, Echo showed him her mother's hairpin and told him the truth about her escape from the jeweller's.

Horace shook his head. 'This sounds dangerous, Echo.'

'We're just looking at books – how dangerous can it be?'

'I suppose.' He looked uncertain. 'But it's not much of a clue.'

'It's the only one I have.'

The desperation must have shown on her face because, after a moment, Horace sighed and nodded. 'Okay, I'll do my best.'

'Thanks.' Echo took a sidelong look at him as he settled down next to her and began to study a book. It did feel good to trust someone. And, besides, Horace knew more than anyone what it was like to grow up without a mother.

Echo went back to searching her book for anything about the hairpin. There was no mention of the robbery or her mother's pin, just endless pages about the Royal Crown Collection.

Horace went to the shelves and returned with another book on royal jewellery and they both read in silence.

'Look at this,' he hissed.

'What?' said Echo, jerking her head up. Horace pointed at a drawing of a brooch in the shape of a beetle. 'It's a Hanson's Nightcrawler! Wonder if there are any butterfly ones.'

Echo huffed and went back to her book. 'We're not looking for butterflies,' she whispered crossly. 'We're looking for my mother's pin.'

As the minutes turned to hours, Echo searched every book about royal jewellery she could get her hands on, but could find no trace of the hairpin. Gilbert had fallen asleep under the lamp, and Horace's eyes were almost shut as he yawned and turned yet another page.

'Those jewellers must have been mistaken,' she muttered. 'It's not one of the Crown Jewels. And that means I'm at a dead end.' She put her head in her hands. There was no way of tracing the pin now. She had come all the way to Port Tourbillon for nothing.

'Is this it?' Horace blinked and sat upright, interrupting her thoughts.

'What?' replied Echo, without looking up.

'*A small gold and emerald pin in a wolf's head design,*' read Horace.

'Ha ha.'

'No, I'm serious.' Horace stabbed a forefinger at the book.

Echo glanced at him and then the book. Her heart almost stopped and the room spun round her. There, on the velvety parchment of the library book, was a drawing of her mother's pin, in black and white. She gripped the edge of the table.

'Are you okay?' asked Horace. 'You look . . . funny.'

'I'm fine.' Echo shoved her chair up to Horace's. 'Better than fine in fact. What does it say?'

'It says it's a minor piece belonging to the Crown Jewels.'

Echo took the pin out of her pocket, checking quickly over her shoulder that nobody was looking, and compared it to the one in the book. She traced the pin's familiar golden curves with her thumb. The drawing in the book was identical, from the wolf's pelt of finely woven golden strands to the gleaming facets of its emerald eye. She ran her finger down the page and found the description, but when she began to read she found herself dizzy all over again.

A small gold and emerald pin in a wolf's head design, one of two identical pieces made for the Crown Princess Serafine by Messrs Evergreen & Spruce. Both were stolen in the Black Sky Wolves' infamous Zeppelin hijack, where jewellery worth seven million guineas was taken. None of the items has ever been recovered.

A Zeppelin hijack? So the jewellers and the professor had been right. Seven million guineas! Every part of Echo's body prickled with excitement. The pin really *was* part of the stolen Crown Jewels. And there was another one out there somewhere.

She flipped the pages over, her heart thudding, but the next chapter of the book was a long and boring essay about wigs and, however much she and Horace searched, there was no more information on the hairpins to be found. But Echo's mind couldn't stop spinning with questions. How had her mother ended up with a stolen pin in the first place? And where were the Black Sky Wolves? It was all still a perplexing mystery, but one that, somehow, she was getting closer to solving.

CHAPTER SEVENTEEN

Echo scanned the streets outside the library for guards before slipping out of the door with Horace, Gilbert curled round her neck. Although her mother's pin was securely tucked away in her pocket, she couldn't help feeling the weight of it. Seven million guineas! People would steal for that kind of money. Or maybe even kill. She thought she caught a glimpse of oily black hair as she looked over her shoulder with a shiver, but, when she looked again, passers-by bustled past without a second glance.

'Are you coming?' asked Horace.

'Yes!' Echo took another quick look around. Her imagination was working overtime! She pushed the pin deeper into her pocket and pulled her scarf more tightly round her face as she hurried after him.

'I just can't believe it,' she said, as they made their way back along a path through the neatly clipped lavender beds of

Clearwater Park. 'It really is stolen.'

Horace nodded. 'The timing works. The jeweller told you the robbery was fifteen years ago. Before you were born. So perhaps your mother *could* have got hold of the pin sometime in between.'

'But how?' Echo stopped, suddenly exasperated. 'Nobody from Port Tourbillon's been to Lockfort, except Professor Daggerwing. And nobody from Lockfort's been *here*. Except us. So how can my mother have had one of the Crown Jewels?'

Horace shrugged. 'Someone must have secretly brought it to her ...'

'Or she came here in secret,' finished Echo. 'If only I could ask her.' A sudden wave of emptiness caught her by surprise and she clenched her fist round the pin. 'One day I will.'

She studied Horace's doubtful face. 'Why are you looking like that?'

'Looking like what?' Horace flushed.

'Tell me,' Echo demanded, stepping in front of him. 'What is it? You don't think I'm going to find her, do you?'

'It's just ... all you've got is a hairpin. How do you even know she's still alive?'

'Of course she's alive!'

'But ... but then wouldn't she have come back for you?' asked Horace.

Echo opened and closed her mouth. She had often asked herself the same question, in the dead of night when everything had seemed hopeless. Had her mother not wanted her after all? Sorrow rose in her throat, but she swallowed it down. 'Something must have happened. I don't know.' Echo shrugged, as if she didn't care. 'She'll tell me all about it when I find her.'

'It's just . . .' Horace trailed off.

'*What?*' Echo scowled.

'Well, mothers don't do things like that. My mother would never . . .'

'Never what?'

'Well, she wouldn't have left me.'

Horace's words stung. Echo's sorrow suddenly turned to anger. 'Neither would mine,' she snapped.

Horace opened his mouth to say something, but Echo interrupted. 'I'm going to the Mech Market. Why don't you go home and talk to your caterpillar eggs.' She stalked off through the rose gardens without saying goodbye.

Echo was still fuming by the time she walked through the cog-encrusted archway to the Mech Market. But the only way she was going to prove Horace wrong was by finding her mother, and that meant somehow tracking down the Black Sky Wolves. Abena had said at the Cog and Gasket that she would ask her brothers. Perhaps she'd learned something Echo could use.

Echo found Abena lying on her back underneath *Smokesister*, surrounded by spanners and frowning up at the mechanical dragon's innards.

'Ah, you've finally returned. Nice haircut.' Abena peered up at her through her goggles. 'You all right?'

'Yes.' Echo rubbed her eyes on her sleeve, hoping Abena couldn't see she had been crying. 'I had to lie low for a while,' she explained. 'Did you find out anything from your brothers about the Black Sky Wolves?'

'Jed said they were rumoured to have raided a load of merchant ships in the Mondegreens last year, so he reckons they're still around. Their captain is a woman called Indigo Lil,' said Abena. 'And Theo said there's still a fifty-thousand-guinea reward for their capture or the return of the jewels, but nobody's ever claimed it. Fergus is away building fancy technology for some explorer called Jefferson and isn't back for a while, but I'll ask him then.'

She adjusted something with a spanner and dodged to one side as a shower of small cogs rained down on her. 'Blast this clockwork.' She pushed her magnifying goggles up on to her forehead and wriggled out from beneath the dragon. 'It's so fiddly. I can't get these back in.' She gathered up a handful of the tiny cogs. She glanced at Echo's hands, then grabbed one and examined it. 'You've got small fingers. Reckon you could give it a try?'

'Sure.' Head still spinning with the new information, Echo shuffled, feet first, under the metal dragon's chest.

'Put these on,' said Abena, handing her the goggles. Echo

strapped them on and blinked as the eyepieces whirred into focus. Abena passed her a cog and a screwdriver. 'It needs to go right in there,' she said, pointing.

'I can see it,' said Echo, putting her tongue between her teeth and wrinkling her brow as she slotted the tiny cog between the others. She aligned the teeth, tightened it in place with the screwdriver and slid back out from beneath the dragon. 'What's next?'

'You've done it?' said Abena, her brown eyes wide. 'Just like that?'

'Yes,' said Echo.

'But . . . how?'

'I just sort of . . . slotted it in.'

'Ha!' The portly man with the handlebar moustache came out from his workshop, a clockwork beetle in his hand, and slapped Abena on the back. 'Poor Abena's been struggling with that all morning!'

Abena blushed scarlet. 'It's too fiddly,' she said. 'Give me a nice bit of welding any day. Clockwork is not my thing.' She took the magnifying goggles from Echo with a gruff, 'Thanks,' and turned back to her blowtorch.

'Oh, don't be cross, Abena,' said the man. 'She's obviously got the gift.' He turned to Echo and shook her hand before inspecting it. 'Yep, good hands for clockwork,' he said. 'I don't suppose you fancy assisting me with these?' He shook the beetle at her. 'I could do with some help.'

Echo gazed at his workshop and its glittering array of clockwork creatures for a moment before breaking into a huge grin. 'Do you mean it?' she said. 'I could learn to make these?'

'Only with top-rate tuition.' He tapped his nose and winked at her. 'I'm Mr Mainspring, but you can call me Jimmy.'

Keen to avoid the frosty atmosphere that had grown between her and Horace, Echo spent the rest of the day in the workshop at the Mech Market, painstakingly assembling and disassembling clockwork under the guidance of Jimmy Mainspring. It was delicate work, but Echo loved seeing all the parts come together into something with purpose – a beautiful creation that flew of its own accord. It was so much better than embroidering all those pointless samplers and handkerchiefs! She found the hours melted away until finally the evening of the meeting at the Guild came.

'Gotta go!' she said, suddenly realizing the time and wiping the oil off her hands with a rag.

Jimmy looked up from his work. 'Wait there. I've got a little gift for you, as payment for all your hard work.'

He rummaged in his workbox and took out a miniature clockwork bird with feathers of copper and gleaming white enamel.

'My own postal pigeon!' said Echo, turning it over in her

hands and carefully stretching out one wing to marvel at the intricate metal feathers. She beamed. 'Thank you, Jimmy.'

'It's not just any postal pigeon,' said Jimmy. 'It's my own design. You enter the coordinates here.' He showed her a series of dials under the little bird's wing. 'Write your message and put it in the bird's claw here, then let it fly. When the message is returned, the bird will navigate its way back to you. You just need to calibrate it to something metallic, something you always keep with you. Do you have anything?'

'Yes,' said Echo, thinking of her mother's pin.

'Well, you just set it, using this dial here, and it can find you wherever you are.'

'Oh, Jimmy, it's the best present ever.' She gave the stout man a hug and her heart glowed. In just a day, she'd learned so much, and not just about clockwork. Making things with her hands had made her feel more real somehow. Not just a grateful ward of the king whose only role was to be quiet and look presentable, but someone who could create things, who could do things, who could change things.

'Thank you, Jimmy.' She carefully stowed the pigeon in her pocket before racing all the way back to Hawthorn Square, Gilbert clinging to her shoulder, and a huge smile on her face.

Echo found Horace and Professor Daggerwing in the parlour. The professor was wearing a white shirt and a crumpled maroon velvet suit that looked like it had been lost in an attic for several years.

'How do I look?' he asked.

Echo took in the frilly white cuffs that dangled from the jacket sleeves. 'Um ... odd,' she said.

Horace looked up from his caterpillar jar. 'She means smart.'

'Do *we* need to dress up?' asked Echo, ignoring Horace.

'No, no, not necessary at all,' said the professor, running his hands through his hair and making it stand up at a peculiar angle. 'I just like to make an impression at the Guild. Are you ready?'

Echo threw her scarf round her face, just in case she was recognized, then she grinned. 'I've been ready all day!'

'Well, chop-chop!' The professor clapped his hands together. 'We must be there at seven. You're in for an absolute treat!'

CHAPTER EIGHTEEN

The Explorers' Guild was a grand green-stone building with wide oak doors and a coat of arms inscribed with a mountain, a dragon and a compass.

'It's a very exclusive club,' whispered the professor, as they rapped on the knocker and waited on the doorstep. 'Members and their guests only. I only gained entry after delivering my ground-breaking paper on the origins of the kibblesnerts of the Verdigris Plains.'

The door swung open and a white-gloved butler ushered them inside. They followed Professor Daggerwing down a corridor lined with ancient objects from explorations gone by – the fossilized tusk of a merwhale, excavated by Captain Mei Fan on her expedition to the far west; a fragment of parchment from the Scrolls of Pomegranth; an ancient-looking wooden sled once hitched to a team of wolves and driven across the frozen wastes of Dark Nordland by the heroic Colonel Femi Fox.

As Professor Daggerwing told them the stories of each object in a hushed voice, Horace's eyes grew wider. 'There's so much out there,' he said, with a shiver.

Echo gazed at the artefacts in awe and delight, imagining the long-ago heroes who had brought such treasures back to Port Tourbillon. They had all been searching for something, and they had found it. She touched the hairpin, still deep in the pocket of her breeches, and it filled her with courage. The world might be big, but that wasn't going to stop her. These brave men and women hadn't given up and neither would she.

At the end of the corridor, double doors opened into a dimly lit lecture theatre with rows of velvet-backed seats. Professor Daggerwing directed them towards the front of the auditorium and they took their places, Echo in the middle, the professor and Horace on either side.

Echo scooped Gilbert out of her pocket and perched him on her knee, where he had a good view of the stage. The air smelled of musty tobacco smoke and old tweed and there was the gentle murmur of voices as the room began to fill. Echo gazed at the explorers and adventurers who had come to listen.

'That's Dr Fitzwilliam, over there in the front row with the grey hair,' said Professor Daggerwing in a loud whisper. 'He was the first man to navigate across the Stony Sea, many moons ago. And that's Evander Jefferson, something of a rival of mine.' The professor shook his head. 'We were both heading to the Violet Isles last time I saw him, trying to catalogue the elusive Greater Brimstone, that huge butterfly variety I was telling you about, Horace. I dare say he'll be talking about them tonight.' He sighed regretfully. 'He's beaten me to it thanks to my detour to Lockfort.'

The professor continued to point out eminent explorers and scientists in the audience until the lights dimmed and the crowd hushed.

The first talk was not exactly what Echo had expected, although Professor Daggerwing listened, rapt, as a pair of women explorers droned on about rock formations and soil composition. It didn't seem very adventurous at all. Echo glanced to her left. Horace had fallen asleep and was snoring softly, his head lolling back on the velvet seat. Even Gilbert, perched in her lap, looked bored.

Echo wriggled in her seat as the two women finally finished. Next a tall dark man with long grey-streaked hair and a bushy walrus moustache lumbered on to the stage to rapturous applause.

'This is it,' whispered Professor Daggerwing, clutching Echo's wrist. 'Evander Jefferson. I wonder if he did manage to spot them? Nobody's presented a photogram of a Greater Brimstone yet!'

Echo stifled a yawn and nodded politely. A hush fell over the room as Evander Jefferson began to speak. Echo slid down further in her seat and let her eyes close. Her body relaxed and she was just slipping into a dream when she felt a sharp nip on her collarbone. She jerked upright to find Gilbert on her shoulder, staring right at her, his scales an urgent red and his crest upright in a way that said, *Listen*.

'What?' she hissed.

'Shh!' said someone in the row behind.

Echo glanced up at the stage. Evander Jefferson was still talking.

'... unfortunately, this meant our trip was cut short due to safety concerns before we were able to see so much as a chrysalis. We would strongly recommend avoiding the area for the foreseeable future.'

Echo frowned. What was so interesting about this?

Jefferson continued. 'As you all know, the Black Sky Wolves became notorious fifteen years ago when they infamously robbed the Royal Zeppelin and have never been seen since. They are considered incredibly dangerous and are known for kidnapping people and enslaving them to work on their ship. Although they haven't been sighted in recent years, people exploring remote regions regularly go missing, and it may well be that these pirates are responsible. We were incredibly fortunate to avoid their notice.'

The Black Sky Wolves! Echo sat up, electricity running through her skin.

Jefferson pulled down a creaking white screen and fired up a steam projector. Echo leaned forward in her seat as he continued.

'We spotted their ship, the very distinctive *Scarlet Margaret*, to the south and were able to take this photogram.'

A grainy image appeared on the screen, showing a huge airship with billowing sails moored above a curved beach of black sand.

'The most notorious of the crew is their current captain, Indigo Lil, so called due to the indigo clay she smears on her face before going into battle. She's known to be savage and heartless and fond of torturing her victims. Her true identity has never been confirmed. However, we did find this old photogram in the Guild Archives.'

The projector clicked and whirred and another much older photogram shuddered on to the screen, showing a fierce-looking gaggle of men and women slouching in front of the same airship. Gilbert scuttled down Echo's arm and peered intently at the image on the screen. At the fore was a ferocious-looking woman with long white curls, clay-smeared cheeks and a gleaming cutlass at her hip. But someone else in the photogram made Echo's head spin.

In the very bottom corner of the photo was a sad-looking woman with her arms behind her back. A woman with a head of wild dark curls like Echo's. And in those dark curls was a hairpin in the shape of a wolf's head, its eye a gleaming emerald.

CHAPTER NINETEEN

'Are you okay, Echo?' asked the professor, as they arrived back at Hawthorn Square. 'You've hardly said a word since we came out of the lecture.'

'I'm tired,' said Echo, kicking off her boots and feigning a yawn before heading up the stairs, feeling more wide awake than she ever had in her life. Her mother was in terrible danger. Kidnapped by the Black Sky Wolves! Echo had to rescue her.

But she couldn't tell the professor about her plans. Not yet. Even if he believed Echo, he'd never agree to a rescue mission, especially one so perilous. No, she had to work out another way to track them down. She raced up the four storeys of stairs, lost in her thoughts, ignoring Horace and the professor's calls for her to wait.

It was only when she'd slammed her bedroom door behind her that Echo stopped to take a breath. She couldn't waste one second. She needed to find the Black Sky Wolves and rescue her mother, however dangerous it might be.

Gilbert emerged from her pocket and shook himself.

'I'm going to rescue her, Gilbert,' she said. 'I don't know how, but I'm going to do it.'

Gilbert gave her an enquiring look.

Echo swallowed. 'I know it'll be dangerous, but I don't care. She needs me.'

She thought back to the lecture. Evander Jefferson had seen the Black Sky Wolves near the Violet Isles. Would their ship still be there? Would her mother still be with them after all these years? There was only one way to find out. She had to persuade the professor to take her there in the *Hummerbird*. But how?

She threw a bag on to the bed and began hurling in her belongings, narrowly missing Gilbert, who scuttled to the safety of her pillow and watched her with a worried expression. If she could just get close to the Black Sky Wolves' ship, she would find her mother. She didn't know how yet, but she would do it. She threw in her set of spanners, Jimmy's postal pigeon and absent-mindedly yanked an indignant Pumpernickel's tail in her haste to cram everything in.

There was a soft knock at the door and she turned to find Horace in the doorway.

He cleared his throat. 'What are you doing?'

'Packing,' said Echo, shutting the bag with a snap. 'I have to go to the Violet Isles right now.'

'The Violet Isles? But the professor says they're infested with pirates.'

Echo shrugged, although her heart secretly sparked at the idea. 'I know.'

Horace continued. 'He even says he's going to have to rechart our course back to Lockfort to avoid getting close to them. It's a shame really. I'd hoped we might see a Greater Brimstone if we flew close by.'

Echo stared at him. That was it! The Greater Brimstone! She raced past Horace and threw herself down the slideway, whizzing down to the parlour. She landed on the cushions, breathless. 'Professor!' she yelled. 'Professor Daggerwing!'

The professor was examining a map with his head in his hands. He looked up as Echo raced in. 'Echo, whatever is the matter?'

She caught her breath. 'We have to go to the Violet Isles.'

'But my dear girl, we can't venture near the Violet Isles until the pirates have moved on. No, we'll need to take a different route to Lockfort.' He stroked his chin, then grabbed his fountain pen and began scribbling furiously in his notebook.

'But . . . but we *have* to go. Now!' Tears welled in Echo's eyes and she crossly wiped them away with her sleeve.

Professor Daggerwing looked up, perplexed. 'You're bamboozling me, Echo. I know you must be keen to get back home, but we'll find another route.'

'What about the Greater Brimstone?' she burst out. 'I

thought you wanted to beat Evander Jefferson. You could be the first to show photogram footage at the Guild!'

'Well . . . well, yes, I do agree that it would have been nice—'

'But now's your chance!' said Echo. 'He didn't manage to see any, and nobody else will be going. They're all too scared of the sky pirates.'

'And with good cause,' said the professor. 'It's a most dangerous situation.'

'But you said yourself that you've had brushes with pirates before, and they mostly just go for merchant ships. They wouldn't bother us! You wouldn't be scared!'

'Well, I . . .'

'You're braver than that Jefferson man, I'm certain of it!'

The professor flushed. 'Well, I don't know about that.'

'And what about Horace?' she said.

'Horace?' The professor raised confused eyebrows. 'He didn't say anything to me.'

'He has his heart set on going,' said Echo. 'He didn't want to tell you himself. He so loves butterflies and it's his one chance to see the Greater Brimstone before you take us back to Lockfort.' She felt a stab of guilt as she lied. 'He begged me to ask you.' She finally let her tears of desperation flow. 'Please, Professor.'

The professor nodded gravely, running a hand through his bushy hair and looking around in search of a handkerchief. 'Oh dear. Oh dear me. Now, please don't cry. You know it makes me nervous. Let's put the kettle on and we will see what's to be done.'

After a cup of the professor's strongest orange peccadillo tea, Echo was a little more composed, but she still couldn't shake the itchy frantic feeling inside that told her she had to get to the Violet Isles right away.

She leaned over the professor's shoulder as he studied his charts. 'Didn't Jefferson say the pirates were to the south of the islands?' she said. 'Couldn't we fly in from the north?'

'I suppose it could work,' he said, wrinkling his brow.

'Yes, look,' said Echo, pointing at the map. 'It's open sky here. If there are any sky pirate ships around, we'll be able to see them before we draw near.'

He frowned. 'I suppose we would be safe enough.'

'We could stop off so Horace can see the butterflies and you can get your photograms—'

'And then onwards to Lockfort by cover of darkness.' The professor rubbed his chin and nodded slowly. 'It's not a terrible plan. Are you sure Horace will want to risk it though? I got the impression he was, well, rather a timid fellow.'

'I told him it might be risky, but he's desperate to see the Greater Brimstone.' Echo tried to keep her voice light and stared resolutely at the map to avoid the professor's gaze.

'All right. We'll do it. The Violet Isles and onwards to Lockfort.'

'Oh, thank you! Thank you!' Echo threw herself at the professor in a huge hug, not telling him that she had no intention of being on the *Hummerbird* when they went on to Lockfort and would instead be hunting for the Black Sky Wolves alone.

The professor patted her back awkwardly. 'We can't be hasty though. There are still preparations to be made. If we're venturing into sky-pirate territory, we'll have to ensure the *Hummerbird* is shipshape and spotless.'

Echo dropped her arms and nodded reluctantly. 'So when *can* we leave?'

'It'll take two days to get the old girl ready.'

'Two days!' Echo exclaimed. 'But can't we go right away?'

Professor Daggerwing shook his head. 'I'm afraid that part of the expedition is non-negotiable. An explorer must be prepared, especially when there are sky pirates around.' He clapped his hands together. 'In the meantime, I think a good supper is in order.'

Over a fireside supper of hot buttered crumpets with slabs of crumbling cheese and a peculiar aubergine pickle the professor had found in the cupboard under the stairs, he explained what he knew about the Violet Isles to Echo and Horace.

'It's a cluster of five islands in the Stony Sea,' he said. 'No population to speak of, with dense jungle. The biggest island,

Amethyst, is where my good friend Doctor Beetlestone has her laboratory. We could even pop in to see her! The others – Mauve, Heliotrope, Tyrian and Magenta – are much smaller.'

Horace looked at Echo suspiciously as the professor described the change in plans. 'Is it really safe, Professor?' he asked. 'I thought you said we had to avoid that area?'

'I think I've found a safe enough route,' said the professor, worry flickering across his face. 'Or at least I hope I have. But I know how keen you are to visit before you return home, Horace, and, as Echo has pointed out, it is only a small detour.'

Horace glared at Echo and opened his mouth to speak. 'But—'

'Why are they called the Violet Isles?' Echo interrupted quickly. 'Is it something to do with the plants that grow there?'

'No, no, not at all. The Violet Isles are so called because of the peculiar purple fog that rolls in off the sea. It's most unpredictable. Makes navigation quite a challenge, I can tell you!'

Echo nodded. 'What about the butterflies?' she asked, licking pickle from her fingers. 'I bet you want to know all about them, don't you, Horace?'

Horace frowned at his crumpet, then shrugged. 'Are they rare?'

'Frightfully rare,' said the professor. 'I've only ever witnessed them once, but unfortunately the plates I took got blown into the water by the backdraught from their wings and all my photograms were lost.'

'Just think what they'll say at the Guild if you manage it this time,' said Echo.

The professor flushed and stroked Fred, who had jumped up on to his lap. 'It would be satisfying to beat old Jefferson.'

Echo smiled and finished her crumpet, avoiding Horace's gaze. She was getting closer to finding her mother, she could feel it. As for her mother's pirate kidnappers, well, she'd work out what to do about them when she got there. For the moment, just getting closer was enough.

Back in her room, Echo threw on her nightclothes and pulled up the soft eiderdown. Gilbert arranged himself on her pillow and closed his eyes, with a sleepy chirrup.

'Scaly dreams, Gilbert,' she whispered, kissing the top of his head.

There was a sharp knock at her door and Echo tensed. Had the professor changed his mind? Was their expedition to the Violet Isles off? Instead, the door opened and Horace appeared, a suspicious frown on his face.

Echo swallowed. Now she was in trouble. 'What is it?'

'What are you up to?' he said.

'Nothing!'

'You've persuaded the professor to stop off in the Violet Isles and I want to know why. You don't care about butterflies.'

Echo put on a hurt expression. 'I thought *you* wanted to see them. Can't I do something nice without you accusing me of some sneaky plan? It's your only chance before you go back to Lockfort.'

Horace flushed and looked at his feet. 'I admit they do sound interesting.' He looked up. 'Did you really do it for me?'

Echo nodded, hoping the flood of guilt she felt didn't show on her face. 'I know how much you love them.'

'Right, well . . .' He paused awkwardly. 'Listen, I should say sorry,' he said, sitting down on the end of her bed. 'For those things I said before about you not finding your mother. Or her not finding you. I didn't mean to upset you. I know how much you wanted to find her and I'm really sorry the pin didn't end up meaning anything.'

'It's okay.' Echo sat up and touched his hand.

'And thanks for persuading the professor to take us to the Violet Isles. It'll be great to see one last wonderful thing before we go home for good.'

'Yes.' Echo nodded guiltily. 'Are you really looking forward to it? Lockfort, I mean?'

'Of course – Lockfort's home! Although it will be strange going back,' he said. 'After everything we've seen.'

Echo nodded again and for a moment they just sat in silence.

There were footsteps on the stairs and Professor Daggerwing popped his head round the door. 'I think you two should get some rest,' he said. 'There are lots of preparations to be made.

Those fluffle valves won't tune themselves, you know. In fact, that reminds me! I must add barnacle grease to my shopping list. Sleep well!' He rushed back out of the room.

Horace said goodnight and disappeared to his room.

But, as Echo lay alone in the darkness, she couldn't sleep for all the thoughts tumbling round her head. She was putting not just herself but Horace and the professor in great danger. And for what? Would she really find the Black Sky Wolves in the Violet Isles? There were five islands after all. And would her mother still be with them? The chance seemed so small. And, if the Black Sky Wolves *did* have her mother, how was Echo ever going to rescue her?

'It seems almost hopeless, Gilbert,' she said to the little lizard.

He gave a sleepy chirrup, which Echo thought might just have meant, *A little hope is all you need.*

'You're right.' Echo yawned and stroked his scales. A little hope had got her this far after all. But, as she finally drifted off to sleep, her dreams were filled with fierce pirates and cannons and ships that sailed away from her before she could catch them, and even in sleep her fists were curled as tight as clockwork.

CHAPTER TWENTY

The next two days passed in a blur of preparations for their trip. Vinegar wafted through the house as the professor stirred a huge steaming saucepan of prickly-pear pickles. Mrs Milkweed hummed as she hunched with a sextant over the sky charts. The cats, somehow knowing that adventure was afoot, mewed and rubbed round everyone's legs, play-stalked Gilbert with new vigour and, when it was all too much, fell asleep in a sevenfold furry heap, usually on top of a map, or in a half-packed suitcase, or among a pile of essential provisions.

Echo couldn't keep still. She'd been to the Mech Market to buy barnacle grease and steam oil, cleaned out the *Hummerbird*'s water tank and helped the professor oil the pistons, hoping to hurry things along, but it all seemed to be taking forever. 'Oh, when will the envelope be ready?' she said, pacing up and down the parlour when she'd finally run out of tasks.

'Please do stop stomping around,' begged Horace, hunched over his caterpillar jar at the table. 'The vibrations are upsetting my chrysalises.'

There was a whirring noise outside the window and Echo looked out to see a brass postal pigeon winging its way towards them.

'This must be it!' she said, flinging the window wide and catching the little bird in both hands. She checked the scroll held tightly in its metallic claw.

'Professor, it's for you!'

She ran through to the kitchen and breathlessly passed the message to the professor, who was spooning pickles into jars. He put down his ladle, unrolled the paper and read it.

'Is the envelope ready?' asked Echo.

'It most certainly is,' said Professor Daggerwing. 'We just need to go to the Mech Market and collect it.'

'Can I come?' Echo said. 'I want to say goodbye to Abena and Jimmy too.'

'Why don't we all go?' said the professor. 'A little outing in the fresh air will do us good. Mrs Milkweed, Horace, the new envelope awaits!'

The *Hummerbird*'s new balloon made a weighty parcel, and it took all four of them to carry it, carefully folded and tied up in brown paper, back through the streets to Hawthorn Square.

'That's strange,' said Horace.

'What is?' said Echo, panting as they rested the parcel on the bottom step.

'Look.' He pointed at the front door, which swung open on the breeze. 'Didn't you shut it when we went out, Professor?'

The professor peered through his glasses. 'I'm sure I did.' He left the balloon envelope where it was and ran up the steps. 'Oh no!' he said, gazing into the hallway in dismay.

'What is it?' Echo and the others followed him into the house. Echo gasped as she saw the chaos inside. The lock to the front door was broken clean off. Maps lay strewn all over the floor, chairs had been turned upside down and the drawers of all the cabinets hung open, their contents scattered across the rug. In the parlour, every one of the professor's pickle jars had been smashed.

'Who's been in here?' she said.

'Is anything missing?' asked Mrs Milkweed in a shaky voice. She stepped carefully between her torn maps, her eyes full of worry.

'No, no, I don't think so,' said the professor. His face was white with shock. 'But they were obviously searching for something. Although what, I have no idea.'

Chills ran down Echo's spine as she squeezed the hairpin in her pocket. She had a horrible feeling that she knew exactly what they'd been looking for. 'Let's check upstairs,' she said.

All of the bedrooms were untouched except Echo's. Her bed

had been moved away from the wall, the mattress slashed and the stuffing pulled out. Every item of clothing in her wardrobe was thrown on the floor. Stargazy shot out from under the bed and wrapped himself round Mrs Milkweed's ankles with a terrified mew.

'Poor puss,' she said, rubbing him behind the ears. 'What's been going on in here?'

There was a hammering of fists on the front door below. The professor peered out of the window. 'It's the Queen's Guard,' he said. 'Four of them, no five. But what are they—'

'Professor!' said Echo, turning to him. 'It's me they're looking for. I'm sorry I didn't tell you before, but I really need to leave. I'm in trouble.'

'Trouble?' said the professor, his bushy eyebrows almost touching in a frown. 'What kind of trouble?'

'There's no time!' she said. 'Please! I have to get out of Port Tourbillon. Right now. People are after me. All sorts of people. I'll explain on the way, I promise.'

The professor looked at her for a moment. 'Okay, you two, get up to the *Hummerbird*. Echo seems to be in grave danger.'

'But what about the new envelope?' exclaimed Horace.

'The old one will have to do,' said the professor. 'Let's go. Follow me.'

'I'll stay here and keep them busy,' said Mrs Milkweed, a grim look on her face.

'But you won't be safe!' said Echo.

'I'll be fine. I've seen off worse than the Queen's Guard in my time, believe you me,' she replied, tapping her diamond nose stud. 'Plus, someone has to stay and look after the cats.'

Echo started as they heard the front door slam and the sound of pounding feet.

'Go,' said Mrs Milkweed, launching herself down the slideway. 'I'll distract them.'

Echo, Gilbert and Horace stared at one another for a moment, then Echo grabbed Gilbert and they pelted up the stairs after the professor, Horace only pausing long enough to grab his caterpillar jar.

When they reached the landing, Professor Daggerwing had already opened the hatch to the roof. He hauled down the telescopic ladder and they scrambled up the shining brass rungs. The professor came last, passing up their bags and pulling the ladder up behind him.

'Get her inflated, Echo! That's the ticket!' he shouted.

Far below them, there were muffled bangs, followed by shouts and the shrill blast of a whistle.

Echo clambered into the airship, ran to the cockpit and hit the inflate button. There was a *whoosh* and the old balloon envelope, complete with petticoat patch, billowed into the air. Echo fired up the engines as the professor had shown her and felt the *Hummerbird* rumble beneath them.

Horace scrambled inside, clutching his caterpillar jar. Then the professor and an assortment of packages fell through the hatch, landing in a heap at the bottom of the ladder.

'Go!' yelled the professor, grimacing in pain.

Echo shoved a lever forward and heard a hiss and a clank as the anchor was released from the mooring dock. She pulled back hard on the throttle and felt the engines shudder as they soared into the air, Port Tourbillon's rainbow rooftops spreading out before them. Gilbert scuttled down her sleeve and positioned himself by the window. Echo glanced at the spinning discs of the gyrocompass, then turned back.

'Which way?'

'Aim for the southern boundary,' said the professor, hauling himself to his feet and clutching his right arm.

Echo turned the wheel until the gyrocompass needle settled on the letter S. She cast a worried glance at the professor. 'Are you all right?'

'Fine, fine. Don't worry about me, just fly.'

'Are they following?' she asked, not daring to take her eyes from the flight-deck window.

'The roof hatch is well disguised,' said the professor. 'They won't find it from the inside. Just keep going, full steam ahead. Get some height.'

'I can't see anyone tailing us,' said Horace from the rear porthole.

'Are you sure?' said Echo, casting a nervous glance at the back of the ship.

The professor pointed to a pair of brass handlebars hanging from the ceiling above her seat. 'Pull down the periscope and see for yourself.'

Echo stretched up and grabbed the handles, pulling them down to reveal a smooth brass cylinder. She pressed her eye to the lens and used the handles to slowly turn the contraption. The skies were clear, just the odd merchant ship or pleasure cruiser in the sky over Clearwater Park.

'There's no time for complacency though,' the professor said, rubbing his injured arm. 'If the Queen's Guard are after you, they may well try to stop us at the city boundary. We need to have our wits about us.'

Echo turned back to the flight-deck window. The city stretched out in a carpet of colourful rooftops and snaking chimneys. Far in the distance she could glimpse hazy greenery, and beyond that she imagined the Violet Isles with their strange fog. And somewhere in that fog her mother. She held her hands steady on the wheel and willed the little ship onwards.

CHAPTER TWENTY-ONE

'Well, that wasn't quite the departure I had hoped for!' said the professor, sitting down heavily in the co-pilot's seat, a dazed look on his face. They had cleared the maze of Port Tourbillon's streets and were out of the city, humming through the sky over wild green moors below.

Echo leaned back in the pilot's seat and flexed her stiff fingers. 'I'm sorry, Professor,' she said. 'I should have told you before.'

'Anyone following?' she asked Horace, who was still looking quite shaken. He peered with his binoculars through the rear porthole.

'No,' he replied. 'I can't see anyone. Where are we anyway?' He put down the binoculars and joined the other two in the cockpit.

'These are the Verdigris Plains,' said the professor, pointing up ahead. 'Known for their wild asparagus and citrus groves.'

He gestured at a glade of trees below. 'I've spent many a night camping in these parts. The fruits are delicious, although rather pungent. I smelled of lemons for weeks after my last visit. The cats were most put out.'

Gilbert flicked out his tongue.

'And what's that up ahead?' asked Echo, squinting in the distance as a terracotta-roofed town came into view.

'Ah, that is the town of Anisett, famous for its confectionery and the annual horse race. It's a shame we can't stop off, but it's such an old city, the streets are too narrow for aircraft. Let's get closer though, so we can take a look.' He took the wheel from Echo, pulled a lever and reduced their altitude.

'Here it is,' said the professor, as they approached. He pointed at a wide square that opened up in the midst of the tightly packed pink-stone buildings. 'That's where the race is held every spring. A most invigorating—'

'Er, Professor, Echo,' said Horace, who was now at the rear of the ship, his voice wobbling. 'Come and look at—'

BANG! The whole ship shuddered and Horace toppled backwards on to the floor.

Gilbert jumped and his scales turned danger red.

'What was that?' Echo yelped.

'A ship,' panted Horace, pushing himself upright. 'I saw a ship!'

Echo grabbed on to the pipework as something whizzed past the porthole.

Gilbert's scales paled to white and he scuttled up Echo's sleeve, gripping her shoulder tightly through her shirt.

'Let me see.' Professor Daggerwing looked into the periscope eyepiece. 'Yes, you're right, young Horace. A Matasan fighter with the royal crest. It must be the Queen's Guard.'

'A fighter?' whimpered Horace.

BANG! Something heavy clattered against the *Hummerbird*'s hull.

'They're shooting at us!' Horace's face crumpled. 'We're all going to die!'

'It's not bullets they're shooting, it's harpoons,' said the professor grimly. 'And they're not trying to kill us. They want to reel us in. You take over, Echo. Full power to the engines. It's a fast ship they've got, but let's try to outrun them. Time for the secondary engines. Hold tight, everyone!'

Echo nodded and kept her hands firmly gripped to the wheel while the professor pulled open a trapdoor in the floor. Echo glanced back and caught a glimpse of pumping pistons in the cavity beneath their feet.

'The main engine's gas-powered!' shouted the professor over the engine noise. 'But when I need a little extra oomph I crack out the old coal burner. She's elderly but effective. Here, Horace, take a shovel, that's a good man.'

Horace grabbed a shovel and, after a brief pause and a deep breath, slipped down into the engine hold to throw scoops of coal into the burner. Echo felt the little ship surge forward as the pistons thrummed beneath her. She stole a glance back at the professor, who was scanning the air with the binoculars.

'Is it working?' she said.

'For the moment,' he said. 'But I'm not sure how long we can keep this speed up.'

Echo held grimly to the wheel with one hand and pulled down the periscope with the other. She looked through the eyepiece and swallowed down a cry as she saw a huge armoured airship surging along in their wake. There was no way they could outrun it. Even after the boost from the coal burner, the ship was gaining on them. They had to think of something else.

She scanned the horizon, but there was nothing there to help her. They'd never shake this ship off. She leaned forward and glanced down at the terracotta-hued city, searching desperately for somewhere to hide. But there was nowhere, just building after building after building. Horse-drawn coaches crawled along the narrow streets like ants.

Horace gave a squawk of fear and Echo turned back to see a huge grey shape looming up at them through the rear portholes. The ship had almost drawn level.

A tinny voice came through a loudhailer. *'Allow us to board in the name of Queen Valberta the Third of Port Tourbillon!'*

The ship had to be at least three times as big as the *Hummerbird*. Echo glanced back down again at the grid of narrow streets below them and was hit by a thought. *Narrow streets.*

'Professor!' she yelled. 'Bigger ships, do they take longer to slow down?'

Professor Daggerwing popped his head out of the engine hatch. 'Well, yes, dear girl. It's a case of basic physics—'

But Echo didn't wait for the rest of his answer. She leaned on a brass lever and the altimeter spun as the little ship seemed to drop out of the sky and dive towards the street.

'Are we hit?' Horace yelped, still shovelling frantically.

'No.' Echo shook her head, keeping her eyes on the streets below. 'Change of plan,' she said. 'We're going down.'

The *Hummerbird* shuddered as it nosedived towards the rooftops. The teacups rattled in their cupboards, jars of pickles and the copper kettle rolled to and fro across the floor.

'Take the periscope, Horace!' yelled Echo. 'Are they following?'

'Hang on,' said Horace, who had climbed out of the engine hatch and was staggering to the cockpit. Echo grabbed his braces and pulled him into the co-pilot's seat. Horace buckled the straps round his middle and yanked the periscope down.

'They're right on our tail,' he said.

'Good,' said Echo.

'Good?' he squawked.

Echo pushed the altitude lever forward even further and the *Hummerbird* dived down between the towering buildings of Anisett's streets, its gondola skimming the street lamps. She caught a glimpse of shocked faces staring from windows, treetops flashing past in a blur and figures below them stopping and pointing as their hats were blown off by the little ship's downdraught.

Horace pressed his face to the periscope. 'They're still following! They're going to—' He broke off with a triumphant squeal as there was an enormous, rubbery, groaning squeak from behind them. 'They're stuck!' he shouted, punching the air with his fist.

'Let me see.' Echo grabbed the periscope and, despite the fear running through her, couldn't help breaking into a huge grin. Unable to stop in time, the Matasan airship balloon had become well and truly wedged between the top storeys of two townhouses, its gondola dangling feebly below. A crowd gathered in its shadow on the street beneath.

Echo steered the *Hummerbird* swiftly away down a side street, guiding it carefully between the dusty-pink buildings, until finally, when she was sure they weren't being followed, she drew back on the throttle and took them back up above the rooftops, slipping quietly away from the city, out of Anisett, and beyond.

Echo held the little ship on a steady course as they left the town behind. Gilbert had recovered his usual yellow shade and sat on the dashboard, peering out at the landscape below. Soon they were flying over golden fields with dark patches of woodland, and then further still over dense green pine forests. Echo gazed out in wonder. There was so much world out there!

'Anyone behind us?' she asked Horace.

Horace peered through the periscope and shook his head. 'There are some ships way out to the east, but they look like ordinary merchant vehicles. There's no sign of the Matasan.'

'Glad to hear it,' said Professor Daggerwing, who was still looking dazed. 'In all my exploring days, I have to say I have never been fired at by the Queen's Guard. Echo, perhaps now you could explain why it was you needed to leave Port Tourbillon so urgently.'

Echo sighed. She couldn't put it off any longer. 'It's all because of this,' she said, taking her mother's hairpin out of her pocket. She explained to him all about the pin, how she'd traced it to Port Tourbillon and discovered it had been stolen, along with its twin. Then she bit her lip. What was it that Martha had always said? A problem shared was a problem halved. But, as much as she wanted to, she couldn't tell the professor or Horace about her plan to track down the Black Sky Wolves. Not yet. They might have agreed to stop in the Violet Isles to see the butterflies, but they would never agree to rescuing her mother from pirates. No, that part of her plan would have to wait.

'There's a reward for it, you see,' she finally said. 'And now all sorts of people are after me, not just the Queen's Guard.' She thought back to the black-haired man and the fifty-thousand-guinea reward for the return of the jewels. 'So I couldn't stay in Port Tourbillon.'

'Well,' said the professor, raising his bushy eyebrows as he examined the pin, 'it's certainly a striking piece. I do wish you'd told me sooner though.'

'I'm sorry,' said Echo.

'Never mind, can't be helped. No point crying over burnt bananas. But the sooner we get to the Violet Isles and Doctor Beetlestone's laboratory the better. Can you help me patch up this arm, please, Horace?'

Echo fixed her eyes on the horizon while Horace followed the professor's instructions to put together a makeshift sling for his arm.

'Do you think it's broken?' he asked.

'No, just sprained. I'll be as right as rain in a couple of days,' said the professor. 'In the meantime, Echo makes a fine pilot.'

Gilbert bobbed his head in agreement and Echo grinned, sitting up a little taller in the pilot's seat. 'Which way now?' she asked.

Professor Daggerwing studied his charts. 'If we head south-west to Sea Lark Bay, we'll be on our way to the Violet Isles,' he said. 'Why don't you put the old girl on autopilot and take a break, Echo? I'm afraid my arm's not up to making tea though.'

Echo glanced back at the hatch where previously she and Horace had held on to the professor's legs, and jumped down from the pilot's seat. 'Let me have a try,' she said.

'Well, I really don't know about that,' said the professor. 'It's very dangerous.'

'You said it wasn't!' exclaimed Echo. 'Anyway, you and Horace can hold on to my boots.' She flipped the hatch open, grabbed the kettle of water and wriggled out.

As the little ship glided onwards, they settled down in their hammocks, chatting lazily and drinking tea while the professor consulted his map. There was no cake today. In fact, their hurried exit had meant the only food onboard was a large jar of pickled sweetroots, which both Echo and Horace graciously declined.

'Gosh, what time is it?' asked the professor a while later, searching awkwardly for his pocket watch with his good hand. 'We must be nearly at the ocean by now.'

Echo raced back to the cockpit, where Gilbert lay snoozing on the dashboard, and peered out to see the pine forests give way to a wide, rocky beach that curved before them. Beyond that the ocean, pale blue and sparkling, stretched out to the horizon. The Stony Sea! She gazed in wonder at the white crests of waves breaking below. She'd never seen such a huge blue expanse. Yet again, she marvelled at the vastness of the world. And somewhere out there in it was her mother. Echo leaned forward on the dashboard and squinted into the distance. 'Where are the islands?'

'Oh, they're miles away yet,' said the professor, with a chuckle. 'Could you two clear these things away? I'm going to have a catnap. We'll have to do the washing-up when we drop anchor.'

He retired to his hammock and Echo skipped over to stack up the teacups. It was a while before she looked over at Horace, who still had a pained look on his face.

'What are you worrying about now?' she said.

'I don't know,' he said miserably. 'Something's not right.'

'What's not right? We escaped the guards! *I* got us out of trouble and we're heading in the right direction.'

'It was you that got us into trouble in the first place!'

Echo scowled. 'Well, everything's fine now, so you can stop worrying.'

Horace shook his head. 'Something's off.'

'Oh, Horace.' Echo threw down her tea towel in frustration. 'Don't be such a pudding heart. We're going to the Violet Isles! Think of the butterflies.'

Horace huffed and cleared away the tea things in silence.

'Maybe you should have just stayed in Lockfort.' As soon as the words came out of her mouth, Echo regretted them.

Horace flushed scarlet. He shoved the teacups into a cupboard and went back to examining his chrysalises without another word.

I didn't mean it like that, thought Echo. But why couldn't he enjoy the adventure? She opened her mouth to apologize, but Horace had already turned away, so she pretended to study the professor's sea charts instead as the uncomfortable silence between them grew.

They still weren't speaking several minutes later when Echo noticed Horace peering out of the starboard porthole.

'What's the matter now?' she said.

Horace sniffed and glared at her. 'You'll only make fun of me if I tell you.'

'No I won't!'

'It's just I'm sure we're going rather slower than before,' he said eventually.

'No, of course we . . .' Echo rushed to the cockpit and felt her heart lurch as she gazed out. They did seem to be losing speed. The little ship gave a jerk as the engine sputtered. She glanced at the speedometer. 'Oh no!'

Horace was right: they *were* slowing down. She stared at the quivering needle. Fraction by fraction, they were losing power, and they were nowhere near land. She frantically pulled the thrust lever, but it was no good. Suddenly the smooth hum of the engine stopped altogether, before faltering back to life.

'Professor!' she called. 'Professor!' She ran over to his hammock and shook him awake. 'Professor, something's wrong!'

CHAPTER TWENTY-TWO

The professor lurched out of his hammock and ran to the control deck. As he pulled levers and punched at buttons with his good hand, the steady hum of the little ship's engine stuttered and ground to a halt.

'What's happening?' wailed Horace.

Gilbert shook himself awake and peered worriedly through the windscreen.

'We appear to have run out of fuel,' said the professor, shading his eyes and scanning the horizon. 'But I can see an island up ahead. We'll just have to hope the wind will get us there. I'll take her down on the first beach we come to.'

'Is it one of the Violet Isles?' asked Echo, squinting hopefully out of the window.

'No, my dear, we're still a few miles off the Violet Isles,' the professor replied, a grim look on his face. 'This is good old Galligaskins.' He took the wheel and steered for the rocky island that had appeared in the haze up ahead. Without the engine to help, steering the *Hummerbird* was down to luck – the wind took the little ship wherever it wanted to. But the professor held her steady, and finally, after several nerve-wracking attempts, they were skimming over the waves and grinding to a halt on the rocks.

'Now, this is something of a predicament,' said the professor, as they stood on the pebbly beach beside the *Hummerbird*. Galligaskins was a large but somewhat bare and windswept island, with plenty of stones, spiky plants and mangy-looking rock rabbits, but not an awful lot else.

A large bluish-grey seabird squawked past overhead, hitting Horace's shoulder with a splat of white guano. 'Yuck!' He grimaced. 'Oh, this is the worst luck.'

'Don't panic,' said the professor, with a smile. 'You know what they say: there is always a way out for an explorer.' He broke into song:

> *'When you're feeling full of gloom,*
> *You are never really doomed,*
> *There is always a way out for an explorer!*
>
> *When you're sure you're out of luck,*
> *You are never truly stuck,*
> *There is always a way out for an explorer!*

When you're trapped,
Your rope's snapped,
There's a spider in your shoe,
Lost your map,
In a flap,
And you don't know what to do,

Do not swerve,
Hold your nerve,
There will be a passage through,
Because there's always a way out for an explorer!'

'Er . . . how far exactly are we from the Violet Isles?' asked Echo when the professor had finished his song.

'It's thirty miles to Amethyst,' he said, with a sigh. 'If only we could contact Doctor Beetlestone. She knows these islands much better than I do. I'm sure she'd have some ideas.'

'Wait!' Echo dashed back inside the *Hummerbird* and riffled through her bag to find the little white-and-copper bird Jimmy Mainspring had given her. She climbed back out and slithered down the ladder. 'How about using my postal pigeon?'

'Perfect!' said the professor, reaching into his pocket for his fountain pen. 'I'll send her a message straight away.' He scribbled several lines on a piece of paper, rolled it up and inserted it into the mechanical bird's claw.

Echo spun the dials under the little bird's wing to set the

coordinates of the laboratory, wound the key and threw the pigeon up into the air. It whirred off into the sky, scattering the local seabirds. Echo watched it fly until it was just a dot among the clouds.

'We'll make camp here and see what's what by daylight,' said Professor Daggerwing, squinting into the thorn-clad trees.

'But . . . how are we to get the airship started again with no fuel?' said Horace.

Professor Daggerwing winked at him. 'Don't worry, dear Horace. I have complete faith in Doctor Beetlestone. She is a most remarkable woman.'

Horace sniffed and hugged his caterpillar jar to his chest. 'I hope you're right.'

The professor nodded. 'For now, let's find something to make a fire. I don't know about you, but I'm famished.'

Echo wandered away from the shore, scuffing her boots through the stones. Why couldn't anything ever run smoothly? It was yet another delay to their journey. Would they ever even get to the Violet Isles? She sighed, gathered an armful of desiccated wood shards and brought it back to the airship, where Horace was still clutching his jar and looking nervously around him.

A cool breeze blew off the sea and down the shoreline and the professor hummed a jaunty tune as he collected driftwood.

Suddenly he gave a shout, scrabbled for a moment in the sand and held up a shiny black rock. 'Look!'

Echo licked the salt from her lips and screwed up her eyes to see. 'What is it?'

'Black gold!'

'Black gold?'

'Sea coal,' said the professor, with a grin. 'I felt it crunching under my boots. Probably broke off a seam of coal out in the water somewhere. If there's more of this around, it'll make a fantastic campfire.'

The sea coal did indeed make a strong fire, although it was rather damp and smelly and occasionally spat salty flares into the air. In the last light of the evening, the professor showed Echo and a reluctant Horace how to spot sea potatoes and starfish in the shallows and spear them with a sharpened branch. They were soon roasting the strange, fleshy creatures over the flames, while Gilbert nibbled with relish on a blue clump of weed he'd dragged back from a rock pool.

'Anyone for a pickled sweetroot?' said Professor Daggerwing, opening the jar with a *pop* and releasing a pungent cloud of vinegar.

'No thank you,' said Horace.

Echo was about to decline too, but, at the professor's hopeful look, she softened. 'I'd love some,' she said, reaching out for a couple of the slippery white spheres. She popped one into her mouth and almost choked as she bit into the crunchy flesh. It was so tangy it made her eyes water.

'Ooh, I think the sea potatoes are ready!' said the professor, turning to take his stick off the fire. Echo swiftly shoved the other sweetroot into her pocket, before retrieving her own spear and taking a mouthful of sea potato. It was strangely salty and as chewy as rubber, but definitely better than a sweetroot.

'How is it?' said Horace, sniffing the charred lump on the end of his spear with suspicion.

Echo continued chewing and considered this. 'It's ... different,' she said, after managing to swallow. 'Like a hairy, salty egg that's been boiled for far too long.'

'Oh,' said Horace, looking queasy.

'It's really quite all right,' said Echo. 'Go on, try it.'

'I don't think I can.' Horace recoiled, as Echo took another bite, squirting briny juices across the sand.

'Adventurers must eat, Horace,' said the professor, swallowing his own in one gulp. 'I think they're quite delicious.'

After hesitating for what seemed like an hour, Horace finally held his nose and put the sea potato to his mouth. He closed his eyes, took a bite, gagged and eventually swallowed.

'Better than the pickles?' said Echo, trying not to laugh in case she upset him again.

'I really couldn't say.' Horace was looking almost as green as he had in the *Hummerbird*, but he forced a few mouthfuls

213

down and soon even he had managed to relax as they lounged companionably in the glow of the fire, drinking mugs of sweet tea and gazing at the luminous pulsing of jellyfish in the shallow waters of the bay.

Echo leaned back on her elbows and took in Horace's face, still smudged with coal dust, and his fingers slick with sea-potato grease. He seemed like a different boy from the pampered prince she'd known back in Lockfort. She smiled to herself, then finished up her mug of tea and stifled a yawn.

'I think it's best if we get some sleep,' said the professor, noticing Echo's eyelids drooping. 'And, with any luck, we'll be on our way to the Violet Isles in the morning.'

They all clambered back into the *Hummerbird* and arranged themselves in their hammocks.

'Goodnight,' said Horace.

'Goodnight,' said Echo, tucking Gilbert into the crook of her arm. But, although she was bone-tired from the adventures of the day, her head was so full of sky pirates and airships and mothers, and her heart was so full of hope, that it was a very long while before she fell asleep.

Echo woke the next morning to a nudge from Gilbert and a strange tapping sound on the porthole near her head. The little lizard scurried to the window with a chirrup.

'What is it?' She struggled out of her hammock,

disorientated, and peered through the glass to see her postal pigeon fluttering at the window, a scroll of paper in its claw.

'A message from Doctor Beetlestone!' Echo opened the airship's hatch and clambered out on to the roof. The little mechanical bird flew up to her and landed in her cupped hands.

'Professor!' she called, scrambling back inside. 'There's a message for you!'

The professor groggily climbed out of his hammock and after a few moments found his glasses. 'Aha!' he said, as he unrolled the scroll of paper and read.

'Is it from your friend?' asked Echo, hopping from one foot to another.

'Yes, yes, indeed,' said the professor. 'And she's on her way!'

The professor relit the coals and they sat huddled on the rocks for a campfire breakfast of slightly charred golden snapperfish. Horace tucked in with relish, having finally got used to the taste of the ocean. Gilbert made do with snapping at flies that landed on the rocks. Seabirds perched warily around them, eyeing Gilbert and the travellers suspiciously.

'*When* will she be here?' Echo shaded her eyes with her hand and scanned the skies for the millionth time. They had to get to the Violet Isles. What if the sky pirates had moved on already?

Then, with a jolt, she saw something. In the southern sky, a small dark dot hovered among the clouds.

'Is that her ship?' Echo jumped up, knocking her half-eaten snapperfish on to the rocks, where the gulls leaped on it in a mass of squabbling beaks and flapping wings.

'It doesn't look like an airship,' said Horace, squinting in the morning sun as the dot grew bigger. 'It looks like a . . . a flying person.'

Echo stared. Horace was right: it did look like a flying person! She turned to the professor, open-mouthed.

'Well, I do declare!' Professor Daggerwing beamed. 'The doc's finally got her jetpack working.' He stood up, waving his arms. 'Edie!' he shouted. 'Edie! Over here!'

CHAPTER TWENTY-THREE

After a few attempts, the flying-suited Doctor Beetlestone made a wobbly landing on the rocks, the flames shooting out of her jetpack sending the gulls squawking into the air. She flicked a switch in one gloved hand to turn off the burners, then took off her helmet and goggles to reveal a tanned face with friendly crinkles around twinkling green eyes. Two thick silver plaits tumbled out over her shoulders.

'Professor Daggerwing!' she said, striding over and slapping him heartily on the shoulder. 'It's been far too long. How are you?'

'Oh please, call me Mangrove,' said the professor, turning scarlet to the tips of his ears. He cleared his throat. 'I see you've got the old burners firing at last.'

Doctor Beetlestone nodded and unstrapped the copper contraption from her back, laying it down carefully on the rocks. 'It's a prototype really. A tricky beast to steer, but it gets me about. Now, you must introduce me.'

She pulled off her glove and stuck out a hand to Echo, who was still staring in wonder at the doctor's jetpack, complete with gas tanks, a propeller and the two burners that had propelled her through the sky. 'I'm Edie Beetlestone.'

After they had all introduced themselves, the professor explained what had happened.

Doctor Beetlestone nodded. 'I've plenty of fuel back at the lab.' She pulled on her jetpack and helmet again. 'You get her aloft, I'll guide you back in and you can refuel at my place.'

Soon the *Hummerbird* was gliding over the sea towards Amethyst Isle, with Doctor Beetlestone clinging to the hull and propelling them forward. Echo couldn't tear herself away from the windscreen, her heart beating a mad polka in her chest as purple mist appeared on the horizon, finally giving way to an island thick with greenery and fringed with sandy beaches. They were in the Violet Isles!

Even Horace was in a good mood at the thought of seeing the Greater Brimstone and hummed along while the professor sang a jaunty song:

> 'Oh, the Violet Isles, the Violet Isles,
> Where the purple mist goes on for miles,
> And the sea potatoes grow in piles,
> In the Vio-Violet Isles.

Oh, the Violet Isles, the Violet Isles,
Where the mantraps snap like crocodiles,
And their sweet hypnotic scent beguiles,
In the Vio-Violet Isles.

Oh, the Violet Isles, the Violet Isles,
Where everyone beams with great big smiles,
Oh, we all are Violet-Isle-o-philes,
In the Vio-Violet Isles.'

As Doctor Beetlestone towed them closer to the islands, Echo's insides fizzed with excitement as the fabled violet mists drew in and clouded their view. As soon as they'd glided on to the sand of Amethyst Isle, she climbed up and released the airship's hatch. She stuck her head out and was met with warm, humid air, rich with the salty scent of the ocean and the heavy perfume of tropical flowers. She wriggled out and jumped down lightly on to the sand. The professor and Horace followed.

Echo couldn't help grinning as she gazed round the island. They were in a curved bay fringed with palm trees, sea foam lapping gently on to the beach of pale pinkish sand. They were in the Violet Isles! And, though she couldn't see any sign of a sky-pirate ship yet, her mother could be close by. Although that meant the sky pirates would be too, she thought with a sudden stab of fear. They'd approached from the north, as the professor had planned, but would they really be safe? Of course they would, she told herself. Doctor Beetlestone lived here, after all.

Gilbert ran down her leg on to the sand and sniffed the air appreciatively, before cocking his head to one side and scuttling off to investigate a rock pool.

'I don't see a laboratory,' said Horace, looking around.

'That's because it's camouflaged,' said Doctor Beetlestone, jumping down from the rear of the *Hummerbird*. 'It can be dangerous to draw attention to yourself out here. Follow me.' She strode off into the trees and they all tramped after her.

'Here we are,' she said when they'd pushed their way through the vines and found themselves in a little clearing.

Echo and Horace looked around, but all that was to be seen were tree trunks hung with dripping vines.

'I don't see anything,' said Echo, confused.

Gilbert chirruped from her shoulder.

'What . . . Oh!' Echo gasped in amazement as she followed his gaze and saw a spherical building of glossy wood nestled in the treetops. 'It's a tree house!'

'Or a tree lab,' said Doctor Beetlestone. She twisted what appeared to be a knot in the wood of the tree trunk and steps sprang out, spiralling upwards until they reached the door to the laboratory. 'After you!'

Echo and Horace scampered up the stairs and found their way into a circular room with windows all around. In the

centre was a gleaming steel workspace with saucepans of bubbling, sweet-smelling liquid. On one side was a curved desk covered with charts and notes, and on the other was a curved bed with butterfly-print blankets and a pillow shaped like a beetle.

'Please excuse the mess,' said the doctor. 'I wasn't quite prepared for your arrival and the lollipops are not quite ready.'

'Lollipops?' said Horace.

'For the butterflies, of course.' Doctor Beetlestone smiled and beckoned him over to the saucepans. 'Here, you two can help. Echo, the moulds are under the worktop. Horace, once the nectar is bubbling, let's pour it in.'

Echo found the moulds, each one with a disc-shaped indentation the size of her head, while Horace hovered over the saucepans with a thermometer.

'With any luck, we'll be able to see the butterflies as they pass by this afternoon,' said Doctor Beetlestone.

'Splendid,' said the professor, rubbing his hands together. Then his face turned grim. 'And on to Lockfort tomorrow.'

'Lockfort? The out-of-bounds, nobody-ever-dares-go-there Lockfort that hasn't been visited for more than a hundred years?' Doctor Beetlestone gaped and almost poured a saucepan of nectar all over the worktop.

The professor flushed and nodded. 'The very same. I owe these two a return trip. They rescued me, you know.'

'Well!' Doctor Beetlestone shook her head in astonishment.

'You'll be needing plenty of fuel if you're attempting that,' she said. 'The sea coal's in the adjoining trunk. Help yourself to however much you need.'

The professor disappeared off to refuel the *Hummerbird* while Horace, with the help of Doctor Beetlestone, poured the sticky liquid into the moulds. Gilbert sniffed greedily from Echo's shoulder as she stood and watched, the enormity of her sort-of-plan suddenly dawning on her. The professor was leaving for Lockfort tomorrow. Then she'd be trying to find the Black Sky Wolves on her own. Worry fluttered in her stomach.

'It's my own special recipe,' Doctor Beetlestone explained, as they filled the last mould. 'The Greater Brimstone only eats nectar from three flowers – the leopard lily, the ginger rose and Foxton's night orchid. But I've found when I harvest all three, and mix them together in just the right proportions, the butterflies can't resist.' She took a handful of huge lollipop sticks, each one as long as Echo's arm, and placed each one in a mould. 'Once these set, we can use them to lure the butterflies to us.'

'Ha!' The professor reappeared in the doorway. 'I bet old Jefferson never thought of that! He might have all those young engineers working for him, building all his fancy technology, but does he have lollipops? I think not!'

Doctor Beetlestone laughed. 'Don't be so competitive.'

Jefferson. Fancy technology. Echo's mind suddenly made

the connections. Fergus! Abena had said he was one of the engineers who worked for Jefferson. He'd be back in Port Tourbillon by now. Perhaps he'd already told Abena something that could help!

Echo raced out of the room, pulling the postal pigeon from her pocket. She shimmied back down from the tree house, scrawled a note on a scrap of paper and released the little bird into the sky with a metallic flutter. She watched it leave with every finger and toe crossed. Abena had to have answers. Time was running out.

Once the nectar lollipops had set, Doctor Beetlestone pulled them out of their moulds with a *pop* and stashed them in a bag. 'Come on,' she said. 'Let's go and find some butterflies!'

They followed her through the jungle until they came to a wide clearing with a gleaming greenish-blue lake. On its surface floated enormous lily pads, each one as wide as Echo was tall. Doctor Beetlestone stepped on to the first one and strode across the lake, using the wrinkled leaves as stepping stones.

Echo followed, hopping from leaf to leaf. The leaves bobbed slightly as they took her weight, but they held. Each plant had a mottled yellow-and-brown flower or a bud as big as Echo's fist.

'Leopard lilies,' the doctor explained, as Horace inched from leaf to leaf to join them in the middle of the lake. 'The butterflies sometimes come here in the late evening to feed, but they're shy creatures. If we're quiet and patient, we may get lucky.'

The four of them arranged themselves cross-legged on a leaf. Doctor Beetlestone handed out the lollipops and they sat in silence, scanning the skies for any sight of a fluttering wing. The purple mist descended on the lake, bringing an eerie hush with it, only broken by the occasional *plop* of a fish or the squawk of a heron.

'But how will we see them—' started Horace.

Doctor Beetlestone put a finger to her lips. She waved her lollipop aloft.

Echo let out a gasp as a black-and-gold butterfly with wings as big as dinner plates loomed out of the mist and landed on Horace's head. Gilbert gave a chirrup of alarm and hid himself in Echo's hair as the butterfly's coiled tongue unrolled to lick the lollipop Horace was holding.

'It's . . . it's heavy!' said Horace, looking up in amazement, a huge grin spreading across his face.

'If only I had my photographic plates,' said the professor, with a groan, as suddenly a whole flock of Greater Brimstones descended on them out of the fog, their velvety wings brushing Echo's arms as she held her lollipop out. She giggled in delight as one landed on her wrist and lapped at the sweet nectar, all the while keeping one huge compound eye fixed on her.

'Aren't they incredible?' whispered Horace, his face glowing.

'Yes,' Echo whispered back, suddenly understanding what Horace saw in these beautiful insects. 'They really, really are.'

Finally, the butterflies dispersed, Gilbert was brave enough to emerge from Echo's hair, and they all followed Doctor Beetlestone back over the lily pads and through the jungle to her treetop laboratory.

She headed up the steps, followed by the professor and Horace. As Echo approached the stairs, there was a rustle of leaves and her postal pigeon swooped down through the branches. Echo caught it in both hands and feverishly unrolled the scroll of paper clasped in its claw. Could this be it? Her hands shook as she read the note:

F says try Tyrian Isle. That's where Jefferson's crew saw them last. Abena

Tyrian Isle. Echo thought back to Mrs Milkweed's charts. That was the largest island to the far south of the cluster. Could Fergus be right?

226

'Come on, Echo!' called Horace from the top step. He peered down at her. 'Who's that from?'

'No one,' said Echo, guiltily shoving the message and the pigeon into her pocket and hurrying up the steps.

'How close are the other islands?' Echo asked Doctor Beetlestone, as she cleaned the lollipop sticks and stashed them away neatly in a cabinet.

The doctor smiled. 'How about I give you a bird's eye view?' she said. 'I've made a few adjustments to the lab since you were last here, Professor. Hold on tight.' She pressed a large blue button on the wall and the whole laboratory shook before sliding smoothly upwards into the air above the treetops. She pressed a yellow button and the others gasped as the roof unfurled like a bud opening. The walls slid down to reveal a glass parapet, leaving them gazing in amazement across the treetops of Amethyst Isle and over the glittering sea.

'Wow!' said Echo. 'This is incredible! Can we see all the islands from here?'

'That's Magenta to the west,' the doctor said, pointing to a tiny, beach-fringed island. 'And the larger one beyond it is Heliotrope.' She walked over to the other side. 'Then, to the north-east, we have Magenta.'

'And what about Tyrian?' asked Echo.

The doctor turned to Echo. 'Tyrian is far to the south,' she said, pointing out a dark shape on the horizon. 'But it's barely part of the Violet Isles really, different flora and fauna entirely.'

'Have you ever been there?'

The doctor shook her head. 'No, and I don't intend to. It's a dangerous place. No butterflies there either! Just poisonous fire ants, porcupythons and worse.'

'Why's it so dark?' asked Horace, squinting through his binoculars. 'The sand looks black.'

But Echo's heart was thudding so loudly in her ears she didn't hear the professor's reply. She thought back to the photogram Evander Jefferson had shown at the Guild. The *Scarlet Margaret*, tethered above a charcoal-dark beach.

'Can I see?'

Horace passed her the binoculars and Echo focused on the island. She shivered as she took it in. Black sand. Tyrian had to be the place.

She needed to get there, and there wasn't much time.

CHAPTER TWENTY-FOUR

The next morning Echo woke at the break of dawn, as the first tendrils of sun crept in through the windows of Doctor Beetlestone's tree lab. She had to get to Tyrian, but neither Doctor Beetlestone nor the professor were going to take her there. She looked at the sleeping forms of her companions and bit back a guilty sigh. No, as much as she'd like the company, she would have to get there herself.

She scooped up Gilbert, who cheeped a drowsy, *Whasssgoingon*, before going back to sleep round her neck, then crept across the room and out of the door barefoot, boots in one hand.

She was almost at the beach when she heard the crunch of a footstep behind her. She spun round to find a rumpled Horace staring accusingly at her.

'What are you doing now?' he hissed.

'None of your business.' She went over to the *Hummerbird* and started to climb.

'You can't take the professor's ship,' said Horace. 'What will he do without it?'

'He'll be fine,' said Echo. She opened the hatch. 'He's safe here with Edie. And I'll have the ship back before he knows it's gone.'

'You can't!' said Horace, scrambling up after her. 'Where are you going anyway?'

'Tyrian,' said Echo. She slipped inside.

'But that's . . . that's the dangerous island.'

'It's the island where the sky pirates are,' said Echo. 'Where my mother is.'

'Your mother? But how can you possibly—'

'She's there. I know it.' Echo faced Horace and told him about what she'd seen at the Explorers' Guild, about what Fergus had said and the black-sand beach. 'The Black Sky Wolves kidnapped her and that's where they're hiding.'

'But that photogram was years old, Echo. How do you know they still have her?'

'I don't, but it's all I have to go on.' Why couldn't he understand? 'This is important, can't you see?' She clenched her fists to stop her voice shaking. 'This is the only chance I have to find her. And anyway, I have a plan.' Echo lowered her gaze, unable to meet his eye. She'd figure one out when she got there anyway.

Horace nodded slowly and folded his arms. After a moment, he said, 'I'm not letting you go. Not alone. It's too dangerous.'

Gilbert gave a wounded chirrup as if to say, *Alone? What*

about me? But, as Echo looked at Horace, an understanding passed between them.

'So you'll come?' she asked. 'Even though it's dangerous?'

Horace nodded stiffly. 'I know what it's like not to have a mother,' he said. 'We've got to bring the ship straight back though.'

Echo smiled at the *we*. 'Promise,' she said. 'Let's go.'

Echo tried not to let Horace see how nervous she felt as she fired up the *Hummerbird*'s engines and they lifted into the air. She barely spoke for the whole journey and didn't loosen her grip on the wheel for a single moment, praying all the way that the damaged balloon envelope, still patched up with her old petticoat, would hold. As they neared Tyrian, fear fluttered in her belly and she frowned in concentration. Her landing had to be more successful than the last time she'd flown or they'd be stranded in this perilous place! But the little ship kept humming forward and, after a slightly wobbly approach, Echo managed to bring them down on to the sparkling black sands without a hitch.

'So, which way do we go?' asked Horace, as they climbed down from the *Hummerbird*.

Echo felt her cheeks flush with heat. 'I don't really know yet,' she said. 'I guess we should look around a bit.'

'But they could be anywhere!' Horace threw up his hands.

'We can't just fly here and expect to find them! *You* said you had a plan!'

'I know!' Echo felt her eyes prickle with tears and she held her breath to keep herself from snapping at Horace. 'But I lied. I didn't ask you to come.'

'You're a fool, Echo.' Horace shook his head in disbelief. 'What are we even going to do if we find them? They're pirates! There are only two of us!'

'Don't you think I know that?' Echo shouted. 'You can't always have a plan, Horace. Sometimes you just have to go out into the unknown and see what you find.'

'Fine,' said Horace, sitting down on the black sand. 'Let me know when you've worked out what to do.'

'I'm going to look at the map.' Echo turned her back on him and stormed back to the airship. Why had she ever thought Horace had changed? He was the same old spoilt prince he'd always been, tagging along and ruining things. She would just have to work this out by herself.

After consulting all the charts she could find, Echo was still in the dark about how to find the *Scarlet Margaret*. She sighed. 'The only thing for it is to explore,' she said to Gilbert, who was also eyeing the maps with a confused expression. 'Let's tell Horace.' She climbed out on to the roof of the *Hummerbird*, shaded her eyes with her hand and scanned the empty black-sand bay. Where *was* he?

Echo wiped the sweat off her brow with the back of her hand and jumped down on to the beach.

'Horace!' she called. There was no answer, just the swish of the tide and the odd melancholy cry of a seabird. 'Oh, where is he?'

Gilbert curled his tail into a question mark and turned a worried shade of white.

'Perhaps he's hiding.' Echo draped the lizard round her neck and circled the ship's gondola, but the sand was empty. 'Horace?'

Nothing. The beach was deserted. She spun round and scanned the bay, a heavy feeling settling in the bottom of her stomach. Horace wasn't on the beach anywhere. So where was he?

Echo retraced her steps to the water's edge. *Think, Echo.* Horace had been sitting right here and then they'd argued and she'd stomped off up to the *Hummerbird*.

Echo flushed as she remembered. Perhaps she shouldn't have shouted at him. Perhaps she even owed him an apology. But, if he'd wandered off, she had no idea which direction he'd gone in.

Gilbert suddenly tensed on her shoulder and scuttled down her leg on to the sand.

'Gilbert, what are you . . . ?' Echo trailed off as she saw him sniffing a set of footprints veering away from her trail to the

Hummerbird and leading towards the trees.

Her heart dropped into her stomach. Doctor Beetlestone had said this island was dangerous! Echo scooped up Gilbert and ran up the beach, her boots slipping on the loose sand, thoughts of vicious porcupythons, whatever those were, filling her head. She followed the footprints until they dried out and disappeared.

'Horace!' she called into the trees, hoping in vain this was some kind of joke. 'Horace, you can come out now!'

But there was no reply, just the papery rustle of the palms and the rhythmic *whoosh* of the sea behind her. Echo stepped forward, out of the sunlight, and peered into the dim green darkness. There were no neat pathways like on Amethyst Isle, but she could see a trampled section in the ferns where someone had pushed their way through.

Oh, Horace! Echo stroked Gilbert's scaly tail. No need to panic. She'd go and find him, and apologize, and bring him and the ship back before Professor Daggerwing even realized they were gone. Horace was right, she *had* been foolish to think that two children could do this alone. She took some deep breaths to steady her nerves. He couldn't have gone far. Could he?

She stepped into the trees. The beach had been hot and dry, with the sun beating fiercely on the back of her neck, but the palm forest was a wet sort of warm, with damp, leafy air and a springy bed of moss underfoot. Echo pushed through the dripping ferns, making her way into the jungle. Something rustled in the bushes, and she jumped backwards, fearing teeth sinking into her ankle, lost her footing and landed on her bottom in the leaves.

She laughed in relief when she saw it was just a glossy red beetle scuttling through the undergrowth with a berry clamped tight in its pincers. It still took a minute or two to get her breath back though, and steady her pounding heart. Once she had, she realized just how quiet and still and Horace-less the place was.

She filled her lungs. 'HORACE!' she yelled, as loud as she could, her voice reverberating through the trees. A flock of bright green parrots exploded from the forest canopy at the sound, but when the leaves settled there was still just that damp, dripping quiet and the thud of Echo's own heart in her ears.

Where was he? Why did he have to run off? Didn't he know how dangerous this place was? Tears prickled in her eyes and she rubbed them away with the back of her hand. No, she wasn't going to sit here and cry. She was going to find him.

Echo got to her feet and turned in a circle, scanning the greenery for any sign of Horace's yellow-blond hair. Up ahead, she could make out the trail of crushed ferns, and so she trudged onwards through the trees, ducking trailing vines and stepping over clusters of brightly coloured toadstools for what seemed like hours. She had almost given up and turned round when a wide clearing opened up before her and she spotted a strange group of huge plants, each with a drooping stem as thick as her arm, and topped with a gaping pink flower as large as an armchair.

'Wow, Gilbert, look at these.' Echo stepped forward to get a closer look.

Pain shot through her shoulder. 'Ow!' She looked down to find that Gilbert had sunk his jaws into her skin and turned a bright emergency red. 'What's the matter? They're just big flowers.'

He raised his crest, but Echo ignored him.

'Don't worry, I'm not going to eat them.'

The flowers were a deep fuchsia-pink and each wide, rounded petal was fringed with a row of needle-sharp thorns, each one as long as Echo's finger. As she got closer, she breathed in a delicious, heady scent, like peaches and oranges and candyfloss all wrapped into one. She licked her lips and moved closer still.

'Or maybe I should. They smell delicious!'

Gilbert scuttled into her hair and nipped her ear with a, *No, Echo!*

'Get off!' She brushed him away and he landed with a *plop* in the leaves as she walked, as if in a trance, closer to that delicious scent. As she got nearer, she realized each flower contained a pool of nectar in its centre that glistened like honey. Her mouth watered.

'Is this what smells so beautiful?' As she reached out to dip a finger in the sticky liquid, Gilbert raced up her leg and bit her hard on the thigh.

'OW! What're you—'

As she snatched her hand back, her fingers brushed a thorn and the flower snapped shut with a fleshy thud.

Echo staggered backwards, her heart racing. What was this thing? She shook her head, trying to get rid of the fug in her brain. Why couldn't she think straight? Had the flower done this to her?

Gilbert scrambled up her back and nudged at her shoulder. Somehow she stumbled away from the plants before collapsing at the edge of the clearing with her head in her hands. It took several minutes for her head to clear, but, once it had, she scooped up Gilbert and put him back on her shoulder. 'Sorry, Gilbert, I should have listened to you.'

Gilbert rolled his eyes in an *I know* kind of way.

'What on earth are those things?' She smoothed his scales. 'Let's get out of here. They're giving me the creeps.' She glanced around. 'Where *is* he?'

As she turned to leave the clearing, there was a muffled cry from behind her.

Echo spun round, blinking. 'Horace?'

CHAPTER TWENTY-FIVE

'*Mmmmph.*'

There it was again. Echo froze, scanning the clearing for any sign of movement. Then she saw it, and her heart dropped. There, in one of the closed plant mouths, was a large, squirming lump. A rather Horace-shaped lump rippling within the fleshy bud of petals. She could make out an elbow, or was it a knee? Whatever it was, it did not seem happy.

She was about to race forward and wrench open the petals when Gilbert's claws tightened on her shoulder and she remembered the plant's strange perfume and its effect on her.

'Horace,' she whispered. 'How in Lockfort am I going to get you out of there?' She glanced round the clearing in desperation and spotted a long, dry branch on the forest floor. She grabbed it, pinched her nose tight with one finger and thumb and, pulse racing, stepped towards the plant. Still holding her nose, she thrust the end of the branch between the tooth-like thorns that fringed the petal mouth. The bud shook slightly and seemed to clamp itself even more tightly shut.

'*Mmmmph!*' A muffled complaint came from inside.

Echo pulled down hard on the other end of the branch, but the plant didn't give. She bounced up and down in an attempt to force the bud open. As she did so, she saw a tiny gap open up between the rim of thorns and caught a glimpse of Horace's hand. Lungs burning, she slammed her body down again.

There was a loud, splintering crack, the branch snapped and Echo tumbled on to the ground. She took an involuntary gasp and felt her head spin with the plant's perfume. She stumbled to the edge of the clearing before daring to breathe again. Glancing back, she saw one end of the branch still wedged in the plant's mouth. But the bud was still tightly closed.

Anger engulfed her. Horace might be irritating at times, but that didn't mean she'd let some overgrown flower have him for supper. How dare it take her friend? She scrabbled around in the bushes for another stick, a shorter, stronger one this time. Gripping it in both hands, she glared at the plant. The edges of the tooth-fringed petals seemed to be curved slightly upwards in a smug grin. Was it . . . was it laughing at her?

Echo took a deep breath and ran at it, beating its thick stem like a wild thing. But it was no use. The flower simply swayed gently, as if being rocked by a light breeze. When her breath gave out, she stumbled back out of the clearing, panting, and gazed at her enemy. The plant didn't have a scratch on it and, worse still, Horace seemed to have stopped wriggling and complaining.

What now? She had to get him out. Could he even breathe in there? Was his mind completely scrambled by the plant's perfume? Panic rose in her chest and she tried to steady herself. She instinctively reached into her pocket for the pin, but instead of firm metal her fingers closed round something round and slimy. She snatched her hand back in disgust. What *was* that?

Very carefully, she put her hand back in her pocket and pulled out a slippery white sphere. She rolled her eyes. It was that disgusting pickled sweetroot she had pocketed after their impromptu picnic on Galligaskins. She was about to fling it into the undergrowth when an idea sprang into her mind. What was it that the professor had said about pickles?

Vinegar is a natural weedkiller.

Would it work? She could only try.

Echo gripped the stick in one fist and the pickled sweetroot in the other. 'Think you can get one over on me?' she snarled at the plant. 'Well, think again, you ... you weed!'

Holding her breath, she stormed over to it and stabbed the stick between the fringe of teeth. The plant shivered a little, but didn't budge. Echo wrenched at the stick with her right hand and levered the petals open.

As quickly as she could, Echo shoved the pickled sweetroot through the gap in the plant's razor-sharp teeth and backed up until she was a safe distance away. She stooped forward, hands on her knees, gasping to get her breath back. Then she gazed up at the plant.

The petals were still firmly closed in what was now most definitely a smug grin. Echo dropped to the ground and put her head in her hands. She had lost Horace. This was all her fault! And now she was all alone on the most dangerous of the Violet Isles. She had never meant this to happen. Why had she ever thought they could do this by themselves? She stifled a sob.

There was a strange rumble and Echo looked up at the sky through tear-filled eyes. A thunderstorm. This was all she needed.

The rumble came again, deep and throaty, and Echo suddenly realized it was coming from the clearing. She looked at the plant where Horace was trapped and saw that, where once it had been stock-still and smug, now it was quivering, its petals convulsing.

As she stared, the plant began to thrash from side to side and let out what could only be described as a big plant burp. As its petals opened and slammed shut again, Echo caught a glimpse of Horace lying curled up, still and sticky with nectar.

She jumped to her feet. 'Horace!' she yelled. 'Horace, you've got to wake up!'

But before she could race forward there was a huge, ground-shaking gurgle as the plant shuddered. Echo froze, gaping, the stick still gripped uselessly in one hand as, with one last mighty groan, the bud burst open, spitting both the pickled sweetroot and Horace out into a high arc through the air.

There was a crash and a muffled cry as Horace landed somewhere beyond the clearing. Echo broke from her trance and ran, careering through bushes and slipping over leaves, in the direction he'd flown.

'Horace!' she yelled.

'*Urrrghhh.*' There was a muffled grunt from a clump of ferns up ahead. Echo plunged through the bushes, jumped a small stream and slithered over the rocks to the other side. She pushed the ferns apart to find Horace sprawled in a heap, groaning and plastered with nectar from head to foot.

Was he hurt? She dropped to the ground beside him. 'Are you . . . are you all right?'

Horace rubbed the goo from his eyes and blinked at Echo. 'I don't know.' He tried to stand, swayed and tottered to one side. Echo got up to steady him and covered her nose at the hypnotic scent of the flower's nectar. 'We need to get that stuff off you. That's what's making you feel funny.'

She took Horace's arm and guided him back towards the stream, where he sat down in the shallow water. Echo waded in next to him and scooped handfuls over his head.

'What happened? What was I even doing out here?' Horace rubbed the sticky nectar off his face and blinked. 'Wait a minute, I do remember! I thought I saw a Lesser Blackspot in the bushes. And I followed it and I found those plants.'

Echo rolled her eyes, but couldn't help smiling with relief. Horace and his butterflies! 'There *are* no butterflies on Tyrian, Horace. Doctor Beetlestone said.'

'That's why I followed it. I wondered what it was doing out here. Anyway –' Horace brightened as he reached into the pocket of his soaking breeches – 'I suppose I should thank you really. If we hadn't argued, I never would have managed to get these.' He took out a little waxed paper packet and peered inside. 'Thank Lockfort they're still dry.'

'What are those?'

'Seeds.' Horace grinned. 'From that big plant. It's called a Goliath's mantrap. I'll be able to grow one at home now.'

'Grow one!' Echo jumped to her feet. 'Why would you want to grow one of those monstrous things?'

'To feed my butterflies.' He showed her the shiny purple seeds, as smooth and iridescent as pearls.

'Careful,' said Horace, as Echo leaned to look more closely. 'They're even more potent than the plants. Send you right to sleep.'

Echo swiftly stood back. 'I'll take your word for it. But now we should get back to the *Hummerbird* – I was crazy to think we could come here without a plan. We'll fly back to the lab and I'll tell Professor Daggerwing everything. He'll know what to do.'

Horace stood up with a squelch and shook the water out of his hair. 'Hey, look!'

Echo turned to see what he was pointing at. 'What?'

'It *was* a Lesser Blackspot.' Horace's cheeks were glowing.

'A Lesser what? Oh . . .' Echo trailed off as she realized Horace was pointing at a little brown butterfly. She shook her head in annoyance. 'This is no time for butterfly hunting, Horace.'

But Horace wasn't listening. 'Most peculiar,' he muttered, half to himself. 'These varieties are city butterflies. They lay their eggs in sailcloth. They don't live out in the islands. How could they have got here?'

'Who cares!' Echo threw her hands in the air. 'This whole trip has been a stupid mistake. Come on, I've had enough of this place.'

But Horace wasn't listening and he resisted Echo's tug on his wet sleeve. 'There are more of them.' He pulled away from Echo and marched off through the bushes after a cluster of fluttering brown shapes.

'I'm not coming!' Echo yelled after him. But Horace plunged onwards and disappeared into the undergrowth. 'Okay, fine,' she said, following his trail. 'But, if you get eaten by another carnivorous plant, I'm not rescuing you.'

Echo almost walked into Horace's still sopping back as he came to a sudden halt. He pointed up at the canopy. A thin plume of blue-grey smoke snaked its way into the sky from somewhere beyond the trees.

'Smoke,' he said. 'But what would make smoke out here in the islands?'

Echo's pulse quickened at the only possible answer. 'Another airship,' she whispered.

'But that means . . .'

'It means we've found the Black Sky Wolves!'

CHAPTER TWENTY-SIX

'Come on.' Echo crept forward through the bushes, Gilbert clinging to her shoulder and her blood pounding in her ears. Could she really be this close to finding the sky pirates? Could she really be this close to finding her mother?

As they reached the edge of the undergrowth, she pushed the damp leaves apart and, suddenly dizzy with a mixture of excitement and fear, sucked in a shuddering breath. Down on the beach a huge vessel, easily five times larger than the *Hummerbird*, bobbed on the breeze. In place of the shining copper gondola, there was an open wooden deck, like a seafaring ship's; instead of a balloon, huge sails billowed from two tall masts. The airship was tethered to the sand, and a rope ladder snaked down the side of its hull to the beach below. On the main deck, Echo caught sight of a huge, bald, tattooed man with great rounded shoulders and seemingly no neck. A gleaming cutlass was tucked in his belt.

'What is it?' whispered Horace, peering over her shoulder.

'Sky pirates,' she breathed.

Horace pushed through the leaves beside her and shook his head, the colour draining from his face. 'No, no, no!' He covered his eyes with his hands. 'Please tell me this is a dream! I didn't think we'd really find them. Let's go.'

'Not yet,' said Echo, unable to tear her gaze away from the ship. 'I want to see if my . . .' Her voice was shaking. She swallowed and composed herself. 'I need to see if my mother—'

There was a metallic swish from behind, and a shriek from Horace, as Echo spun round to find a small, buck-toothed, eyepatched girl brandishing a cutlass as long as her arm.

'Stop right there!' she snarled, stamping her peg leg. 'Don't move a muscle.' The girl glared at them with the eye that wasn't concealed by a patch. 'Who dares try to approach the *Scarlet Margaret*?'

Gilbert froze on Echo's shoulder.

Echo licked the salt from her lips. 'We're looking for the Black Sky Wolves.'

'And what business have you maggots got with the Black Sky Wolves?'

'Maggots?' spluttered Horace. 'I hardly think—'

'*Shh*,' said Echo, silencing him with a look.

'But she's only about eight. How dare she . . .' Horace trailed off, as the girl stalked towards him, cutlass raised.

'Something to say, *maggot*?'

247

'No, no, I . . . er, no. Do carry on.'

'Walk,' the girl snarled, gesturing towards the beach with the tip of her blade. She marched Echo and Horace through a cluster of rock pools towards the sooty stretch of sand where the airship was moored. Out in the open, the ship looked even larger than it had from the safety of the bushes. Gilbert squinted up at it from his perch on Echo's shoulder and her pulse quickened as she caught sight of the rows of cannons studding its hull. She took a deep, shaky breath and scanned the deck, but the thick-necked pirate had disappeared from view.

They stepped into the ship's shadow and Echo gazed up at the rope ladder swaying in the breeze.

'Up there,' snarled the girl, prodding Echo between the shoulder blades with the tip of her cutlass. 'And no funny business.'

Echo grabbed the coarse ropes in both hands. She put her foot on the first rung, swallowed and shot a last nervous glance up at the hull. What was waiting for her at the top? Could her mother really be on the ship? Was she locked below decks somewhere, chained up and forced to work? Would she recognize Echo, when she hadn't seen her for so long? A prickle of fear ran up her spine as she remembered the cutlass glinting behind her. Would she even get a chance to find her mother?

She set her jaw and willed her hands to stop trembling. She could do this. She swung herself up on to the first rung.

'What's going on down there, Flora?' A man's voice rang out from above. Echo looked up to see a skinny man with a shock of white hair aiming a catapult at her from the deck of the ship.

'Got us some prisoners!' yelled the girl. 'Two kids with a . . .' She flipped up her eyepatch and squinted at Gilbert. 'Some kind of frog.'

Gilbert raised his crest and hissed in disgust, but the girl simply snapped back her eyepatch and ignored him.

'What business do you have here?' the man shouted.

'Well, I . . .' Echo's voice had dried to a croak.

'It's a personal matter,' interrupted Horace, a slight tremor in his voice.

Echo swallowed, grateful for the interruption.

'Personal?' The white-haired pirate snorted. 'What'll we do with 'em?' he shouted to the girl he'd called Flora. 'Gut 'em here or take 'em up to walk the plank?'

Echo glanced at Horace, who had turned as pale as Gilbert, beads of sweat forming on his upper lip. She found her voice. 'I'm looking for my mother.'

The two pirates looked at each other, then broke into laughter.

The white-haired pirate's grin turned to a glare. 'I'll give you five seconds to tell me why you're really here, and then I'll let Flora here loose with her cutlass, understand?'

Echo's words tumbled over each other in her panic at the talk of gutting. 'My mother *is* on your ship. Or at least she was. You . . . you kidnapped her!'

The pirate raised his eyebrows. 'Nah, not us. We don't do that any more. Not since Indigo Lil took over. More's the pity.

I used to enjoy a good kidnapping.' He smiled dreamily for a moment, before remembering himself and fixing Echo with another glare. 'Right, let's see what the captain makes of yer.' He pointed to the rope ladder. 'Bring 'em up, Flora.'

Once they'd climbed to the top of the ladder, the white-haired pirate reached over and hauled a shivering Echo on to the deck. Horace followed, his face tinged with grey, then Flora, her cutlass gripped expertly between her teeth. Echo looked around. The ship was just as vast as it had looked from below, and the crew bustled here and there, busily sloshing soapy water over decks, scrubbing masts and polishing metalwork.

'Bulkhead! Beti!' yelled the white-haired pirate. 'Got two spies here to walk the plank!'

Echo swallowed as the bald, thick-necked pirate they'd seen earlier climbed out of a hatchway to the main deck and thudded over. He was joined by a gap-toothed woman with long skirts that clinked with bottles. 'Maybe I should take their organs first, in case they come in handy,' she said, drawing out a little saw from one of her pockets and putting her face up to Echo's with an evil sneer.

Echo shrank back at the woman's hot, cinnamon-scented breath.

'What crew you from?' said the bald man, who must have been Bulkhead, putting one meaty hand to the hilt of his cutlass. He narrowed his eyes and leaned in. 'You after the Tyrian pearl too?'

'The Tyrian . . . ? We're not from a crew,' said Echo. 'We're—'

'Reckons we kidnapped her mother. Or that was her story anyway,' said the white-haired pirate.

'You *did* kidnap her,' said Echo, glaring at him. How could she convince them? She put her hand in her pocket and found the hairpin, and it filled her with courage. 'I saw a photogram of her on this very ship. You're the ones who stole the Port Tourbillon Crown Jewels, aren't you?'

Bulkhead puffed up his chest, making the octopus tattoo that coiled across his collarbone swell to twice its former size. 'We are indeed. One of my proudest piratin' days.'

'Then you'll recognize this.' Echo drew the pin from her pocket, trying to steady her shaking hands, and the pirates' eyes grew wide in recognition.

'You little thief!' Bulkhead grabbed her wrist as a crowd of heckling pirates gathered round.

'I'm not a thief!' Echo's voice trembled. Was she going to walk to her death after coming so close to finding her mother? She had to convince them. Her voice rose in desperation. 'It's my mother's, I swear on my life!'

'You know what we do to thieves?' the woman called Beti snarled.

'Gut her like a fish!' yelled Flora, waving her cutlass in the air.

'Gut her! Gut her!' they all chanted.

'Chop off her toes!' screeched Flora.

'Chop them! Chop them!'

'Slice off her fing—'

There was the clunk of boots on the deck and the yells of the gathered sky pirates suddenly hushed as they all turned. The boards creaked as the footsteps came closer.

'What in all the seven skies is going on here?' It was a woman's voice. An angry voice that made all the sky pirates stand nervously to attention.

Echo shrank back as a woman in a tricorne hat with a huge cream plume came storming through the crowd in buckled boots. Bulkhead licked his lips nervously. Echo tightened her grip on the hairpin and swallowed. Was this the dreaded Indigo Lil? The captain of the Black Sky Wolves, who smeared indigo clay on her face and liked to feed enemies' fingers and toes to cloud eels? What had this woman done with her mother? What was she going to do to them?

'To the plank!' yelled Flora, with a whoop.

The crowd of sky pirates began shouting again, leering at Echo, pulling her this way and that.

'To the plank!' they roared. 'To the plank!'

Horace's face was frozen in fear as they marched him across the deck.

'No!' shouted Echo. 'I can explain. I didn't steal it, I promise you!' But her voice was drowned out by the baying mob.

'It's my mother's pin, I swear it!' said Echo with a sob. She jerked away from the hands grasping her and the pin went skittering over the boards, landing by the woman's boots.

Indigo Lil froze. 'Stop, all of you, stop!' she bellowed. She bent down slowly and picked the pin up, turning it over in her hands. She turned to Echo with a frown. 'Where did you get this?'

'It ... it was my mother's. She left it for me when I was a baby.'

Lil grabbed Echo's chin, tilting it to look up at her, and examined her with piercing grey eyes. 'Left it where?'

'In ... in my basket, pinned beneath the blankets.'

Lil's frown turned to a look of utter shock, and then, as she looked again at Echo, one of wonder. 'Echo?' Lil said, her strong voice suddenly weakening to a croak. She shook her head and took off her hat, revealing a mass of dark curls pinned with an identical hairpin. Her eyes, stormy grey with flecks of gold, met Echo's. 'Echo, is it really you?'

Echo stared back in astonishment, trying to take in every detail at once. Lil's eyes, grey and gold, were like a mirror of Echo's own. Her skin was freckled even darker than Echo's and her hair flowed to her waist in a wild black mane. *Impossible hair*, thought Echo, *like mine.*

'M-mother?' Every muscle in Echo's body felt like it might burst. '*You're* Indigo Lil? But the woman in the photogram had white hair ...'

For a long moment, Lil just stared at her, and Echo faltered as a wave of fear washed over her. Her mother, a sky pirate?

And not just any sky pirate, but the terrible Indigo Lil. A violent thief! A murderer!

'Let me look at you.' Lil took Echo's face in her hands and stared into her eyes, oblivious to the rest of the sky pirates, who looked at one another in confusion. 'My Echo. Is it really you? But how?'

Echo could hardly move as Lil touched her hair, her face, mesmerized. She breathed in cinnamon and gunpowder. Was this really happening?

'Of course it is. As if I could ever doubt it. I don't need proof.' Lil threw her arms round Echo, her voice muffled in Echo's hair. 'I'd know you anywhere, Echo. My darling Echo.' She pulled back and stared into Echo's eyes again. 'How well you've grown.'

'I came to find you.' Echo scrubbed her eyes with her sleeve. Her head was spinning so fast she couldn't take it all in. Was this where she belonged? With thieves and murderers?

'A proper adventurer!' Lil smiled for the first time, and her own eyes filled with tears. Then she shook her head and her voice cracked as she said, 'They told me you were dead. They told me . . .' She took a deep breath and anger suddenly flashed in her eyes. 'That no-good *Alfons* told me you were dead. I should have known he was lying.'

Echo swallowed. So Lil *hadn't* forgotten her. She hadn't even known she was still alive. 'They lied to me too,' she said. 'All I had left of you was the hairpin.'

Lil turned it over. 'I used to hide it in your basket so King

255

Alfons didn't take it away. He didn't like me having anything that was different.' She passed it back to Echo. 'It's yours, Echo.' Then she enveloped Echo in a hug again and, despite Echo's fears, despite her shock and worry and confusion, Lil's arms somehow felt like home.

CHAPTER TWENTY-SEVEN

Echo and Lil finally drew apart, and Lil stepped back, wiping her eyes on her sleeve. She turned to the rest of the pirates, who were shuffling their boots nervously and looking at the deck. 'Right, you lot, I think Echo here is owed an apology.'

Bulkhead, the huge, thick-necked pirate, stepped forward. 'Yes, Cap'n. Sorry about the mix-up,' he said, flushing all over his bald head. 'I'm Bulkhead, first mate and chief navigator. Honoured to meet you.' He thrust out a huge hand with fingers as big as sausages. Echo grabbed one and shook it.

'And this is Beti,' said Lil, as the woman with the skirt full of bottles stepped forward. 'She's the ship's doctor.'

'I was just joking about yer organs.' Beti grinned, showing her gapped front teeth. She took a little corked bottle from one of the many pockets sewn into her skirts and waved it at Echo. 'I've got tonics for whatever ails yer. Any aches or pains, just come find me.' She gave Horace a wink. 'Although you do have a bit of a bruise on that arm, young man.' She examined the scrape on his elbow. 'Sure you don't need me to ...' She reached into another pocket and brought out the little saw again.

'No thank you!' Horace's face turned ashen and he stepped backwards in horror.

Lil waved Beti away, as the rest of the crew giggled. 'Put it away, Beti. The lad's fine.'

'Yes, Cap'n.' Beti shuffled back in place, her skirts clinking.

Bulkhead bent down and whispered in Echo's ear. 'She's dying to cut a limb off. Never done it before, see.'

Lil continued. 'Where were we? This is Flora, the ship's boy. 'Cept she's a girl, of course.'

The peg-legged girl who'd found them on the beach took one hand out of her breeches pocket to wave shyly at Echo and Horace.

'You've met Slingshot.' Lil pointed at the white-haired pirate. 'He mans the crow's nest and keeps the rigging shipshape. And these are the kitchen boys, Spud and Skillet.'

Two identical-looking men in grimy white overalls stuck their heads out of the hatchway and grinned at Echo.

'Hello,' said Echo to all of them. 'I'm Echo, and this is my lizard, Gilbert, and my friend, er ...' She shot a nervous glance at Lil. If Lil hated King Alfons, then she wouldn't want his son aboard. She thought quickly. 'Bob.'

'Good to have you aboard, Gilbert and Bob,' said Lil.

'Any friend of Echo's is a friend of ours.' She clapped her hands together. 'Right, lads, we need to prepare a feast,' she said. 'A feast worthy of a new member of the Black Sky Wolves.' She looked at Echo, then remembered Horace. 'And new friends.'

'Spud, Skillet, get to the galley. Flora, you can help too. Slingshot, Bulkhead and Beti, get down to the beach and see what you can forage from the rock pools. I thought I saw some juicy urchins down there among the seaweed.'

The crew all marched off and Lil turned to Horace. 'You can help Spud and Skillet,' she said. 'They always need a hand skinning sea urchins.'

Horace glanced at Echo in panic, but she shrugged.

'If you need me or Echo, we'll be in the captain's quarters.' Lil patted Echo on the shoulder. 'We've got a lot to catch up on,' she said softly.

As the crew and Horace headed off to prepare the feast, Echo followed Lil to the captain's quarters, a dark, wood-panelled room lit with flickering gas lamps and a wide oak desk littered with sky charts and treasure maps. Echo was still dizzy with the turn of events. This version of her mother was so different to the one she'd dreamed of. What if Lil was thinking the same? What if Echo wasn't tough enough to fraternize with sky pirates? What if she was a big disappointment? She tried to push her worries away, but still they lingered as she shyly sat down at the captain's desk.

'I suppose I should explain a few things,' said Lil, taking the seat opposite. 'I don't know how much you know.'

Echo cleared her throat. 'I don't know anything. They told me you abandoned me when I was born. I was found on the steps of the castle in a basket of almonds.'

'Abandoned?' Lil's eyes narrowed and she slammed her fist on the desk. Echo flinched in alarm.

'Who told you?' snarled Lil. 'That no-good Alfons, I'll bet.'

Echo cast a guilty glance back outside at the deck, but Horace was deep in conversation with Flora. Lil's eyes were still fixed on Echo.

'I... I suppose he must have,' said Echo. 'I mean, I don't really see him much. It's Martha who looks after me.'

Lil shook her head in disgust. 'He's always hated me, from the first moment your father brought me back to Lockfort. Alfons can't stand outsiders, you see. Prefers to pretend they don't exist.'

'My father brought you to Lockfort?'

'I can see him in you.' Lil smiled sadly. 'Although I still think you're more Quickthorn than Lockfort.'

'Quickthorn?'

'That's our name.'

Our name. Echo turned it over in her mind. She'd always been Echo, or Lady Echo, or Echo of Lockfort. But Echo Quickthorn! It seemed to fit.

Lil continued. 'I met your father Edmond in Port Tourbillon.

260

He'd developed Lockfort's first airship and was on a mission to explore the outside world. Lockfort had been a strange, secretive sort of place ever since the Great War when they put that wall up. They didn't welcome outsiders and everyone out here knew to keep well away. But when the old king, your grandfather, died and Alfons became king, his brother Edmond persuaded him to change things and venture out to Port Tourbillon to form ties with their royalty. He dreamed of opening up the gates of Lockfort and making it a free city.'

'Wait, my father was a prince?' Echo's eyes widened.

'You mean you didn't know that either?'

'But ...' Echo's mind was spinning. 'But ... that makes King Alfons ...'

'Your uncle,' said Lil. 'More's the pity.'

All this time, Echo had thought the king had taken her on as a charity case, and he'd been family all along! Why had he done it? Separated her from her mother. Lied! She felt dizzy with it all. And, if King Alfons was her uncle, then that made Horace her cousin. There was so much she didn't know!

She turned back to Lil, her head still swirling. 'So what happened? How did you meet my father?'

Lil flushed and stared intently into the distance. 'Well, he ... he got sidetracked on his expedition. Edmond never met the queen of Port Tourbillon. Instead, he bumped into me. The Black Sky Wolves were on the run after holding up the royal coach, you see, and when Edmond heard what we'd done he helped hide us. Of course, Indigo Vi was captain then. I was just a deck-swabber and pot wash.'

Echo swallowed, her bubble of happiness suddenly bursting. Her mother was a sky pirate. A murderer and a thief! And Echo's father had helped her. Echo's hope that there had been some kind of mistake, some kind of explanation for her mother having the stolen pins evaporated. Heaviness settled on her. 'So . . . it's true. You did steal the Crown Jewels.'

Disappointment must have shown on her face because Lil suddenly frowned. 'We had good reasons,' she said.

'*Are* there good reasons for stealing?'

'Plenty, unfortunately,' said Lil. 'Princess Serafine wanted a new solid-gold fountain in the royal gardens and Queen Valberta had decreed that the city orphanage be closed to fund it. It wasn't the first time they'd pulled a stunt like that either. Under their rule, everyone in Port Tourbillon was suffering. Children didn't eat! Well, the Black Sky Wolves don't stand for that sort of thing. We relieved Princess Serafine of her jewels, melted them down and used the proceeds to build a brand-new orphanage on Harris Avenue. Vi gave me this for my bravery,' she said, putting a hand to her hairpin.

'Wait, so you didn't keep the treasure for yourself?'

'Steal for good, that's our motto,' said Lil, rolling up her sleeve to show a tattoo saying the same on her upper arm.

Echo frowned. 'But why is everyone scared of you then? If you're so honourable?'

'We have to keep up appearances,' Lil said. Her face grew serious. 'There's plenty of other bands of sky pirates out there who aren't like us. If they knew the truth, they'd be hunting us down and plundering our treasure.' She leaned back. 'Flora's great at spreading all those gory rumours!'

'So you don't really cut your enemies' fingers and toes off?'

'And feed them to the cloud eels?' Lil laughed. 'That one's certainly got around! No, and we don't burn their bones to run the ship's engines either. Bulkhead would faint clean away if he ever had to cut off so much as a toe. He's very delicate.'

Echo's mind wouldn't stop spinning. Was anything as she'd thought? Although it was a relief to know her mother wasn't a murderous criminal, stealing for good was still stealing.

'Anyway,' Lil said, 'your father and I got married after that and a good pirate knees-up that was! I left the Black Sky Wolves so we could travel the world together, but I agreed to go back and visit Lockfort with him first. He was loyal to his brother and I was in love with him. I was expecting you by this point, of course.'

Echo shook her head. No wonder she'd always had this burning desire to be free. And no wonder she felt so at home out here. Exploring was in her blood! But royalty was too. There was so much to think about. 'No one ever told me my father was an explorer.'

'Alfons never liked the idea,' said Lil. 'He wanted Edmond

to explore in secret until they were sure they wanted to connect with the outside world.'

'And so what went wrong? Why didn't they connect?'

Lil looked down and cleared her throat. 'By the time we got back to Lockfort, your father . . . he was sick. He'd caught frost fever out in Port Tourbillon and he just couldn't fight it off.' Lil looked away into the distance and took a deep breath before continuing. 'Alfons blamed me, of course.'

'But it wasn't your fault!'

'For all his weaknesses, Alfons did love your father and, when Edmond died, Alfons just couldn't see straight,' said Lil. 'He vowed that nobody would enter or leave Lockfort again. He came up with that silly prophecy to explain why the gates could never open.'

'He made it up?'

Lil nodded. 'And the people bought it. Nobody wanted to leave. He spread rumours of a sickness out beyond the walls.' She sighed. 'But he was terrified that I would tell everyone about the real world outside. And so he kept me a prisoner.'

'And that's when you escaped?' asked Echo.

'Not exactly. He threw me down that chute of his and I found my way back to Port Tourbillon and the Black Sky Wolves. But you've got to understand, Echo.' She took both of Echo's hands in hers. 'I thought you were dead. They took you away from me soon after you were born. Alfons told me they were putting me into quarantine, but I ended up in the dungeons.' Her voice cracked. 'Then they told me you'd died of frost fever too!'

Echo nodded, the lump of sorrow in her throat stopping her from speaking. The king had lied about so much. Her mother. Her father. Everything! She clenched her fists. He'd made her feel like an outsider when he was part of her own family. 'I believe you,' she finally whispered.

Lil stared off into the distance. 'At one time, long ago, I vowed to go back to Lockfort and finish what your father started.'

'Opening the gates?'

'Yes,' said Lil. 'Throwing them wide open and showing the people of Lockfort what Alfons was keeping from them.' She shook her head sadly. 'I had grand plans, Echo. I was going to liberate the people. Show them freedom. I thought Alfons would see sense once he got over Edmond's death. But he didn't; he just became madder and madder. When I tried to go back, I was met with cannon fire and fury. And if I'd known you were alive . . .' Her voice cracked and she swallowed. 'I thought I had nothing left in Lockfort. After everything that had happened, I was glad to be out. I never wanted to see that place again. The Black Sky Wolves were the only family I had left.'

She squinted out to sea for a long moment, then looked back at Echo and smiled. 'But that's all history. Tell me about you, Echo. I want to know *everything*.'

So Echo told Lil everything: about the castle, about finding the professor's airship and the hairpin and Port Tourbillon, about Abena, and the Explorers' Guild, about their escape to the Violet Isles and rescuing Horace (or rather Bob) from the mantrap.

'And then we saw your ship,' she finally said.

'And here you are,' said Lil, gazing at Echo with piercing grey eyes, as if trying to take everything in at once. 'And where is this borrowed airship of yours?'

Echo swallowed, guilt suddenly swirling in her stomach. 'On the other side of the island. I ought to take it back to the professor. I owe him an apology.'

'Why don't we go and get him?' Lil said. 'You can invite him to your party.'

'Party?'

Lil grinned. 'You're home, Echo. I think it's time to celebrate that, don't you?'

CHAPTER TWENTY-EIGHT

The sky pirates prepared a spectacular feast, but it was only once Echo had eaten her fill of salted fish and seaurchins that the real celebrations began. It was late evening now, and the sun had almost dropped below the horizon, casting an orange-pink glow over the water.

After collecting a rather bemused Professor Daggerwing from Doctor Beetlestone's laboratory, Lil had steered the *Scarlet Margaret* back to the beach on Tyrian where Echo had landed the *Hummerbird* and they had tethered it several feet up above the bay. Now Echo sat between Horace and Beti at a huge makeshift table that had been set up on the main deck of the airship. Gilbert perched by the edge of her plate, nibbling at some chargrilled squid. Professor Daggerwing sat opposite, enthusing about pickles to Spud and Skillet.

A hush fell over the crew as Indigo Lil, two stripes of indigo clay on each cheek, climbed up to the prow of the ship, a tankard of grog in one hand. She stood silhouetted against the night sky as the ship swayed gently in the warm island breeze and cleared her throat.

'Listen up, you lot. Tonight is a momentous evening!' She waved her tankard and sloshed foam on to the deck. 'It's not often we initiate a new member into the Black Sky Wolves, and never have we welcomed one as important as Echo, the daughter I thought I'd lost. Come up here.' She smiled proudly down at Echo.

Echo scrambled out of her seat and up on to the bow where she perched beside her mother, her chest strangely full. From their seats at the table, the crew of the *Scarlet Margaret* raised their tankards and Echo couldn't help grinning back. She caught Horace's eye and blushed with pride. *The daughter I thought I'd lost.*

Lil put down her tankard and drew out a battered old tin from her pocket, dipped two fingers into the blueish-purple gunk and swiped them on to Echo's cheeks. 'Welcome home,' she said, her voice shaking.

Echo's heart swelled. She was a Black Sky Wolf! The crew banged their spoons on the table.

'Now, let's clear the table and show Echo how sky pirates celebrate!' Lil took a swig of grog and wiped her mouth on her sleeve. 'And don't forget to stow your cutlasses below deck – we don't want any injuries this time!'

The sky-pirate crew erupted into cheers and clashed their

tankards together before draining their mugs, shoving back their seats and heaving the table aside. The ship's foredeck suddenly buzzed with activity as they ran here and there, lighting gas lanterns, rolling barrels and clearing the floor. Then, from every corner of the ship, pirates emerged with fiddles, accordions, whistles, a double bass; one even wheeled out a little steam pianola, complete with an array of brass horns snaking their way skywards from the keyboard.

Once the deck was clear and the musicians had arranged their instruments, the bassist let out a whoop and the music started – a wild, raucous tumble of noise that made Echo grin all over again. Then the Black Sky Wolves took to the floor and soon the whole ship shook with the stamp and shuffle of booted feet on the boards, the *plunk-plunk-plunk* of the double bass and the wild, soaring melody of the fiddles and pipes.

Echo sat on the prow, taking it all in, not yet ready to plunge into the sea of dancers. She still couldn't quite believe what had happened. She was a sky pirate. A real sky pirate. And she had a mother, a mother who wanted her, and who—

'Come on, Echo!' yelled Lil, as she flew past, grabbing Echo's hand and pulling her down on to the deck. 'It's your party!'

'But I don't know how to—'

But Lil had spun away across the floor and Echo found herself jostled into the tide of dancing bodies. A huge hand grabbed hers and she was lifted off her feet and whisked across the deck. She looked up to see Bulkhead grinning down at her.

269

'Welcome to the gang!' he yelled over the music. 'You're one of us now!'

Echo grinned. She *was* one of them. She grabbed Bulkhead's other hand and let him spin and whirl her across the ship, stamping her feet to the rhythm like the others.

'You got it!' Bulkhead shouted. 'Just follow the beat! Ain't no rules at a pirate dance!'

The music played faster and faster, and Echo danced ever faster too, the whole world rushing past her in a blur, her head spinning and her cheeks aching from smiling so hard.

By now, the whole crew had emerged on deck. The kitchen boys had deserted their posts down in the galley and were galloping up and down in their grease-spattered white jackets. She spotted Beti whizz past with a dazed-looking Professor Daggerwing in tow, while Horace was trying vainly to keep up with Flora, who despite her peg leg was far nimbler than him. Gilbert perched on the ship's wheel, rocking his scaly body from side to side with the music. Even Slingshot had abandoned his watch in the crow's nest to join in the festivities.

They danced for what seemed like hours, only stopping to take a swig of grog or to collapse, exhausted and dripping with sweat, on a barrel for a few moments, before beginning the whole thing all over again. The musicians never seemed to tire and neither did Echo. *I am one of them*, she thought. *I'm a sky pirate, and I'm home.*

Bulkhead swung her across the deck to switch partners and

she almost collided with Horace, who had prised himself out of Flora's grasp and was lurking behind the foremast. She grabbed his hand before he could protest and spun round him until they were both dizzy. The worse they danced, the more they laughed, until she finally gave in and they tumbled down in a heap under the airship's wheel.

'I think I've got a stitch,' gasped Horace, clutching his side.

Echo nodded, attempting to get her breath back. Gilbert scuttled down the wheel and flopped down on to her shoulder with an exhausted chirp.

'I don't think I've ever danced so much,' Horace said.

'Me neither. I don't think I've ever danced like *this*.' She looked at him for a moment. Was this the time to tell him? 'You know, my mother told me a few things about my father—'

'Look.' Horace pointed across the deck, the smile slipping from his face.

The music had stopped. For a moment, nobody noticed and the dance continued with a strange ring of boots on boards as everyone shuffled and creaked to a halt.

Echo saw Bulkhead turn pale beneath his stubble. Indigo Lil's smile froze on her face.

They were all staring across the deck into the purple fog that had surrounded the ship. Echo turned to see what they were looking at.

In the noise of the dance and the darkness of the evening, nobody had noticed another airship glide silently up alongside them through the mist. There was a murmur in the crowd as the pirates reached for their weapons, then yells as they realized their sheaths were empty. They scrambled for the stairs to the quarterdeck to retrieve their cutlasses, but it was too late.

A group of uniformed soldiers brandishing swords appeared out of the shadows.

CHAPTER TWENTY-NINE

One by one the soldiers jumped nimbly on to the deck of the *Scarlet Margaret*.

Echo threw herself flat behind a nearby barrel, pulling Horace and Gilbert with her. She stared as a tall, rat-faced man with a thin, greasy moustache stepped forward and unsheathed his sword. Echo's eyes widened even further as she recognized Crawley, one of King Alfons's senior guards.

'Put your hands where we can see them,' he said. 'We are taking control of this ship in the name of King Alfons of Lockfort.'

'But how?' whispered Horace. 'They don't even have airships in Lockfort . . .'

Echo shook her head. 'My father invented one,' she whispered back. 'Lil told me. They must have kept it.'

'Your father? What do you—'

'Shh.' Echo shrank further behind the barrel.

'Where is he?' continued Crawley. As he stepped into the light of the gas lanterns, Indigo Lil strode forward, but another guard stopped her, pressing the tip of his sword to her breastbone. She gently pushed it to one side with a gloved finger.

'I'm the captain of the *Scarlet Margaret*,' she said. 'Who exactly are you looking for?'

'Prince Horace of Lockfort.'

'Oh no,' muttered Horace.

'There's no prince anything on this ship,' replied Lil.

'He was kidnapped several weeks ago and transported here. We traced him to the Port Tourbillon Butterfly House, and a clerk there informed us he was travelling to the Violet Isles.'

Horace gripped Echo's hand. She squeezed back. 'Don't worry,' she whispered. 'None of them know who you really are. And I won't give you away.'

'What if they find me?'

'They won't!' She glanced nervously at Horace. He might be in disgrace if they were taken back to Lockfort, but it would be nothing like the trouble she'd be in.

Horace let out a small whimper and clamped his other hand over his mouth.

Echo watched as Crawley sheathed his sword and addressed his men. 'Gallion, Rothschild, you stay up here and restrain these ... these people. Mortlake, below decks with me to search the ship.'

He strode to the stairs and disappeared down them with a second soldier. The guard he'd called Gallion held a sword to a struggling Lil's throat.

'Gerroff me!' yelled Flora, as Rothschild grabbed her. But it was no good. She and the others were swiftly tied back to back to the masts.

'What are we going to do?' whispered Horace. 'Father is going to be furious!'

'I'll think of something,' said Echo, frantically trying to come up with a way out. They could never overpower the soldiers or take their ship, not just the two of them. She turned and peered over the side. It was a long way down to the beach where the *Hummerbird* was tethered. Echo looked to the stern of the *Scarlet Margaret*, where the long rope ladder snaked down into the mist.

Could they make it? Echo ignored the fear that swirled in her stomach. They'd have to. But first they would need to rescue the others.

'Psst.' She nudged Horace and put Gilbert securely round her neck. 'I'm going to sneak over and let Lil loose.'

'How? They've got swords, in case you hadn't noticed.'

Echo swallowed, fear prickling her spine. 'Well, at least they won't slice *you* up.'

'I don't want anyone to be sliced!' Horace put his head in his hands. 'I'm so sorry, Echo. I should never have come with you. The professor will be in real trouble now. And the sky pirates.'

'Don't be stupid, you're my friend.'

He looked up in surprise. 'Really?'

'Really. And friends stick by each other, no matter what. Stay here and keep quiet until I come for you. Okay?'

Horace swallowed and nodded, his face ghost-white.

'And wait for my signal.' Echo crawled behind the barrels until she was as near as she dared to Lil and the others. Gallion stood, his back to her, shifting up and down on the toes of his boots. Even in the dim light, Echo could see that his sword was sickeningly sharp. She pushed thoughts of blades out of her mind and glanced over at Lil, tied back to back with Flora against the mast. Echo gritted her teeth. She could do this.

There was a bang and the whole deck rocked. Echo jerked her head up to see that another smaller airship had butted up alongside the *Scarlet Margaret*. A man leaped on to the deck. As he stepped into the light of the gas lanterns, sword drawn, she recognized the oily black hair of the man who had been in the jeweller's.

'I'm looking for this girl!' he yelled, holding up a tattered wanted poster with Echo's description. 'She's in possession of stolen jewels.'

Echo clamped her lips together to stop herself from crying out.

Gallion unsheathed his sword with a *swish* and strode towards the man. 'We're in charge of this ship, and any jewels upon it belong to us. Who *are* you?'

'I am in the service of Queen Valberta of Port Tourbillon,' snarled the man. 'I've been following this girl for days. The jewels are mine.'

'That's no royal ship,' said Gallion, squinting through the mist.

Echo glanced over at her mother as the two men argued. Perhaps this was the distraction she needed. There was no time to waste. She scuttled over to Lil and Flora.

Lil blinked in surprise. 'Echo!' she hissed. 'What're you doing?'

'Rescuing you,' Echo said. She crouched down and worked at the rough coils of rope with her fingers, scrabbling for purchase on the tight knots. There was a loud sneeze from the barrels where she'd been hiding. She jerked her head up and saw to her horror that the black-haired man had dragged Horace out from his hiding place.

'*You* know where she is,' he snarled, shoving the wanted poster in Horace's face. 'I saw you with her outside the library in Port Tourbillon.'

'Prince Horace, by the king's seal!' Gallion pointed his sword at the black-haired man's throat. 'Unhand him at once.'

Echo gulped. Oh no, this was not going to plan at all.

'*Prince* Horace,' said Lil, eyes wide. She turned to Echo. 'You told me his name was Bob.' She shook one hand free of the loosened rope and grabbed Echo's wrist. 'Did you know? You did, didn't you—'

'Hey!' Rothschild raced over to Echo, grabbing her by the arm and yanking her away from Lil. 'Gallion, are you keeping an eye on these captives? One's about to escape!'

'That's her!' snarled the black-haired man, letting go of Horace and pushing past an astounded Gallion to grab hold of Echo's other arm. 'Where are the jewels?'

'Get off me!' Echo shouted, but the black-haired man shoved a hand roughly into her pocket and grabbed the pin.

'That's mine!' she yelled, scrabbling at him. He couldn't take it now, not after she'd come this far.

'Where's the rest of them?' he snarled.

Crawley emerged from the hatchway, followed by Mortlake. 'All secure below . . . What *is* going on up here?'

'I've found him, sir,' said Gallion, with a look of astonishment on his face.

'You've found . . . Oh!' Crawley stared at Horace. He suddenly remembered himself and bowed deeply before racing over. 'Are you hurt, my prince?'

'No,' said Horace, flushing. 'I'm fine. Please let them go. That man's going to hurt Echo.'

Rothschild pulled Echo away from the black-haired man, took a closer look at her and his eyes widened. 'By the seal, it *is* Lady Echo. With an urchin's haircut!' He shook his head in disbelief.

'He's got my pin!' shouted Echo. The man was going to get away with it and none of them were going to do anything! She wriggled out of Rothschild's grip. 'Stop him!'

The black-haired man looked from her to the three sword-wielding men, then dodged past Rothschild and ran for his airship.

'Stop!' yelled Echo, but it was no good. With a buzz of engines, the ship pulled away and disappeared into the fog.

'Are you hurt, my prince?' said Crawley, turning back to Horace. 'What have these rogues done to you?'

'They're not rogues,' said Horace. 'They're my friends.'

'Brainwashed.' Crawley shook his head sadly. He addressed Gallion. 'Tie them all up, including her,' he said, pointing at Echo.

As Gallion strode towards her, Echo scrambled to her feet and ran. She couldn't let them take her back to Lockfort again, she just couldn't. Who knew how King Alfons would punish her this time? And she wasn't about to be separated from her mother again. She staggered forward, tripping over coils of rope and abandoned fiddles, dodging past the ship's wheel and towards the bow of the ship, where she knew the ladder was attached. But Gallion was too fast. She heard the thud of boots behind her, hands grabbed her roughly and she fell hard on to the boards.

'Get off me!' she yelled, scratching and scrabbling like a wild cat. Gilbert hissed and turned an angry shade of red, nipping at Gallion's hands. But it was no good. Gallion knocked Gilbert away on to the deck, then threw Echo over his shoulder as if she was no more than a doll.

'Gilbert, run!' Echo beat her fists against Gallion's back. In return the soldier flung her down in a heap and put his sword to her throat. Gilbert hesitated for a moment before scuttling away into the shadows.

'I suggest you stop wriggling,' he said. 'And keep that . . . that thing away from me or I'll throw it overboard.' He turned to Rothschild. 'I'll put her below.'

Rothschild nodded. 'We'll take the young prince back on to the *Star of Lockfort*. This way, Your Highness. There's a most comfortable cabin already prepared for you.'

He marched to where the other airship's gangplank was resting on the *Scarlet Margaret*, then turned when he realized Horace wasn't following. 'Your Highness?'

'I won't go,' said Horace.

'You won't . . . ?'

'I want to stay here with my friends. You can tell Father I said that.'

'But Your Highness, with the greatest respect—'

'I am not going.' Horace sat down where he was with a thump. 'You can let us all go or . . . or tie me up with the others.'

Rothschild raised his eyebrows. 'I cannot do either of those things, Your Highness. I have orders from the king—'

'*I* am ordering you to tie me up with them.' Horace's lower lip was wobbling. 'Or I'll tell Father you disobeyed me.'

Echo stared open-mouthed at Horace, too defeated to

struggle as Gallion finished tying her hands behind her back. How had this happened? Everything she'd ever dreamed of had evaporated before her eyes.

Gallion shrugged and stepped forward with another rope. 'Shall I?'

'No!' Rothschild slapped it out of his hand. 'This is the crown prince of Lockfort. He's obviously deeply traumatized and doesn't know what he's saying.'

'I know exactly what I'm saying,' said Horace, his voice firmer now. 'Let us all go or tie us all up. We're together.'

Crawley sighed and threw his hands up. 'As you wish,' he snapped. 'Rothschild, put Prince Horace and Lady Echo in that small cabin on the starboard side, and secure the door. They can't get up to any mischief in there.' He glared at Echo. 'And perhaps they'll have seen sense by the time we get back to Lockfort.'

CHAPTER THIRTY

'Do you think Gilbert's all right?' asked Echo, her head in her hands. She and Horace had been pushed rather firmly into a cramped little cabin in the *Scarlet Margaret*, which, along with the *Hummerbird* and the *Star of Lockfort*, was being piloted north-westwards across the sky by the guards. The thought of the little lizard alone and frightened and lost was more than she could bear.

'He'll be all right,' said Horace, sitting down beside her on the Jolly Roger print covers of the bunk. 'He's clever. He'll find his way back to you.' He gave her shoulder a gentle nudge. 'Remember that time he fell in the moat when we were looking for mud monsters and we thought he was gone for good? He climbed all the way back up to your bedchamber.'

Echo smiled sadly at the memory of a bedraggled and weed-covered Gilbert appearing at her window.

'In the meantime,' said Horace, 'what are we going to do?'

'I'll have to think of something,' Echo replied. 'But I don't know what.'

'If only I hadn't chased after that butterfly,' Horace said. 'I should have stayed on the beach and waited for you, then we wouldn't be in this horrible mess.'

'But then you wouldn't have found that Goliath's mantrap,' said Echo.

Horace nodded. 'And you wouldn't have found your mother.'

'I bet she's wishing I hadn't found *her*,' said Echo, with a sigh. She couldn't help thinking of the expression on Lil's face when she'd realized Echo had brought King Alfons's guards on to her ship. Lil's look of shock and disappointment haunted Echo and she flushed with shame at the thought. She would just have to make things right, and to do all that she could to get them out of this mess.

'We've got to try something. Maybe one of the windows?' Echo stood and rattled a porthole, but it was tightly shut. She thumped it in frustration, dislodging a dead spider from the curtains on to Horace's lap.

Horace squealed in alarm and knocked the dessicated creature to the floor, then his face crumpled and he stifled a sob. 'Oh, it's hopeless! We'll never escape. We're trapped and we're being taken back to Lockfort and my father's going to be furious and we'll probably all get sent to the dungeons forever and ever and ever.'

Echo sighed and sat back down on the bunk beside Horace.

As much as she didn't want to admit it, he had a point. Even if they did get out of the cabin, where could they go? Nowhere while they were soaring through the air. And what about the rest of the crew? The professor? Her mother? No, she had to wait until the time was right. She drew her knees up to her chest and hugged them tightly, not quite able to meet Horace's eyes. 'You know, Lil told me my father was Edmond, your uncle,' she said.

'My uncle?' Horace stared at her. 'But that means we're . . . we're—'

Echo looked up at him. 'We're family,' she said.

She told him everything as they continued to travel into the night, and soon Echo's head nodded and the rumble of the *Scarlet Margaret*'s engines lulled her to sleep. But her dreams were full of dripping dungeons, locked doors and manacles.

And a mother who was so disappointed with Echo she couldn't bear to look her in the eye.

The first weak light of morning was shining through the portholes when Echo woke suddenly and found herself sliding sideways across the bunk. A sky chart vibrated on the wall and all the gas lamps jingled. She sat up and shook a confused-looking Horace awake. The whole ship shuddered and, after a few moments, the deep rumble of the ship's engines softened into a purr before disappearing entirely. They had stopped.

'How long have we been asleep?' Echo said, peering out of the porthole at the grey stone ramparts of Lockfort Castle, dull in the weak morning light. There was a thud followed by the sound of heavy footsteps. She and Horace both looked nervously at the door.

Echo flinched as it swung open and Rothschild, in his gilt-corded breeches and scarlet jacket, appeared. He beckoned to them. 'Come with me.'

Echo remained frozen next to Horace. She wasn't quite sure whether it was Horace who was quivering or her. Perhaps it was both of them. How on earth would she manage to get them out of this? She took a deep breath. If she couldn't, then Lil would. At least they had her now.

'Out,' said Rothschild, 'and don't try any funny business. There are armed men waiting for you outside the ship.'

It was getting light as they climbed down from the *Scarlet Margaret* on to the castle ramparts. As they passed the *Star of Lockfort* and the *Hummerbird*, which were tethered alongside, Echo glanced out across the battlements to the streets of Lockfort. How long had they been away? Just a few short weeks, but it felt like a lifetime. There was so much world out there, so much more than these ordered streets, and the people of Lockfort knew none of it.

She automatically put her hand to her shoulder to stroke Gilbert's tail and remembered with a jolt that he was lost. Where was he? Had he found a place to hide on the *Scarlet*

Margaret? She scanned the deck and ramparts for any sign of the little lizard, but to her dismay he was nowhere to be seen. Had he tumbled overboard somewhere along the way?

'Keep moving,' snapped Rothschild.

Echo pushed the terrible thoughts from her head and let herself be marched inside. A guard holding a lantern led her and Horace through the eastern turret door and she remembered with a pang of sorrow how Gilbert had unlocked it for her just a few short weeks ago. They trudged down the castle's familiar corridors, past paintings of Lockfort nobility and the little bronze bear, until finally they reached the ceremonial doors and stepped down into the dungeons.

King Alfons was waiting for them at the cells. He turned as they approached, his maroon, ermine-trimmed robes swinging round with a *swish* as they brushed the stone floor.

'Horace! My precious son! I feared you were lost forever!' King Alfons spread his arms wide. His brow crumpled into a frown when Horace remained standing beside Echo. 'Are you hurt?' He strode forward, pushing Echo out of the way. 'What have they done to you?'

'They haven't done anything,' Horace said, brushing his father's hands away. 'You . . . you shot at us!'

The king chuckled. 'A silly mistake, my son. A misunderstanding! I didn't realize *you* were aboard.'

'But you knew Echo was.' Horace glowered as King Alfons

put a bejewelled hand on his shoulder. 'She's my cousin! Why didn't you tell us?'

Echo stared at him. Was this really Horace, standing up to his father?

'Now, now, you're clearly upset, Horace.' The king forced his lips into a smile, but his eyes remained steely. 'Let's get on with the business of identifying your kidnappers and then we'll go upstairs for a celebratory dinner. Nutmeg custard, your favourite!'

Horace folded his arms. 'You lied to me. To all of us. You knew about the world out there. You knew who Echo's parents were. You even had an airship!'

The king shook his head. 'It was for your own protection, dear boy. It's my duty as king. One day you'll understand. Now, who was it that took you?'

'I went by myself.'

'You don't have to protect these people. They can't hurt you now.'

'They *haven't* hurt me, Father. They're my friends.'

'But Horace—'

'No, Father. I'm not going to get them into trouble. Not for you and not for anyone. You need to let them go.'

'I see.' The king took his hand off Horace's shoulder. 'Well, if you can't identify the guilty ones, then we'll have to lock them all up.'

'You can't!' shouted Echo, but the king was already leaving.

'Did you want to see the prisoners, Your Highness?' asked the guard, trotting behind. 'They're just down this way.'

'No.' The king waved a dismissive hand. 'I have no interest in giving that riff-raff any more of my time. Come, Horace.' He marched off down the dripping corridor, his footmen scurrying after him. Horace remained rooted to the spot.

The king turned when he realized Horace wasn't following. 'Come on, Horace. Step to it,' he said.

Horace folded his arms. 'I won't.'

Echo's eyes widened in amazement at Horace's courage. She hardly recognized him.

King Alfons laughed uncertainly. 'What in all Lockfort do you mean, boy?'

'I'm staying here.'

'Here?' King Alfons's eyes bulged and he looked round the dank walls. 'In the dungeons?'

'With my friends,' said Horace.

Echo's heart swelled. She took his hand and noticed it was shaking.

'These ... these people are not your friends,' said the king, glaring at Echo. 'They're sky pirates! Thieves and liars. Whatever they've told you—'

'Echo is family. And the others took care of me. I'm not abandoning them. Not for a warm bath, or a steaming hot custard, or ... or ... anything.'

'That's right,' said Echo. 'Horace wouldn't leave us even if you offered him a Greater Brimstone in a jar. Would you?' She squeezed his hand.

King Alfons looked at her in disgust. 'You always were just like your mother.'

Echo glared back at him as he turned to Horace. 'Well?' he said.

Horace hesitated for a moment, then grimaced. 'No.'

King Alfons shook his head, his eyes turning steely again. 'As you wish,' he said. 'I'm sure a night in the dungeons will make you realize where you really belong. Lock him up,' he said to the guards. 'With his *friends*.'

Echo and Horace were marched down the corridor by Mortice, the dungeon master, and shoved into a small, dank cell. Behind them, the door clanged shut and Echo heard the metallic rattle and clunk of a key turning in the lock.

Echo turned to look and found Mortice staring at Horace appraisingly, his gold tooth glinting in the flicker of the wall-hung torches.

'Hope you don't mind me saying, Yer Highness, but it beats me as to why you'd choose to be down here,' he said, fastening the huge ring of keys to his belt. 'Most people can't wait to get out of here, and that's not just the prisoners!'

His footsteps faded away, leaving Echo and Horace alone with just the gentle drip of water on stone and the occasional faraway shriek from somewhere else in the dungeons.

Echo shoved her hands in her pockets. 'Thanks,' she said. 'You were really brave, standing up to your father like that.'

'S'okay,' croaked Horace, his eyes still focused on the corridor outside.

'I mean it,' said Echo. She shrugged. 'Maybe your father'll see sense tomorrow. When he realizes you're sticking with us, he'll have to let us all go.'

'Or keep us all locked up.'

'He can't do that. Not forever.'

'Can't he? Remember what he did to your mother.' Horace sighed and sat down in a corner with his head in his hands.

Echo flopped down next to him on the damp flagstones. At least her mother was here, somewhere in the dungeons too. She would know how to get them out. The very thought of it calmed her. They had nothing to worry about with the fearless Indigo Lil on their side! She patted Horace's shoulder. 'Lil will get us out of here,' she said. 'Just you wait.' After all, if anyone could get them out, it was the captain of the Black Sky Wolves.

CHAPTER THIRTY-ONE

And wait they did. As the days trickled by in the dingy cell, long, dark days only punctuated by the arrival of Mortice with bowls of disgusting grey gruel, Echo became despondent. 'Where is she, Horace? Why isn't she coming to rescue us?'

'We'll get out of here somehow, Echo,' he whispered, as they sat next to each other in the corner of the cell. Horace swallowed his last spoonful of gloopy porridge and put down his bowl.

Echo shook her head. 'We won't. It's hopeless. We'll be stuck down here forever.'

She took a shuddering breath and reached to her shoulder for Gilbert before remembering yet again that he was lost. Without him, she felt like a part of her was missing. He'd been with her for as long as she could remember, longer even than Horace. She'd lost him and she'd ruined her mother's life too.

Lil probably wished Echo had never found her. Echo bit her lip to halt her tears.

'What is it?' said Horace.

'I bet Lil hates me,' she said, with a sob. 'I bet she's still furious about me bringing you on to her ship and getting her crew locked up.'

'She doesn't hate you,' said Horace.

'Why isn't she coming to rescue us then? She's a sky pirate. She should know how to fix this.'

'But mothers can't fix everything, Echo. Not even sky-pirate mothers. They're just people.'

Echo wiped her nose on her sleeve. 'Do you remember *your* mother?' she asked softly.

'A little.' Horace thought for a moment. 'I remember she was kind, and she read me stories, and she loved butterflies.' He paused. 'But she got cross sometimes too. It didn't mean she didn't love me.'

Echo swallowed. She'd been so selfish. Horace had lost his mother, but she'd been so desperate to find her own that she'd never thought to ask him about losing his. 'Do you miss her?'

'Every day,' he said. 'But thinking about her helps keep her alive somehow, in here.' He touched his chest. 'I feel like she's still with me in a way.'

Echo nodded, her mouth suddenly dry. 'Well, if you ever want to talk about her . . .'

292

Horace smiled. 'I will.' He blushed and examined his fingernails. 'Anyway,' he said, 'we really should get on with planning our escape. There's always a way out for an explorer, you know.'

Echo couldn't help smiling as she turned to him. What had happened to pudding-hearted Horace? He'd changed somewhere along the way. Then her heart dropped again. 'How though? My mother isn't coming to help.'

'Since when did you need anyone's help?' Horace exclaimed. 'We've got this far without Lil, and I think you've done a pretty fine job.'

Echo shrugged. But a little spark of something lit deep down inside her. Horace was right; they *had* done it, together. They'd come a long way since those few weeks when she'd crept off to the *Hummerbird*.

Horace went on. 'Lil didn't help you pilot an airship, escape a Matasan fighter or rescue me from that Goliath's mantrap.'

Echo nodded slowly. 'I suppose we could *try*.'

'I really think we can,' said Horace. 'You and me together.'

'You and me together.' Echo smiled. 'You're right, Horace. We can't give up, not now.' She sprang to her feet and paced the cell, a new determination blazing within her.

The walls of the cell were high and completely windowless, the dungeons being deep underground below the castle. Echo walked to the bars and casually leaned on them, then gripped them with both hands to give each one an experimental pull.

To her disappointment, they were just as solid as they had been the first time she had tried. There was no way out.

Mortice looked up from his guard post and tapped his tankard. 'Don't think you'll be getting away with any funny business. Eyebright tea to keep me awake, see.'

Echo shrugged and wandered back to Horace's corner.

'Any luck?' he whispered.

Echo shook her head, and turned to check that Mortice wasn't listening. He'd gone back to cleaning the grime from beneath his nails with the tip of a huge iron key.

'The cell door's the only way out,' she whispered. 'If only they hadn't taken my clockwork tools, we could have distracted Mortice and I could have tried to pick the lock.'

She inwardly cursed the guards for emptying her pockets.

'Maybe we can get his keys,' said Horace, his eye on Mortice. 'If he falls asleep, perhaps we could reach through . . .'

'I don't think that's going to happen. Not with that eyebright he's drinking,' said Echo, with a sigh.

Horace nodded glumly. 'That'll keep him awake for hours.'

'What is it anyway?'

'It's the traditional drink of nightwatchmen. You make it from the seeds of the eyebright plant.'

Echo stared at the tankard by Mortice's boot. *Seeds*. Suddenly an idea occurred to her. She nudged Horace excitedly. 'Seeds!'

'What?'

'Do you still have them?'

'What do you mean?'

'The mantrap seeds. Do you still have them? The guards didn't dare turn *your* pockets out, did they?'

Horace riffled in the pocket of his breeches and, checking that Mortice wasn't watching, plucked out a tiny waxed-paper packet. He opened it and showed her the three shiny purple seeds. 'But what are you going to—'

'Leave it to me,' said Echo, carefully taking a seed between her thumb and forefinger. 'Give me the packet too.'

Horace shrugged and silently handed it over. Echo unfolded the paper and smoothed it out on the stone floor, then rolled it into a thin tube. She slipped the seed into the end of the tube. 'Now do you see?'

A smile crept across Horace's face. 'I do.'

Echo grinned back and tucked the makeshift pea-shooter into her palm. 'Let's capture the castle.'

'So, what made you go into dungeon keeping?' said Horace, nonchalantly lounging against the cell door a few minutes later.

'Eh? What?' Mortice jerked round on his chair and stared at him.

'Um ... dungeon keeping.' Horace gulped. 'What, er, why ... I mean ...'

'I was conscripted,' said Mortice. 'By yer father.'

'Oh,' said Horace.

As Mortice glared at Horace in the awkward silence, Echo, unnoticed, took a deep breath and blew hard through the paper tube. The tiny purple seed flew in a high arc through the air, hit a cell bar and ricocheted off under Mortice's chair.

Echo clenched her fist in disappointment and almost crushed the paper tube. Still, two seeds left. Her tummy fizzed with fear and excitement.

Horace was still vainly trying to engage Mortice in conversation. 'So, what would you say are the perks of the job?'

'Perks?' exclaimed Mortice, leaping to his feet and slamming a fist on the bars, inadvertently crushing the first seed under one huge, hobnailed boot in the process.

Horace staggered backwards. 'I just mean—'

'There are no perks,' snapped Mortice. He settled himself back on his chair. 'Finally cracked, I reckon,' he mumbled to himself. 'Mind, a lot of 'em do.'

Echo took the second seed and slotted it into the end of the pea-shooter. *Come on!* This one had to go in. She aimed at Mortice's tankard, inhaled and blew. The seed flew upwards, through the bars and hit Mortice square on the temple. He jumped up.

'What the . . . ?' he shouted, glaring at Horace. 'Did yer throw something at my head, boy?'

Echo shoved the pea-shooter behind her back.

'N-n-no!' stuttered Horace.

296

Echo interrupted. 'Did you feel a drip, Horace?' she said, peering up into the gloom. 'Think I did.'

'What?'

'A drip,' said Echo firmly. She looked pointedly up at the ceiling.

Horace followed her gaze. 'I . . . I think maybe I did,' he said, his voice trembling. 'Feel anything?' he asked Mortice.

Mortice followed Horace's gaze and began squinting at the ceiling for the source of the leak. Echo fixed her aim on the tankard. One seed left.

She took a deep breath and fired.

CHAPTER THIRTY-TWO

Echo held her breath as the last seed dropped into Mortice's tankard with a gentle *plip*.

As Mortice turned away from the bars, she gave a quick thumbs up to Horace, who scuttled back over to her.

'Did you get one in?' he whispered.

'Yes!' Echo shoved the pea-shooter back in her pocket with a grin. 'How long do you think it'll take?'

Horace shrugged. 'I don't know ... Look, he's drinking it!'

Echo glanced back at Mortice, who was taking a swig of tea. He wiped his mouth on the back of his hand and set the mug back down on the floor by his chair. He glanced over and his eyes narrowed as he noticed them watching him.

'What're you two up to?' he said, getting to his feet. Echo gasped in horror as his right boot caught the mug and sent it clattering along the flagstones, spilling the rest of the tea all over the floor.

'Ah, blast and bother it,' Mortice cursed, as he chased the mug across the corridor.

Echo's whole body froze. She shot a panicked look at Horace. 'Has he drunk enough?'

'I don't know!'

Mortice was wandering back to his chair with the empty tankard. He took a staggering sidestep and Echo held her breath. Mortice stopped, grimaced and clutched his forehead.

'It *is* working!' whispered Horace in wonder, as Mortice swayed where he stood. Then his face fell. 'But if he collapses over there . . .'

'We'll never reach the keys!' Echo jumped up, ran to the cell bars and rattled them. 'Mortice!' she shouted. 'Come here!'

'Wha—?' Mortice turned towards them, his eyelids drooping.

'Mortice!' Horace joined Echo at the bars.

Mortice stumbled towards them. 'What d'yer . . . whyooo all fuzzy?'

'Quick, Mortice!' they both yelled. 'Over here, we need you!'

Mortice took another clumsy step, then his eyes closed and he fell, as if in slow motion, his mug slamming to the ground and smashing into a hundred pieces on the flagstones.

Echo watched, breathless, as Mortice slumped in front of their cell. After a few moments, he began to snore where he lay, a thin dribble of drool running from the corner of his mouth and puddling on the floor.

Echo dropped to her knees and reached for the ring of keys on Mortice's belt. She pressed her shoulder against the bars and stretched her arm as far as she could, but her fingers barely grazed the cold metal. 'I can't quite reach it,' she said through gritted teeth.

'Let me try,' said Horace, but he had no luck either.

Echo sat back on her heels in desperation. If only Gilbert was here! He'd be able to run straight through the bars and get the keys. But he was lost. No, this was it: she and Horace would be stuck down here forever. Tears of frustration suddenly welled in her eyes. 'Oh, Gilbert!' she cried.

There was a faint chirrup from the corridor and Echo froze. Had she dreamed it? Had all these days in the darkness of the dungeons finally made her lose her mind?

'Did you hear that?' she hissed to Horace.

'Hear what?'

'Quiet.' Echo leaned forward and listened.

There it was again, incredibly faint, but most definitely a lizardy chirp.

'Gilbert?' she shouted. 'Gilbert, is that you?'

There was another chirrup, louder this time, and a splash, and then Echo saw a flash of yellow in the dimness of the corridor. It was him! He was safe!

Gilbert sprinted across the floor towards them and wriggled through the bars, scampering up Echo's body and flinging himself round her shoulders.

'Gilbert, are you all right?' Echo took him in both hands and nuzzled his snout.

He rolled his conical eyes in a way that seemed to say, *Of course I am.*

'I thought I'd lost you forever!' she said, smothering him with kisses until he turned fuchsia. 'How in Lockfort did you find us?'

After a moment, Horace cleared his throat. 'Um, Echo . . . It's great that he's back and I'm really sorry to interrupt your reunion, but the keys?'

Echo looked into Gilbert's eyes. 'Can you get them?'

In answer, the little lizard took a flying leap on to the floor, scampered over and clamped his jaws round the ring of keys. Every muscle in his little scaly body straining, he dragged them back to the cell.

'Brilliant!' Echo took the ring of keys, the metal weighty and cold in her hand, and tried each one in the lock until she found the one that fitted. It turned with a satisfying clunk and the cell door swung open.

'Come on,' she said, stepping carefully over Mortice. 'Let's find the others.'

She darted down the corridor, Horace following close behind and Gilbert zigzagging over the walls beside them. Soon she saw a familiar, frizzy-haired head in a gloomy cell up ahead. 'Professor!' she shouted.

'Echo!' exclaimed the professor, scrambling to his feet and bounding over to the cell door. 'How did you manage to—'

'We drugged the guard.' Echo unlocked the cell and swung the door open to cheers from the sky pirates. 'Quick. We need to go before he wakes up.'

Behind him in the cell, Bulkhead, Flora and the other sky pirates jumped up. All apart from Lil, that was. Instead, she sat alone in a corner, her head in her hands.

'Nice piratin'!' said Bulkhead, giving Echo a friendly slap on the back.

'Good work, mateys!' Slingshot high-fived Echo and Horace as he passed.

The others all filed out of the cell, but Lil remained sitting, her back against the stone wall.

'Cap'n?' said Bulkhead. 'You comin'?'

'Mother?' said Echo tentatively.

Lil shook her head and got to her feet with a sigh. 'Being back down here makes me realize how stupid I was for believing Alfons. I should have fought harder to get you back.'

'But . . . but you didn't know I was alive!' said Echo. 'We've all believed his lies.'

Lil nodded. 'I know. But I shouldn't have.' She looked up at Echo. 'I'm sorry.'

'It's okay.' Echo took her mother's hand. 'None of that matters now. We can't let King Alfons take our freedom away again. We can get out, all of us. But we need you to lead the way.'

Lil smiled, her eyes full of tears. 'You make a pretty fine

leader yourself.' Her chin quivered as she spoke. 'I am proud of you, Echo. So proud.' She smiled. 'You're a true Black Sky Wolf.'

Echo felt her cheeks grow hot and she beamed with pride.

Lil cleared her throat and rubbed her eyes with the back of her hand for a long moment. 'Right then.' She turned to face Echo, her expression deadly serious. 'We need to move before the guard wakes up. But, before we get going . . .' She took off her hat, unpinned her wolf pin from her curls and fastened it to Echo's. 'Lead on, Captain Echo,' she said. 'I think *you're* in charge of this adventure.'

CHAPTER THIRTY-THREE

Once Bulkhead had dragged Mortice into the cell and Echo had locked the door, she and the others followed Gilbert back through the tunnels, only stopping to retrieve Echo's postal pigeon, which lay among Mortice's belongings under his chair. As they raced through the dripping corridors, they passed cell after cell of inquisitive prisoners.

'What're you lot doing?' yelled one man, his beard yellowed and straggly.

Echo shoved the ring of keys deeper into her pocket and kept going. But they weighed heavy in her heart. Didn't *all* these people deserve to be free, instead of being locked up down here? To see the world beyond Lockfort?

'Hurry, Echo,' said Horace, urgently tugging at her sleeve. 'As soon as one of the other dungeon keepers finds Mortice, they'll be looking for us.'

Echo sighed and marched onwards. Eventually, they left

the cells behind them and the corridor widened out into the huge ceremonial chamber. They gathered by the skull-ringed entrance to the expulsion chute and everyone fell silent as they stared at the engraved hatch.

'Well,' said Horace, 'I suppose this is it.'

Echo nodded, her throat dry.

'It'll be a long journey without our airships,' said Lil, her brow creased with worry in the torchlight. 'I only just made it across the Barren on foot last time.'

'That chute is a bumpy old ride too,' said Professor Daggerwing, as he heaved open the hatch, releasing a blast of chilly air. 'All those rivets. Most unforgiving on the derrière.'

Echo peered through the opening into the darkness. She could just make out the brass sides of the start of the chute, before the tunnel snaked away into the gloom. It looked steep, and uncomfortable too. The cool breeze coming out of the opening made the candles flicker and Echo stood back.

'Do you want to go first, Echo?' asked Lil.

Echo swallowed. Something was nagging at her.

'Come on,' said Horace, looking around anxiously. 'The guards might come in. They'll be getting ready for the Gate-opening Ceremony tonight.'

'Tonight?' said Echo. 'How do you know?'

Horace shrugged. 'Mortice said.'

'A Gate-opening Ceremony. Tonight.'

'Yes,' said Horace, looking at her as though she was stupid. 'That *is* what I just said.'

Somewhere, deep in Echo's mind, a spark of an idea flickered.

'Maybe we *could* let everybody out,' she said slowly.

'What do you mean, everybody?' said Horace.

But Echo was already racing back to the cells, the keys jingling in her hand.

'They'll never make it across the Barren on foot, Echo!' shouted Lil after her.

'They won't need to!' Echo yelled back. 'We're going back through the castle!'

She sprinted out of the hallway and back into the dimness of the corridors, Lil and the others racing after her. 'What are you doing?' called Lil.

But that spark of an idea was smouldering, burning, setting fire to a raging inferno inside Echo that couldn't be stopped. 'Remember how my father wanted to open the gates and let the people of Lockfort discover the world?' She paused to open one of the cell doors. 'Here,' she said, throwing the bunch of keys to the goggle-eyed prisoner, 'let everyone out and follow us.'

'Echo, I still don't understand,' said Lil, as Echo set off again down the corridor.

'You said you wanted to finish what he started.'

'But what about the prophecy?' said Lil. 'People believe in it.

306

It doesn't matter what you or I say to them. They won't leave without it being fulfilled, and that's impossible.'

Echo shook her head. 'Nothing's impossible. What day is it today?'

Lil shrugged. 'No idea.'

'Does anyone here know?' she asked the sky pirates.

They all looked at one another and shook their heads. Echo ran to the bars of the nearest closed cell and rattled them. 'Hey!' she yelled. 'Hey, you!'

The woman inside looked up from where she was slumped. 'What is it?' she grunted.

'What day is it today?'

'Dunno. Er, the fifteenth? Gate Ceremony, innit?'

'No, I mean the day of the week.' Echo shifted from foot to foot in exasperation.

'Well –' the woman counted on her fingers – 'I been in here three days. And the night *before* I came in I had dumplings for dinner, and I always have dumplings on a Thursday, so that makes it—'

'Sunday,' interrupted Echo, her heart thudding. 'Sunday night.' Ideas spun through her mind like a whirlwind. A she-wolf, a dragon, Tuesday, blood. Somehow they were combining into something solid.

'But . . . but Echo, even you can't make Tuesday come on a Sunday night,' spluttered Horace.

'Can't I?' Echo reached into her pocket, drew out the postal pigeon and ran back towards the expulsion chute.

'What are you doing?' cried Horace after her.

'Sending a message!' Echo yelled back over her shoulder.

She scrawled a note on a scroll of paper, spun the dials to set the coordinates and hurled the little bird down the chute. The whirr of its mechanical wings died away as it disappeared into the darkness.

'I just hope there's enough time,' she muttered to herself, slamming the lid of the expulsion chute closed. She raced back down the corridor, almost crashing into Horace coming in the other direction. 'Come on,' she said. 'We're going this way.'

'Echo, what are you doing?' said Horace, staring in horror at the prisoners bursting from their cells. 'There *is* no other way out of the dungeons, you know that!'

Echo kept going. 'Of course there is.'

Horace shook his head. 'I must have looked at Father's map a million times. The only way out is the expulsion chute, or the ceremonial gate, and that's locked.'

Echo stopped for a moment. 'How did we get in here?'

'They brought us through the ceremonial gate.'

'The *first* time.'

'Through the kitchens,' said Horace. His face fell in horror. 'But we can't get *out* that way. There's too many of us. Someone will see!'

Echo smiled. 'I don't care if anyone sees. This isn't the time for sneaking about. This is the time for making a stand.'

CHAPTER THIRTY-FOUR

Getting into the kitchens was the easy part. Bulkhead hoisted the sky pirates up in the dumb waiter one by one, before squeezing in himself and being pulled up by Slingshot, the professor and Lil. The rest of the sky pirates and a steady stream of prisoners followed after them.

At first the kitchen staff hadn't even noticed. The whole place was in a frenzy of feast preparation, with chefs shouting orders, ladles clanging on pans, boys stirring great tureens of soup, rolling barrels of mead or winding the handle of a spit where a glistening hog was roasting in front of the fire. Echo stood, Gilbert clinging to her shoulder, and breathed it all in. After days of gruel and bread, her mouth watered. But there would be no dainty slices of roast swan or quince pie for her tonight. No, tonight she had something far more important to do.

Little by little, the noise clattered to a halt as the chefs and the kitchen boys and girls stopped what they were doing and turned to stare at the motley crew emerging from the dumb waiter. For a moment, everyone just stood and stared in silence, the only noise the bubbling of hot liquids and the crackle of fat in the fires.

The kitchen children turned and looked at each other, then back at a chef with a round ruddy face beneath his tall white hat. The fingers of one of his huge hands curled round a meat cleaver. He fixed Echo with furious eyes, then let out a growl and advanced towards her, his hatchet raised.

'What is the meaning of this?' he roared.

Echo swallowed and glanced over at Horace, who was staring white-faced at his boots. The professor twisted his hands together and began to whistle tunelessly. She looked in panic at Lil, who gave her a nod.

'You can do it!' Lil whispered.

'Well?' bellowed the chef.

Gilbert trembled on her shoulder, but Echo took a deep breath and stepped forward. 'I've come to open the gates,' she said.

'The gates?'

'Yes, sir. Of Lockfort.'

The chef's face suddenly cracked into a smile. Echo frowned. Had she said something funny?

'I'm *going* to open the gates,' said Echo, firmly this time. She put her hands on her hips and glared back at the chef.

'And how *exactly* are you planning to do—'

'Haven't you ever asked yourself if there's more than this?' she asked, gesturing around the kitchen.

The chef shrugged. 'Nope.'

Echo raised her voice and turned to address the children. 'Haven't any of *you* wondered what's out there?' she said, looking at the kitchen boys and girls, who had gathered round her, staring. The white-aproned workers muttered and looked at one another as if someone else might have the answer.

The red-faced chef frowned. 'Out where?' he said.

'Beyond the city walls.' Echo climbed up and stood on a nearby workbench to address the whole kitchen. She raised her voice. 'Beyond the Barren.'

'There's nothing beyond the Barren,' said the chef, with a laugh. 'Everyone knows that. You lot have been down in the dungeons too long. All that damp has turned your brains to mush.' He folded his arms across his chest. 'Why should any one of us listen to you?'

Echo paused for a moment. Why *should* he listen to her? The bench wobbled as Horace emerged from the back of the group and scrambled up next to her.

'Will you listen to your prince?' he asked.

A look of recognition flashed across the chef's face and his expression suddenly turned from fierce to fearful. 'Your Highness,' he stammered, 'is that really you?'

Horace, who Echo noticed was shaking very slightly, drew

himself up to his full height. 'I suggest you listen, all of you. What Echo has to say is important.'

'*Lady* Echo?' The chef squinted at her and his jaw dropped.

Hundreds of faces turned to stare up at Echo from across the kitchen. She took a deep breath and began again.

'Outside the city walls,' she said, 'there's a whole world. A world you've never been to or seen, or even heard about in stories. But it's there, I promise you. We've been there.'

Horace nodded in agreement and a murmur rippled through the crowd.

'There are cities and mountains and oceans,' she continued, glancing across at Professor Daggerwing. 'All just waiting for you to explore them.'

'Explore?' said the chef. 'What if we're happy where we are?'

Echo clenched her fists in frustration. 'But how will you know if you never try?' She scanned the room for a familiar face and spotted One-Eye in the crowd, listening intently. She raised her voice. 'Some of you must be curious.'

'No time to be curious. There's work to be done,' said the chef. 'The king needs us.'

'When did King Alfons last give you a day off?' said Echo. 'You all slave away down here so he can feast on swan and quinces. When do you get *your* freedom?' She stabbed a finger towards the floor. 'You're no better off than the prisoners down there.'

Here the prisoners let up a cheer. The chef seemed to consider this for a moment. 'I suppose you're going to tell us there's roast swan for everyone out there, beyond the Barren?' he said. A kitchen girl with two blonde plaits stifled a giggle behind her hand.

'Roast swan?' said Echo. 'No, there's no roast swan. But there are –' she glanced at Bulkhead and Lil – 'there are sea urchins and saltweed and golden snapperfish.'

'Snapperfish?' The chef suddenly looked interested. 'Never heard of them.'

'Of course you haven't! That's the whole point. You haven't seen or heard of half of what there is in the world. But if you roast them on an open fire, with your best friends around you, I promise you nothing tastes better.'

Echo was in her stride now. She looked again at Professor Daggerwing. 'And there are pickles! Pickled squibnuts, pickled lily livers.' She turned and grinned at Horace. 'And pickled sweetroots.'

'Sounds weird,' grunted the chef.

'Oh, it *is* weird,' said Echo. 'It's weird and it's new and it's utterly, utterly wonderful.' She turned to the children. 'Isn't there even one of you who's curious?'

One-Eye thrust his hand in the air. 'I am!'

Another hand crept up at the back. And another. And another. A grin spread across Echo's face as she looked down on a whole sea of hands, a sea of laughing kitchen boys and girls with bright, excited eyes, chattering to each other about this whole new world they dreamed of seeing.

'Quiet!' yelled the head chef. He banged his cleaver on the table, but the kitchen children didn't hush and he was soon lost in a crowd of excited faces as they pushed forward.

'Let's go,' Echo said, jumping down from the bench. 'To the gates!'

There was a roar of young voices shouting, 'To the gates! To the gates!' and the kitchen children of Lockfort surged through the castle in a wave, leaving the open-mouthed chef standing in an empty kitchen, his cleaver still dangling uselessly in one hand.

CHAPTER THIRTY-FIVE

With the castle dignitaries busy feasting in the banqueting hall and the castle staff busy waiting on them, Echo and her merry band of prisoners, pirates and kitchen children marched through the castle and onwards into the city unimpeded.

As they travelled through the streets, Echo told tales of explorers' guilds and libraries, islands and airships, and her little band of followers gradually became a large one.

'King Alfons is a liar and a fraud!' she shouted to the curious crowd that gathered round them. 'His prophecy is a fake. He told me my mother abandoned me when he'd stolen me from her and sent her to the dungeons. He says there's no world out there, but he's lying to you all.'

'Ridiculous!' cried a man.

'Poppycock!' shrieked another.

But the children of Lockfort hung on every word. By the time the sun was setting, and they'd nearly reached the city walls, Echo had a small army on her side. She explained her plan to them as they marched onwards.

As they approached the gates, the royal coach clattered past and the crowd parted, cheering and waving, to let it through. Echo spotted the king's jewel-laden hand waving to the crowd. It was almost time. She scanned the sky. Still no sign though. Had her message got to Port Tourbillon?

The square filled with people. Echo saw Miss Brittle and Arthur, the fencing tutor, pass by without giving her a second glance, thanks to her new haircut. Martha stood in the crowd, wearing her best dress, and Echo almost raised her hand and cried out in greeting before stopping herself. She couldn't lose focus now. There would be time to talk when this was all over.

The bugles blared, announcing the arrival of King Alfons, and she shrank back, concealing herself. Horace squeezed her hand. 'Now?' he said.

Echo felt fear rise up inside her, but she swallowed it back down. She quickly searched the sky again and felt a rush of adrenaline flow through her as she saw a tiny speck out past the north beacon. It was far away, but it was coming.

'Now,' she said. 'NOW!'

The children and pirates and prisoners gave a war cry and surged forward through the crowds. The castle guards tried to stop them, but the ragtag group barrelled past, catching them by surprise as they rushed, whooping and chanting, to surround King Alfons's throne.

'What is the meaning of this?' he spluttered, getting to his feet. Then he saw Echo and Horace, and his face dropped.

'Echo, Horace,' he whispered. He put his goblet of mead down, composed himself and forced a smile on to his face. 'My dear son Horace,' he announced to the crowd. 'He has recovered from his terrible illness.'

He turned to a guard. 'Remove them,' he snarled between clenched teeth.

Gilbert stiffened on Echo's shoulder and let out a hiss.

'With pleasure, Your Highness.' The guard thudded forward, but was immediately pounced upon by at least ten of the prisoners.

The sky pirates formed a protective circle round Echo and Horace. The king's face paled and his mouth opened and closed like a goldfish as he saw Lil. 'Y . . . you!' he said. He drew himself up. 'I should have known you were behind this.' He turned to Horace. 'This . . . this woman killed my brother.'

'I loved your brother!' said Lil, her curls bouncing angrily. 'It was frost fever that killed him, and, if you'd have let me take him back to Port Tourbillon, he could have been cured.'

'I should never have let him leave.' King Alfons shook his head. 'I always said going beyond the Barren would end in disaster.'

'But you can't blame Lil for what happened,' said Horace. 'I know it must have hurt you terribly, but it wasn't anybody's fault. It's not a reason to hide the world from everyone. To lie to them.'

'I'm keeping them safe from the outside,' muttered the king. 'It's my duty—'

'You told me my daughter was dead.' Lil jabbed a finger at him.

'So you didn't come back,' said the king. 'I wanted to forget you existed.'

'Then why keep me here at all?' said Echo. 'Why didn't you let Lil take me with her?'

The king shook his head. 'You were the only thing I had left to remind me of Edmond. I hoped you'd grow up to be a little like him.' His sadness turned to disgust. 'Sadly, you've turned out to be more like her.'

Lil put her arm round Echo's shoulders. 'Edmond would have been proud of the daughter Echo has become.'

The king trailed off as the rest of the sky pirates, Professor Daggerwing and the ragtag group of prisoners stepped forward to surround him.

'It's over,' said Echo. 'All the lies, all the deception. Now, hand us the keys.'

'But these are royal keys,' spluttered the king, clutching the chain around his neck. 'They may only be used by those with royal blood.'

'I have royal blood and so does Echo.' Horace put out his hand. 'Pass them to me, Father.'

'You're making a mistake, Horace—'

Bulkhead stepped forward and silenced the king with a growl.

King Alfons turned pale. With shaking hands, he took the chain from around his neck and passed it to Horace. 'I don't know what you hope to achieve,' he said.

'It's very simple really,' said Echo. 'We're going to open the gates and show all these people –' she gestured to the staring crowds and raised her voice – 'what you've been hiding from them for all these years.'

The king shook his head. 'Hiding?' His voice rose as he turned to the crowd. 'Preposterous! I've been protecting them, from death and disappointment, and from . . . from outsiders!'

There was a whoop and a murmur of agreement from the adults in the crowd and Echo faltered. Would she be able to convince them? She took a deep breath. 'But what if they don't want to be protected? What if they want to be free to discover things for themselves?'

The king bristled. 'It's all beside the point when there's no way out of the city. As you well know, the prophecy—'

'Yes, your prophecy,' said Echo. She turned to the crowd. 'Everybody knows about the prophecy, don't they?'

There was a shuffling of feet and a murmur of agreement.

'And, if the prophecy is fulfilled, the gates of Lockfort open, for good.' She turned to King Alfons. 'Agreed?'

The king twisted his rings. 'Yes, yes, of course. *If* it is fulfilled.'

Echo turned to the Royal Reader. 'Please do start the reading. I think we're ready for the Gate-opening Ceremony to commence.'

The Royal Reader, pale-faced and surrounded by a ring of baying children, cleared his throat and hushed the excited crowd. Over his head, Echo could see the speck in the sky growing larger and larger, until she could make out two gleaming copper wings, a snout that breathed fire and a tiny, goggle-wearing figure astride its back.

The Reader began.

> '*When Tuesday arrives on a Sunday night,*
> *When a she-wolf soars by dragon flight,*
> *When the king's blood turns from red to white,*
> *Then the gates of Lockfort shall open.*'

King Alfons, seemingly recovered from the shock of Horace standing up to him again, pushed himself out of his throne. 'As we all know,' he addressed the crowd, 'the prophecy cannot be fulfilled.'

'Can't it?' said Echo.

There were jeers from the crowd and the king laughed. 'Where are your wolves?'

'Remember my mother?' said Echo, gesturing to Lil. 'The one you told me was dead? She's the leader of the Black Sky Wolves.'

320

There was a ripple of surprise in the crowd.

The king snorted. 'And I suppose my disloyal son is the dragon?'

'Let's make an agreement,' said Horace. 'If we can fulfil the prophecy and open the gates, you step down as king.'

'And if you don't?' said the king.

'You can do whatever you want,' said Echo. 'Lock us up again. Throw us in the Barren. You choose.'

King Alfons glanced across at the other dignitaries, smiled and rolled his eyes as if humouring the two children. 'If you insist.' He grabbed Echo's and Horace's hands and shook them with a smug grin. 'Now do tell me –' he said – 'I am intrigued to know: just when *is* Tuesday going to arrive?'

'Right about now,' said Echo. 'In fact, she's behind you. On that dragon.'

There were shrieks and gasps as Abena Tuesday steered *Smokesister* through the square and swept elegantly to the ground, skimming over the petrified king's head and landing before him, the dragon's metal talons rattling on the stone.

She pulled off her goggles with a whoop. 'That was some ride! Wait till I tell my brothers about this!'

'Please welcome Abena Tuesday!' Echo grinned. 'Have you ever seen anything like this in Lockfort?' she yelled to the crowd.

The children shuffled forward, but then One-Eye stepped out of the crowd and stretched out a tentative hand to touch

321

Smokesister's metal scales. He turned to the others, a huge grin on his face. 'I believe her! Ain't nothing like this in Lockfort.'

'I do too!' shouted a girl with a long blonde fringe.

Even their parents had started to murmur to one another behind their hands, looking from Abena, with her black and green plaits, to the great steaming copper dragon, back to Echo.

'Now we need a she-wolf to take flight,' Echo said, turning to Lil. 'Over to you, Mother.'

But, to her surprise, Lil shook her head. 'No, Echo. Not me.'

For a moment, Echo stood, frozen. 'But . . . but you have to!' she finally said. 'You said it yourself – we have to show the people that the prophecy has been fulfilled so the gates can open.' Her voice shook. 'Otherwise they won't believe. You're the next part of the prophecy. You're the she-wolf.'

Lil shook her head again. 'No, Echo. I'm not.'

The king, who had regained his composure, looked over at Echo with a smirk. 'You almost had me there, young lady, but it appears your plan has a small flaw.' He looked around at the gathered crowd. 'Who'd have thought a sky pirate wouldn't be brave enough to fly?' He let out a snigger.

'That's not what she means, Father,' a small and slightly shaky voice came from behind them. Horace stepped forward and joined hands with Echo. 'The she-wolf in the prophecy isn't your mother,' he said, turning to Echo.

'Then who, exactly, is it?' asked the king, still smirking and winking at the crowd.

322

But Echo suddenly realized what Lil and Horace were saying. She squeezed Horace's hand. 'Thanks, Horace,' she said. Then she raced towards the dragon and hauled herself up behind Abena.

'Go!' she yelled. 'Fly!'

Abena flicked a switch and the dragon's huge wings flapped, blowing the king's hair back and sending his goblet flying.

'Horace was right!' Echo yelled down at King Alfons, grinning as the smirk finally fell from his face. 'It wasn't my mother in the prophecy. It was me!'

'Hold on!' cried Abena, and at once they were soaring into the air, the dragon's mechanical wings beating rhythmically, the king's words lost on the wind. Echo clung to Abena and laughed in delight as her hair whipped back. Down below, face after face turned up to watch her. The gasps from the crowd turned to cheers as they soared skywards, and the buildings of Lockfort shrank to tiny grey doll's houses as they climbed ever higher.

'Shall we do a circuit?' shouted Abena.

Echo grinned and nodded into the leather of Abena's jacket. She felt the dragon's metallic scales slide over one another as *Smokesister* banked and wheeled to the left in a great arc over the city. The world rushed by in a blur and Echo looked down to see the grey little streets fly by below them. Her whole life had been in Lockfort, she thought with a sudden pang. It all looked so small from up here.

Abena pulled back and took the dragon higher, almost into the clouds, and Echo looked out across the city walls, across the Barren and to the horizon. She smiled. Lockfort *was* small, a small part of the great, wide world. And now the prophecy was being fulfilled. They were going to open the gates and let everyone explore that world for themselves. Echo's heart was full to overflowing, and she couldn't stop herself from grinning as they dived and swooped, looped and soared over the circular streets of Lockfort.

By the time Abena steered the dragon back down and they landed near the gates again, Echo's face was stiff from smiling. She unpeeled herself from Abena's back and sat up. The people of Lockfort cheered as she slid down the dragon's flank and landed, legs trembling, on the flagstones. She took a moment to get her breath back before storming over to King Alfons, who took a quick step backwards as she approached.

'You said that the prophecy could never be fulfilled,' she said, jabbing a finger at him. 'But Tuesday's arrived on a Sunday and a wolf has flown with a dragon.' She turned to the Royal Reader. 'Please remind us of the last part of the prophecy.'

The Royal Reader cleared his throat. 'When the king's blood turns from red to white, then the gates of Lockfort shall open.'

Fear was etched on the king's face. He composed himself

and addressed the crowd. 'And how are you going to turn my blood white? Even you have to concede *that* part of the prophecy is impossible.'

Echo thought quickly and turned to Horace, who was still clutching the three jewelled keys. 'Horace is your son, isn't he?'

'Of course,' said the king.

'Then he is the king's blood,' said Echo, taking her place between Lil and Professor Daggerwing. 'Go on, Horace. You know what to do. Turn the keys from red to white.'

Horace nodded and walked over to the gates before taking the glittering red key and turning it in the lock.

Echo held her breath. Was it her imagination or had there been a tiny click?

Horace looked at her and nodded. He inserted the next key, the pink tourmaline. As he turned it, Echo heard the mechanism engage.

Gilbert clung to her shoulder and Echo gripped her mother's hand as Horace took the final key, encrusted with its gleaming white diamonds, and turned it in the lock. The crowd grew silent. There was a symphony of clicks and whirrs as the locks engaged.

And, as if in slow motion, the gates to Lockfort swung open.

CHAPTER THIRTY-SIX

For a moment, nobody knew quite what to do, and an eerie hush descended over the crowd. But then the hush turned to whispers and the whispers turned to murmurs and the murmurs turned to a whole hubbub of people, curious people, excited people, chattering and questioning and wondering, and craning their necks to look at the world that had opened up outside the gates.

All of a sudden, one small blond-haired boy, released from his distracted parents' arms, tottered forward and took a step through the gateway. His mother raced after him and swept him up and then stood, staring, amazed by herself and where she was standing.

'No!' shouted the king. 'You can't go out there!'

Another child walked through the archway.

'It's not right!' The king's face was flushed now and his crown askew. 'It's not safe! You can't . . . Please!'

Another ran through, and another.

'No!' yelled the king. 'No! NO! NO!'

But the people weren't listening, and suddenly there was a rush as the whole crowd surged towards the gates and out they spilled, laughing and whooping and cheering, into the Barren, as King Alfons screamed and wept and raved unheard behind them.

'Thank you!' said a woman, as she rushed past Echo, dragged by her three small children.

'Thank you!'

'Thank you!'

'Thank you!'

Hundreds of voices rose in a great clamour, as the citizens of Lockfort clapped Echo and Horace and Abena on the back, lifting them into the air and carrying them along with the tide of people.

'To Echo! To Prince Horace! To the Beyond!' they shouted.

And so the celebrations started. People brought out musical instruments and food and jugs of mead. One family packed their belongings into a pony cart straight away, the children waving excited goodbyes as they clopped off northwards. Another small boy sketched out maps with his fingertips in the grey dust of the Barren. Yet another spun round with his sister in giddy circles, too excited to do anything else. The chatter was contagious. Everyone's heads and hearts were full of plans – plans for adventures and expeditions and new

discoveries beyond the city walls. Plans to escape and explore
and see the whole wide wonderful world beyond the Barren.

As Echo stood on the castle ramparts the next morning,
Gilbert slung round her shoulders like a scarf, and the wind
whipping across her face, she gazed out across the city and
beyond its walls to the Barren. How long had it been since she
had been here, playing games with Gilbert? Only a few short
weeks, and yet so much had changed. The whole world had
opened, and not just to her but to everyone.

In the distance, she could already see a line of people,
as small as ants, weaving their way out of the open gates
and across the Barren. Away from Lockfort and beyond, to
explore and return richer perhaps. Wiser, without a doubt.
And, although she couldn't see beyond the Barren, she
knew that soon others out there would be making their own
journeys inwards to explore their unknown – the unknown
of Lockfort – for themselves. She sighed and absent-mindedly
stroked Gilbert's tail.

'Why does it feel like our adventure's ending?' she said.

'On the contrary, Echo, my dear.' Professor Daggerwing
appeared at her side. 'I think you'll find that your adventure
is just about to begin!'

'But we're all leaving.' Echo turned and watched the sky
pirates loading up the *Scarlet Margaret*. Over by the eastern

turret, Abena was putting a final polish to her dragon's scales. Gilbert bobbed up and down on Echo's shoulder and chirruped in greeting as Horace emerged from the staircase with his butterfly net and a jar.

'Will *you* come with us?' she said to him, as he walked over to them.

Horace blushed and shook his head. 'Maybe one day,' he said. 'But for the moment I'm going to stay.' He met Echo's eyes. 'I want to make sure Father really does do what he said he would, and the gates stay open.'

'Where is he?'

'Hiding in his chambers. He'll have to come out sometime though. I think he knows that things can't stay as they were.'

Echo nodded. It was the right thing. Of course Horace should stay. She would do the same if she really belonged here. But still. 'I'll miss you,' she said softly. 'We'll see each other again, won't we? Especially now we're family.'

Horace nodded hurriedly. 'Of course.'

Echo glanced down at Horace's butterfly jar. It was empty. 'Oh no! What happened to your chrysalises?' she said. 'Didn't they make the journey?'

'They hatched.' Horace shrugged. 'But I let them go.'

'But what about your collection?'

Her cousin shook his head. 'I've decided – butterflies are wild things and wild things should be free. I'll always find more.'

Lil strode over to join them and put a hand on Echo's shoulder. 'The ship's nearly ready to sail, Echo.'

'Great,' said Echo. 'Where will we go next?'

'I hadn't really thought,' said Lil.

Professor Daggerwing flourished his map. 'Would this be of assistance?'

Lil smiled and took the map. 'What do you think, Echo? I've heard there's treasure to be found in Dark Nordland, and there are always people in need of help from the Black Sky Wolves.'

Echo studied the map with a soaring heart. Dark Nordland! Treasure! Now *that* sounded like an adventure. But why stop there?

'What's here?' she said, pointing at the edge of the map, past Lockfort and Port Tourbillon. Past the Violet Isles and the Stony Sea. Past even Dark Nordland.

'There? Well. Let me see.' Professor Daggerwing studied the map and frowned. 'I'm not sure anyone's ever been *beyond* Dark Nordland before. That's known as the Dragonlands. Completely uncharted territory.'

Echo grinned. 'The very best kind,' she said. 'We'll go there.' She looked up at the professor. 'Will you come?'

'No, Echo.' Professor Daggerwing cleared his throat and rubbed at something in his eye. 'I need to get back to Port Tourbillon and present my butterfly findings at the Explorers' Guild. I'm sure they'll be most interested to hear all about the opening of the gates of Lockfort too. And those cats won't feed themselves.' Here he blew his nose into a huge purple handkerchief. 'I fear there is a limit to even the good Mrs Milkweed's patience.'

Echo nodded, all her words suddenly seeming to have dried up inside her. Then she threw herself at both Horace and the professor and enveloped them in a hug. 'Goodbye,' she said.

Goodbye, Gilbert chirruped.

'For the moment,' said Professor Daggerwing. 'There's no doubt that three great adventurers such as ourselves will cross paths again one day.'

It was much, much later, when they'd all finally said their goodbyes, that Echo took the wheel of the *Scarlet Margaret*, Gilbert perched on her shoulder. Lil cast off the tethering ropes and they set off into the sky with the rest of the crew, waving and grinning and shouting promises to meet again soon to a waving Horace and Martha.

Echo turned to Lil and smiled. Lil was an explorer, a fighter, a sky pirate, with adventure in her heart. Perhaps she wasn't quite the mother Echo had dreamed of, but dreams were dreams and mothers were ... well, they were more complicated than that. Lil was a real mother, *her* mother, and she was here.

'Ready?' asked Lil, looking up from her sky chart.

'Ready,' said Echo, tightening the hairpin in her curls and settling Gilbert on her shoulder.

And they soared off into the sky, away over the walls of Lockfort. Beyond the Barren. Beyond Port Tourbillon, the Violet Isles and the Stony Sea.

Setting sail for the Dragonlands.

And for the Great Beyond.

ACKNOWLEDGEMENTS

I would like to give a hearty Sky Pirate thank you to the following people:

My editor, Lucy Rogers, who completely understood Echo from the very beginning and helped me get my convoluted ramblings airship-shape.

Thérèse Coen, agent extraordinaire, *Sky Pirates* champion and all-round good egg.

Mark Chambers, who has brought *Sky Pirates* to life more beautifully than I ever could have imagined.

Jesse Green for her design wizardry.

Jane Tait and Emma Young for their eagle eyes.

Joanna Nadin, my tutor at Bath Spa University, for her insight, hand-holding and inspirational word-nerdiness.

All the rest of my tutors at Bath Spa University – Julia Green, for her wisdom and encouragement; CJ Skuse for saying 'what about a prophecy?' and telling me about the Traquair stuck gates; Janine Amos for teaching me to write a synopsis (however painful it was at the time) and Steve Voake, in whose workshop this book first started.

My fellow Bath Spa alumni – especially the Aubergines and Lucy Cuthew.

Team Swag for advice, all-round moral support and the gifs (you know which ones).

The Scattered Authors Society, for the blissful writing retreats and creative inspiration.

The many SCBWI pals I have made over the years – particularly Tania and Miriam.

The librarians at Reigate library and the American Library in Paris, where much of this book was written.

And last but most definitely not least, my family, for the ideas, silliness and the space to write.

Recipe for Pickled Squibnuts

Ingredients:

100ml rice vinegar
150ml water
2 tablespoons caster sugar
500g squibnuts (or a 567g tin lychees, drained)
2.5cm piece of fresh ginger, peeled and grated

Method:

In a small, nonreactive saucepan, combine the
vinegar, water and sugar and bring it to a boil
(make sure you have an adult helping you!).
Pack the squibnuts (or lychees) and ginger into
a clean jar.
Carefully pour the hot brine into the jar, seal
and let cool at room temperature.
Refrigerate overnight.
Eat on adventures!

SKY PIRATES QUIZ!

 How many cats does Professor Daggerwing have?

   a) Five
   b) Seven
   c) One

 Where do Echo and her friends get stranded on the way to the Violet Isles?

   a) Galligaskins
   b) Trombones
   c) Bonneville

 Complete the lyric from Professor Daggerwing's song.

'Pickles are not fickle they will always be...

   a) . . . disgusting'
   b) . . . your friend'
   c) . . . far too vinegary'

 What is the name of Abena's mechanical dragon?

   a) Smaug
   b) Draco
   c) Smokesister

Where do the Violet Isles get their name from?

    a) The purple butterflies
    b) The purple fog
    c) The purple trees

 What shape is Echo's hairpin?

    a) A wolf's head
    b) A wolf's paw
    c) A dragon's claw

 What colour is the sand on Tyrian Isle?

    a) Blue
    b) Purple
    c) Black

 What is the King of Lockfort's first name?

    a) Albert
    b) Alfons
    c) Alpacino

TURN TO THE NEXT PAGE FOR THE ANSWERS!

QUIZ ANSWERS:

1) B, 2) A, 3) B, 4) C, 5) B, 6) A, 7) C, 8) B

How many did you get right?

1–2 There's a way to go before you're ready to sail the seven skies. Perhaps you're better off on land!

3–5 Getting there. With a bit more map reading and cutlass rattling, you could be a top-notch sky pirate!

6–8 You are a true-blue sky pirate. Join the crew of the Black Sky Wolves immediately!

ARE YOU READY TO JOURNEY TO...
THE DRAGONLANDS?

SET SAIL ON ANOTHER
SKY PIRATES ADVENTURE.

COMING SOON!

Alex English is a picture book author and a graduate of the Bath Spa University MA Writing for Young People. She currently lives with her family just outside Paris. *Sky Pirates: Echo Quickthorn and the Great Beyond* is her first middle-grade title and the start of a swashbuckling series.

www.alexenglish.co.uk